My Accidentally Fun Summer
Book 1 in the Camp Eerie Series
By: Suzette Emilia

Original Copyright © 2011 Suzette Emilia
Revised and Re-Published Copyright © 2013
All Rights Reserved.

ISBN-13: 978-1466364141

ISBN-10: 1466364149

This book is a work of fiction. Names, characters, places and incidents are products of the author's imagination or are used fictitiously. Any resemblance to actual events or locals or persons living or dead is entirely coincidental.

**Other books by Suzette Emilia
Don't miss the rest of the adventure!**

Sofia's Magical World : Book 2 in the Camp Eerie Series

Charlie's New Sister : Book 3 in the Camp Eerie Series

This book is dedicated to my four brothers, my mom and dad.

This is what I was doing locked in my room when I was younger.

To my husband, who is my best friend, and our three beautiful children.

Most importantly, I dedicate this to you; my reader.

This could not have been done without the Lord by my side.

Author's Note:

To my Reader,

As a writer, sometimes an idea sticks out and refuses to be ignored. I was very excited as I was writing book 3. *Charlie's New Sister* was turning out great. However, in the middle of the story, an idea popped out. What if Charlie told the story herself? So I tested a few sentences switching from third person to first. It was amazing how much more easily the story flowed! What worked best was that by the end I knew everything about Charlie. Not just her quirks, but her fears and her dreams. I even knew what kind of food she'd stock in her fridge. I was just so proud of book 3 that I got to thinking again. What if book 1 was told in Callie's POV? Again, I tested the first chapter and my, oh my, I wasn't disappointed. The story is much better now that Callie is telling it. If this is your second time reading it, I hope you enjoy the little changes. Same story, words changed around a bit! If this is your first time reading the story, be prepared for adventure and fun!

Happy reading!

Suzette Emilia

Table of Contents

Chapter 1: Fun in the Sun with a Cherry on Top
7

Chapter 2: I Want to be in Pictures!
13

Chapter 3: Welcome to Camp Eerie
21

Chapter 4: I Think You're Onto Something
31

Chapter 5: That's Going to be Hard to Top!
45

Chapter 6: As Long as it's Only One Time
58

Chapter 7: I Look Forward to Our Next Meeting
68

Chapter 8: This Could be Bad
80

Chapter 9: It's Funny How Things Work Out
93

Chapter 10: What's the Catch?
103

Chapter 11: I Love That I Can Laugh At Myself
109

Chapter 12: She's A *What*?!
114

Chapter 13
127

Chapter 14: How Did She Do That?
128

Chapter 15: Who *Cares* What We Think?
134

Chapter 16: It's the Best Music Ever
147

Chapter 17: Everybody Likes *You*
157

Chapter 18: Life is Too Short for Grudges
166

Chapter 19: I Think You Should Sit Down
174

Chapter 20: Hello
186

Epilogue
195

Chapter 1

Fun In The Sun With A Cherry On Top

Note to Self: *Never* make a deal with your parents about planning your summer break. *Never*.

THINGS WERE about to get worse for me. And really, that's saying a lot. I mean, I already had to deal with an annoying little nine year old sister named Adele and her little friends (one named Jelly Bean). They stormed my room, pranked me and basically made my life miserable. I really had no one to back me up since I'm pretty lousy at making friends which Adele reminds me of every other nano-second. I really think Adele needs her own talk show which would work out great for me because I'd see less of her. But I digress.

"Ow." *Seriously?* That had to have been the thousandth time I bumped my head on the ceiling of this big drafty old school bus. I wish I at least had a pillow to rest the back of my head. The hard brown seat was getting really old really fast. I mean, this is like a three and a half hour ride from Massachusetts all the way to Maine. I looked out of the window at the beautiful scenery outside. Did I say beautiful? I really meant *awful*. And when I say awful I really mean *terrible*. Hundreds of trees, dark gray skies and an old scary road. I thought about the conversation that brought me to this moment. I was sitting in the kitchen with my arms crossed (because that's what I do when I get really mad) and frowning at my mom and dad. "This is *so* unfair! I can*not* believe you *both* planned *my* summer. What kind of punishment is this?"

"It's not that bad Callie." My mom, Rose, walked by me and tweaked my nose. *Tweaked* my nose! Come on, I'm thirteen years old. So I most definitely sniffed and scowled at my mom's pretty face.

"But we made a deal, remember?" I placed some hair behind my ear (because that's something else I do when I really get mad) and plopped myself onto the kitchen chair.

"Yes, we did make a deal. If you pass all of your exams, you plan your summer. You fail just one subject and we do the planning. Do you remember that?" Dad couldn't help but sound so sure of himself. He sat down across from me and gave me that know-it-all look, even though he *did* know a lot.

"But it wasn't my fault!" Really, I was whining at this point. "Math is brutally hard! I would have murdered those exams if Mr. Currie didn't kill us with an insane amount of homework!"

Mom looked at Dad. "Hey Chris, is she talking about math or an unsolved police crime?"

"Okay, I get it. You guys win fair and square. Where am I going?" I asked with a large amount of misery with a dash of sadness.

I wondered why mom and dad started glowing. They were literally beaming with excitement. I wanted to literally gag when dad answered. "Camp Eerie."

"Camp *What's*-It?"

Really, it was the worst conversation I'd ever had with my parents. Last night, while I folded my clothes (which was a lot of clothes since I had to be there for eight weeks!) mom came in my room.

"You okay Cal?"

I took a really deep breath and stopped folding. And when I say folding I really mean *throwing*. "A deal is a deal." I folded my arms again and tried to avoid mom's piercing blue gaze. To make it known that I was really, really mad, I grabbed my fuzzy gray pillow, squeezed it tight and sat down by my window.

"Your father and I only have you best interest at heart." Mom walked up next to the window and leaned back against the wall. From the corner of my eyes, I saw her tuck some of her blondish-brown hair behind her ear. I realized where I got that from. "Cal, I mean that."

I finally looked up. "I know mom. I'm just..." I sighed. I knew I had to tell her what I was really thinking. "I'm not good with other people. And now I'll be forced to live with strangers."

"They'll only be strangers on the first day." Mom had that really patient look on her face which made me realize how hard a time I must have been giving her.

So I couldn't help but sigh in defeat. "I'm not good at making friends, mom."

"Cal, that's the best part about making friends; you don't have to try so hard."

"So why don't I have any?" I couldn't help the tears from turning mom all blurry. I wiped them away with the palm of my hand and threw my pillow on the bed."

"If you'd just be yourself-"

"I'm sorry mom, but I really don't want to talk about it anymore. I know the problem is me."

Mom straightened from the wall. "The problem is not you Cal, the solution is you."

I had to admit that if anyone knew what the solution was, it would be mom. She was so popular and beautiful and really how could I compare with that? I didn't even look like her, I looked more like dad. I'm not saying that dad is ugly, dad is actually handsome. But I wished so badly that I looked like mom. Adele was her twin.

Speaking of the little booger, she decided to poke her little nine year old head into the room. "I *SO* can't wait to raid this room once you're gone."

"You *SO* better stay out! I'm putting a padlock on the door!"

"I can *SO* crack the code. Jelly Bean knows how to pick locks!" She ran out of the room.

"You have friends with weird names!" I called out.

"At least I *have* friends!"

That stung. But I had to remember that I was dealing with a terminally annoying nine-year old.

So then three and a half hours ago, mom and dad dropped me off at the bus station. Mom hugged me and then frowned. "You're acting like this is a punishment."

"Isn't it?" I asked defiantly. Can you guess what I was crossing at this point?

"It's too late," Adele walked up to us with Jelly Bean standing by her side. "Mom and dad won't be able to get a refund."

I tried to shoot venom from my eyes and realized that it was impossible. "This is the last summer we're making any kind of deal okay? Next summer, whether I pass the exams or not, no one is planning my summer."

"Fine," mom smiled. "Who knows? You might want to go back again next year."

"*Mom*," I whined.

"Everything's loaded!" Dad exclaimed with a little too much enthusiasm. "We're going to miss you Cal." He hugged me tight and I couldn't help but hug him back. He was *dad* after all, but I couldn't help but say, "Yeah dad, okay."

"Aw, come on Cal! You're going to have so much fun, you won't even remember us."

"That's what I told her," mom gave me a knowing look.

"Fine you guys. I'll try." And I really meant that I would try. It was just really hard to believe it. We said our goodbyes and I went into a large blue bus and sat by the window. I saw dad put his arms around mom as they smiled and waved at me. "Okay mom and dad. Here I go…"

And so this is how I'm here at this moment. And I threw the 'I'll try' out of the bus window. The ride was just horrible. Everyone was chatting at the same time. I just wanted to drive back home. I reached for the brochure mom had given me and read the headline. 'Camp Eerie, Fun in the Sun with a Cherry on Top'. I rolled my eyes. "Lame." I kept reading. "Make new friends-' Okay, I had to stop there. *Ha*. Make new friends. Sure, it's *so* easy. I stuffed the brochure back into my backpack. "I don't think so."

I so wished that I had my headphones. I loved listening to that old fashioned swing music. However and this was a *huge* however, headphones and electronics were not allowed. My blonde imaginary-self taunted me. "If you looked more like me honey you'd have some friends." I groaned. Maybe if I stopped having imaginary versions of myself I might have at least one friend. "I'll never forgive my parents," I muttered in frustration.

"Why?"

All I heard was gum smacking in someone's mouth. The voice was right by my ear so I turned around and saw a face looking back at me from over the seat. The voice belonged to a blonde girl with pigtails and braces. "Were you...were you talking to me?"

"Why won't you forgive your parents? I mean," *smack, smack,* "that's kind of mean you know what I mean?" *Smack, smack,* POP!

I cringed at the sound. I didn't really want to explain anything to this girl but for some reason I still tried. "Well...I mean..."

"It's none of your business Rachel."

I looked at the seat in front of me and saw the face of another girl. This one had rich brown hair and light freckles. Rachel, the Gum Smacker, pursed her lips so tightly it looked as if she'd just tasted something really sour. "Who made *you* the boss?" She blew a bubble and when it popped I squeezed my eyes shut.

"Nobody Rachel, just leave her alone."

I looked back and forth between the two girls and hated feeling so helpless. I thought that I could stand up for myself so I started to say something, but it was lost when Rachel spoke louder. "So you just made yourself boss then?" The smacking got even louder.

The composure of the brown-haired, beautiful girl was starting to crack. "What if I am?"

Smack, smack. "Whatever Charlie!"

Charlie? That was an interesting name. Either way, I was glad to put a name to the girl. Charlie opened her mouth after a frustrated snort, but the argument was over when a whistle sounded loudly in the air, making all of us jump.

"Alright ladies, settle down." The voice was stern, yet calm. I peeked over Charlie and saw a sporty looking lady wearing a blue Camp Eerie cap complete with matching sweatshirt. Looking out of the window, I realized that during the argument, the bus had stopped and everyone on the bus was looking in my general direction. "Welcome to Camp Eerie! Off to the rec hall now, come on. You're the last bus to get here."

Everyone got up and when Rachel passed by my seat she stuck her tongue out at me and Charlie. I clutched my purple bag and followed Charlie outside where everything was still gray and gloomy. As a matter of fact, I could barely even see the sky since it was blocked by really tall trees. "Hey!" I called out to Charlie. She stopped and adjusted her own blue backpack over her shoulder. Her ponytail whipped as she turned around to face me. I had it in my head what I was going to say to her, but really, does it ever come out the way you mean it? "I can stand up for myself you know…well, you don't know, but *now* you know."

Charlie shrugged and smiled. "Okay." She glanced at the other campers walking ahead of us and looked back at me. "I'm Charlotte."

"I guess I'm Calliope," I gave her a handshake. A handshake! That was totally something my dad would do! And really, why would I *guess* what my name is?

"Nice to meet you Calliope. If your guess is right that is." There it is. Okay, I just had to shake it off. "Dude, your face is like really red."

Embarrassing much! I knew I was bad at this. I also knew that I had to change the subject and do it like five minutes ago. "You can call me Callie."

"Call me Charlie. And hey, I've got your back if you ever need it."

I smiled at her and together, we walked through a scary looking path. Both sides of the path were lined up by extremely tall trees and hovered over us like a canopy.

"I'm sure you can stand up for yourself," Charlie said as she walked, "but I had to say something to Rachel. She's my neighbor back home and she can be just a little annoying."

"Just a little?" A*ha*! My first joke. And Charlie totally laughed which made me laugh and I knew my dimple was showing which meant that this was my first real smile since leaving for this place. Did I make a friend? Was it really as easy and painless as mom explained?

Chapter 2

I Want To Be In Pictures!

Note to self: Don't talk with exclamation marks.

ABOUT FIVE minutes later I was standing in a very crowded room in the recreation center. There were so many campers that I lost sight of Charlie and was jammed against the wall by a giggling group of delighted girls. "Excuse me," I actually grunted. Applause suddenly rang out and I looked to the front of the room as an older couple, clapping along, entered. The woman was very tall with blonde hair combed into a fancy hair style behind her head. The man was the same height and had graying blond hair, but he looked very muscular and healthy. They both wore 'Camp Eerie' shirts and huge smiles. I noticed a lot of grown-ups along the sides of the walls and they made us all sit down pretzel-style.

The man began to speak. "Welcome to Camp Eerie!" Applause rang out again. I would have been left out if I didn't clap as well. "I'm Greg Reeves, owner and director of the camp and this is my lovely bride of twenty-seven years, Elsa. We'll be here for anything you campers may need. We want you to have a fun time so let's make this summer even more memorable than the last!"

Applause.

"Let's make it count!"

More clapping.

"We have a fun summer planned for you all don't we Elsa?"

"Oh yes, we have great times. There's kayaking, horseback riding, hiking and don't forget the many art projects and our nightly hymn sing by the bonfire!"

"We'll end with our annual dance and obstacle course race!"

"And don't forget the annual camp play!" There were a few extra rounds of applause for that last announcement. My hands really hurt at this point.

Mr. Reeves continued. "We want you all to have a fun time. There are quiet, sitting down activities in the morning.."

"And fun physical activities in the afternoon."

"There will be fun-"

"Fun-"

"Fun!"

"Oh and did I mention fun?" Elsa joked and they both laughed together. I thought *my* parents were corny? This couple took the prize.

"Hey now we've got something special planned for tonight. This is no Fourth of July if it doesn't have fireworks or a barbecue! Isn't that right Elsa?"

"It sure is. We always take pride in being Americans so when you go to your trunks make sure you pull out the red, white and blue and join us tonight for the Welcome Party! Let's get to it!"

"And hey, if you're not having fun," he looked at his wife and they both said together, "than our job isn't done."

The entire room broke into a rowdy applause and Mr. and Mrs. Reeves started to sing…

"Oh our Camp Eerie,
We hold you in our hearts!
And we can't live without you,
We never want to part!"

Most returning campers and teachers began singing the song and I had to fight off the urge to sing along.

***

After I got my welcome packet, I looked through the papers. Most talked about the rules and the dos and don'ts and the main paper told me which bunk I'd be staying in.

"Bunk thirteen," I whispered to myself and looked up at the cloudy sky, convinced for sure now that I'd never see the sun again. I held onto my packet and backpack and started my walk towards the bunks. Surprise, surprise, it was another long and scary path. But this one was even *scarier* because the trees were really black and old. I followed a random group of girls as they entered the thick forest. I suddenly wished that I was walking with a big group of girls. After walking for about five minutes, I started to see short wooden posts planted into the ground.

The first one was on the left and it said that Bunks One through Six were that way and several girls broke apart from their group and went down the left path. As I passed the opening, I noticed six pink and tidy little bunks. So. The bunks weren't as bad as I thought. They even had cute shutter thingy's and pots of flowers. I was so happy that I wouldn't be sleeping in a cave!

A few minutes later, on the opposite side of the path, I saw the same sign for Bunks Seven through Twelve. Girls started cheering excitedly as they bounced down the road. I continued walking and realized that I was all alone now. The hair on the back of my neck stood up, but I tried to shrug off the feeling of loneliness.

Five minutes later I saw a tiny little sign that read Bunk Thirteen. *Finally*! But that was it; just Bunk Thirteen. A really bad feeling entered my stomach at this point. I ducked under a thick branch and finally saw my bunk house. If I said 'Oh my goodness!' it would totally be an understatement. This had to have been the scariest bunk I'd ever seen! And I saw twelve so I would know.

The bunk looked taller...older...very old. The white paint on the wood was chipped and worn down. There were no cute little blue shutters or hanging flower beds below the windows. It didn't help that it stood at the top of the hill like some sort of fortress. It *also* didn't help that sitting right in front of it was a mammoth of a tree.

I didn't think it should even be considered a tree since it was so thick and twisted. The branches lay over the roof of the bunk and reached out like claws as it ended on the other side. It wasn't even brown...it was more black than anything. Just as I backed away and turned around to run for my life, the screen door squeaked open and a ball of sunshine came barreling out.

"Hello! You must be Calliope." An older girl by maybe three or four years walked onto the big, wide wooden porch.

"How did you...how did you know my name?" I was starting to think that mom and dad put me on the wrong bus.

"Be*cause*!" She took a pen out from her bright blonde hair and checked the clipboard in her hands. "You're the very last one to get here. We've been waiting for you! Come on in!"

I took that moment to try and relax and told myself to keep it together. I was just too tense from my first look at the bunk. I really hoped the inside wasn't as scary. I walked up the stairs and onto the porch and the girl smiled even wider. I'd never seen so many teeth on one person. "I'm Mary, your honorary bunk captain! I'll be helping you get settled in. So put on that shiny smile and get ready to have a great-tastic day!"

Really, the enthusiasm was a bit much, but nonetheless I took a deep breath and walked inside. Thankfully, the inside of the bunk looked nothing like the outside. The floors were polished hardwood and the walls were lined with scenic pictures taken around the camp grounds. There were pink lacy curtains on the windows and it smelled like pine.

On the left wall, there was a bunk bed, on the right wall, there was another bunk bed and straight ahead there was another bunk bed. My luggage was tucked on the bottom of the bunk bed on the right wall. I immediately sat down on it and sighed. Really, I've never sighed so much in my life.

"Why so glum?" came the chirping bird Mary. Her voice was high, musical and at the moment, *oh-so* annoying! "You know what they say? Turn that frown upside down, but not too long or you'll get a head rush!" Mary laughed at her own joke and continued on to check on another girl. I shook my head and started to unpack my things.

"Hey there Ca-*lee*-oh-*pee*."

I looked up and saw a face hanging upside down from the top bunk. I couldn't believe who it was. "Charlie, we're bunk mates? Cool."

"I know." Charlie jumped down and sat next to me. "I saw your name on the list and basically jumped with delight.

"We should have stuck together. I felt so alone." I couldn't believe I actually admitted that, but there it was.

Charlie scratched her cheek. "I suggest we stick together from now on or one of us is bound to become another missing camper."

"Missing camper?" Did she really just say that?

"HEY there camper Charlotte!" Mary came over…*again*. "I've got your camp hat, here ya go! *Oh*! Here's yours too Calliope!"

"Yeah thanks," Charlie muttered. "So anyway, we stick together, pinky deal?" She stuck out her pinky.

I stared at it for a moment and hesitated, but then I thought of what my mom said, to just be myself, and really, it was working for me so far, so I wrapped my pinky around hers and smiled, "Pinky deal."

"Besides," Charlie reasoned, "I don't think this is going to be so bad after all."

"Okay! Listen up all you sunny *faces*!" Mary shouted over the six chattering girls. "It's time to put on your designated shirts and hats and make your way to your first mag-*tastic*, awe-so-*riffic* Camp Eerie activity!"

Charlie's face looked pinched and she muttered to me, "I could be wrong sometimes."

"Did she say that all in one breath?" We heard someone whisper.

The door swung open and all of our breaths stopped when another older girl walked inside. She was thin and her hair was long and full of soft black curls. "Hi, sorry I'm late." She placed her thumbs in the front pockets of her jean shorts and looked at all of us.

"No problem!" Mary chirped. "I was just introducing myself to the girls." She faced us. "I'm Mary Matthews, camp counselor extraordinaire!"

"I'm Madison Ramirez, your other camp counselor."

I couldn't help but admire Madison's pretty face. She had a small brown beauty mark in between the left side of her mouth and chin. I watched as she took the clipboard from Mary and looked it over. Mary took that moment to sing. "Tonight we'll meet up for the Welcome-To-Camp-Eerie party! And this is not just *any* welcome party; it's also a Fourth of July Extravaganza!"

"I can actually see the exclamation marks when she talks," Charlie whispered to me.

"Complete with *fire*works!" Mary continued.

"Why don't we have everyone introduce themselves," Madison said to Mary as she looked at us. The thick black lashes that lined her bright gray eyes turned towards a girl with chin length, dark blonde hair and silver glasses.

"I'm Lane. Nice to meet yo-"

"I'M *Sheila*! *Star* extraordinaire! This is my *third* year here and *I'm* always the star of the annual Camp Eerie play!" Big and loud both inwardly and outwardly; I admired her self-esteem. However, I didn't admire her rudeness to Lane, even though Lane didn't seem to mind. "What's *your* name?" She suddenly turned to me.

I was taken by surprise, but answered, "Callio-"

"*Well* Callio, *I* want to be in pictures!" All of a sudden, Sheila shouted as a flash of light lit up her face. "Ahh!"

Charlie held a Polaroid camera and handed Sheila the picture that slid out. "There ya go. You're in pictures." She let the camera rest around her neck and smiled smugly.

Sheila held the picture and lifted her head high with dignity. The sides of her mouth twitched up and down until finally she recovered and her face became animated again. "We'll be *such* friends!" She said to me, ignoring Charlie completely. "But *please* save yourself some time and embarrassment and *don't* try out for the lead in the play," she looked at the other girls, "you will just be disappointed when I get the roll."

She finally turned to Charlie. "Charlotte; isn't it? You have such *beautiful* brown hair." She flipped some flaming red hair off of her own shoulders and I noticed silver stars dangling from her ears. "*I'd* have brown hair too, but red hair is *much* more interesting." She suddenly turned to another girl. "You like my glitter clip? You know…"

As Sheila continued on and on…and on; all of us girls and the two counselors stood helplessly still. "…and imagine my surprise when I realized that *I* was the best singer in the group!" At the silence that followed, Sheila gasped lightly. "Oh heaven's *me*! The time got away from me." She shrugged at Madison and Mary with a delicate shoulder. "Sorry." Sheila didn't look so sympathetic in my opinion.

Madison raised her perfect black eyebrows. "It's okay. So you're Lane, you're Sheila," she pointed at each girl and then looked at me.

"Calliope Thornton, but everyone can call me Callie."

I looked at Charlie since she was next to me and she introduced herself. "Charlotte Mackenna. Call me Charlie," she pointed at herself with her thumb and looked at the girl beside her, who looked very graceful, almost regal.

Her black hair was in a French braid that started on one side of her head and ended over the shoulder on the opposite side. It fell down until it reached the front of her waist. Her eyes had to have been the brightest green I'd ever seen.

"I am Sofia de V-" she cut herself off and mysterious looks passed between her and Madison. I wasn't sure if anyone else noticed since she quickly continued. "Sofia Smith." She looked at the pretty black girl next to her.

"Saliesha Washington." She had black, chin length hair and large dark brown eyes. She looked very athletic and when she smiled I noticed braces planted proudly on her teeth. She adjusted the sunglasses on the top of her head.

"Good. Now that we're all introduced, we'll lay a few ground rules," Madison announced as she and Mary walked to the dry-erase board and grabbed markers. There was another board next to it with papers thumb-tacked to it; like the rules, words of encouragement and drawings of hearts and stars. "Rule number one." Madison underlined the number one with her blue marker. "You must be in the bunk by ten o'clock. No exceptions."

"Rule number two," Mary sang as she held up two gingers and wiggled them and her eyebrows at the same time. I didn't think anyone could really do that at the same time, but I was just proven wrong. "Cleanliness is friendliness! You'll each have a chore to do for each exciting week. There's a chart on the closet over there which contains all of the cleaning products."

She pointed to a small door with her yellow marker and sang even higher, "Every morning after breakfast is the time to clean your area. So those tummies will be nice and filled and you'll be energized!"

"Rule number three," Madison continued, ignoring Mary's energized speech and sticking to a calm voice. "Respect each other's property…"

For five more minutes, the two counselors continued down the list. There were a lot of rules, but I tried not to think about it too much or I'd start to feel suffocated.

"Finally, we're here to guide and help you through the next eight weeks." Madison's face showed understanding and experience as she spoke and it made me really believe her. "If you ever have a problem or need someone to talk to, you can come to me." Madison's beautiful gray eyes connected with my boring brown eyes.

"Me too!" Mary chimed triumphantly.

"I believe you all have different schedules." Madison put the marker back down and made her way to the door, Mary followed. She placed her thumbs in her jean pockets again and smiled at everyone. "We hope you girls have a great first day. We'll see you at the dining hall so you can energize."

After she walked out of the door, Mary exclaimed, "Have an amazing, *fab*-tastic day!"

All of us started to dig into our bags to find some red, white and blue jeans or shorts. They had given us a bunch of different colored Camp Eerie t-shirts, so I kept it simple and put on my white one with some light blue jean shorts and I tied my mousy brown hair with a red hair band.

Charlie and the rest of the girls kept it simple as well, except for, of course, Sheila. She had stars on every piece of clothing and completed her ensemble with a starry red scarf she tied around her neck. Sheila ran to the mirror to fix up her big, curly and wild red hair. "I have to admit that I would die for Madison's hair…not that there's anything wrong with *mine*, I mean *really,* whoever is thinking *that*?" She quickly snapped her fingers. "Let's be gone Laney."

Lane quickly followed behind without complaint and as Sheila swept out of the cabin, she seemed to have taken all of the sparkle along with her…which might have been a good thing. "Time to get to the main camp for some food," Charlie stated firmly as she put her big camera away and grabbed a smaller, slimmer camera and slipped it into her pocket.

"We'll walk with you guys," Saliesha offered as Sofia nodded behind her. "I do *not* wanna walk down that long path alone."

I so agreed. All four of us kept up a steady chatter on the way back to the main camp grounds; which made the scary, lonely path, not so scary and lonely any longer.

Chapter 3

Welcome to Camp Eerie

Note to Self: Always hold onto your lemonade cup.

AS IT turned out, Sofia and I had our first activity together. The gathering was located in the gardens. To get to the gardens, we had to go through a complicated maze, which consisted of high grassy hedges. Sofia thought it was fun, but I didn't like the feeling of getting lost.

"You just have to trust that the path will bring you to the right place," she explained in a light Spanish accent.

I shook my head. "I can't do that so easily."

"It is not as hard as you think it is. One time, I was lost in the royal garden maze, but I closed my eyes and calmed down a little and soon I was in the right place."

I stared at Sofia. "Did you just say '*royal* garden maze'?" Because I know that's what I heard her say.

"Um…" Sofia looked a bit panicked, "never mind. We will be late, let's go!"

A few minutes later we entered the garden. There was a beautiful fountain surrounded by a skinny little stone path and surrounded by neat patches of grass. The scenery was actually kind of beautiful. There were flowers growing everywhere and the smell was earthy and fresh. I knew that my mom would have loved this place. I stopped myself for a second, realizing that I've been calling a lot of things here 'beautiful'. It was just the first day and I didn't want to like the camp as much as I was.

"Callie."

I snapped out of my thoughts and saw Sofia nodding over to a shady spot on the grass under a tree. I sat down crisscross applesauce and started to poke at the holes in my jean shorts. An older woman fluttered in with a boy camper carrying a folding chair behind her. He set it down in front of the fountain, facing all of us and made his way out.

She sat down primly and properly, crossing her ankles and clasping her hands in her lap. She reminded me of a warm and loving old grandmother. She even had on a high collared, long-sleeved dress that looked too thick to wear in the summertime. "Okay dearies, shall we begin?" She asked in an upper class English accent. I sat up straighter, feeling the need to be proper all of a sudden.

"Yes," the campers all said at once.

Her pointy nose stuck into the air as she furrowed her white eyebrows and asked, "What?"

Some of the campers looked at each other.

"Oh dear me, yes of course," she clicked her tongue and gave a warning glance and a smile. "I knew what you all meant. Shall we begin?"

This time none of the campers said anything.

"We shall start with me. I am Edina Copperpot, nee Hollingsworth of Chipping Campden, Gloucestershire, England. I am not ashamed to say that I am sixty-four years young," she giggled to herself. "I have two wonderfully grown children and four delightful grandchildren…er, or is it six?"

"Piece of gum?" Sofia whispered in my ear. I nodded and she handed over a stick of gum while Mrs. Copperpot continued. I noticed that the wrapper was different than what I was used to seeing. It was designed with stripes and polka dots and the words were in Spanish. I looked up at her curiously and she tried to hold back a laugh. "It's from my home. Strawberry flavored."

"Cool, yeah, thanks."

"OH! Thank you for volunteering young lady! Go ahead now and stand up."

I looked up and saw that Mrs. Copperpot was talking to me and everyone was looking…at *me*. And since the word 'me' was the last word on my mind, "M-me?"

"Why yes dear. You *did* just volunteer did you not? Stand up now and tell us all about yourself. Don't be shy!"

Slowly... *very* slowly, I stood up, feeling like one of those frogs in science class. I placed some hair behind my ear and cleared my throat. "I'm Callie." I sat back down quickly.

"Oh no, no, *no* dear!" Mrs. Copperpot complained. "Tell us some *more* about yourself."

I really didn't like that all of the campers were still looking at me. *Really*? Why did they have to look? I thought they got a good look the first time. "There's not really much to tell." There wasn't really.

"Nonsense! What it your full name? Age? What are your dreams and aspirations?" Her voice sang out in wonder.

I sighed because that's what I did best in stressful situations and stood back up. I tried to talk with the speed of lightning. "Calliope Thornton, thirteen and I really have no dreams or aspirations." I sat back down with a thump and I think I sat on a rock.

Giggles came from two girls and one of them raised her hand. "Mrs. Copperpot, may I?"

Still confused about what just happened, Mrs. Copperpot opened and closed her mouth like a fish out of water. "Er...by all means dearie..."

The girl stood up, folded her hands neatly in front of her and stood as straight as could be. Pushing black straight hair behind her shoulder with disgusting feminine grace, she started, "I am Gwendolyn Mariella *Merchant*. *I* am thirteen," she looked at me, "and a *half*." She looked back at Mrs. Copperpot. "My dream is to be a loving mother and lawyer and prosecute against unruly and rebellious people to serve justice for one nation under God."

A resounding round of applause came from Mrs. Copperpot. "*Very* well done dearie. And *that* is how an introduction is to be made!"

I briefly wondered how I got myself into this situation. I glanced over at Gwen and saw a smug grin on her face. Okay then, if they want an introduction, they're going to get one. I cleared my throat, stood up and with my head held high I began. "I am Calliope Thalia Thornton. I am thirteen years, six months and nine days old," I threw a pointed look at Gwen. "My dream is to be a defense attorney so I can prove innocence against the gruesome and disorderly prosecution, indivisible, with liberty and just for all." I placed my hand over my heart and sang, "Oh say can you see, by the dawns early light, once so proudly we held…"

Sofia stood up and placed her hand over her heart as well. Slowly, the rest of the campers did the same and Mrs. Copperpot (still looking confused) stood up as well. And as I continued the song and hit every note (in my opinion) correctly, it was apparent to everyone exactly who I was.

*****

I walked into the dining hall and almost collapsed with relief when I saw Charlie and the others girls at the lunch table a few hours later.

"Callie!" Charlie called out. "Over here!"

Wow, I was so amazed that I was actually being called over to a lunch table. Back home at school…well…there's no need to think about my school. Not here. I waved, got my dinner tray and made a bee-line straight for my bunk mates. I couldn't believe I made a few friends; it happened so fast. "I'm so happy to see you guys." I sat across from Charlie and settled next to Saliesha.

"First activity that bad?" Charlie asked in her dry tone of voice.

Sofia cut in and said softly, "Not a chance, you all should have seen Callie during our first activity when we had to introduce ourselves. She was amazing."

Swallowing the bite of her apple, Charlie said, "Well fill us in. Don't leave us in suspense."

"Come on, it was nothing!" I was pretty sure that my face was a blotchy shade of red. I looked down right away.

Saliesha piped in. "Oh please Sofia, forget Callie. Why don't you tell them how 'amazing' you were during swimming?"

"Please, don't." Sofia looked down at her macaroni salad and turned a slight shade of pink. I wondered how our table looked with all of these different colored faces.

Saliesha ignored Sofia and decided to fill everyone in. "We had a 'trust' session before actually swimming, you know, to teach us to trust our partner before we get in the water. I had to close my eyes and fall backwards with the *trust* that Sofia would catch me." Saliesha rolled her eyes.

Mouth filled with apple, Charlie had to ask, "Did she catch you?"

Sofia squeezed her eyes shut. I had never seen anyone turn so pink before. "You did catch her...*right*?" I knew that was a dumb question by the look on her face.

Sofia's green eyes flew open. "It was an accident! I thought I saw something across the river and I became distracted." I gasped and Charlie almost choked on her apple.

"Oh, it was *so* important that you *had* to send me flying to the ground," Saliesha shook her head as she spoke.

Sofia looked uncomfortable. "No...I thought I saw someone..."

"Give up the goods, will ya?" Charlie asked with interest. "Who did you see?"

Sofia took a deep breath. "I have been hearing a lot about a missing girl. She went missing more than twenty years ago."

Charlie rolled her eyes. "They tell ghost stories to all the new campers. It's just to get them too scared to sleep on the first night."

"Look, I know what I saw."

"Why don't we change the subject," Saliesha suggested. "We'll be mingling with the boys tonight after all." She wagged her brows up and down.

"What are you talking about?"

Saliesha answered me, "The Camp Eerie Welcome Party, duh." She rolled her eyes...*again*.

"I am so tired, I do not feel like going to a party," Sofia said softly.

"Oh come on, there's going to be music and dancing and games," Saliesha explained.

"Yeah, really crazy party," Charlie agreed.

Backs leaning on the wall in the recreation center; Sofia, Charlie and me drank our lemonade from little foam cups. "Some 'crazy' party." I glanced at Charlie and smiled.

"Well I didn't know their idea of music was easy listening. I feel like I'm standing in an elevator." No one was dancing; the teachers and camp counselors were laughing and mingling on one side of the large room. On our side, different groups of campers chatted.

"This has to be the most boring party I've ever been to and I have been to many," Sofia said quietly.

Charlie took her small black camera out of her pocket and snapped a picture of Sofia standing with me. When she pulled the camera away from her face she whined. "Come on, it works way better when you guys smile."

"Great memory of The-Most-Boring-Party-Ever. Come on Callie, let's smile." The small dimples under the sides of Sofia's lips came through as she smiled.

"Well if it's boring than I don't think we should be smiling." I made a plain, bored looking face. Sofia couldn't help but laugh and tried to copy me as best as she could. "Come on Charlie, take the picture," I said through my clenched mouth. Sofia's eyes were shut tight as she tried to hold down her laughter and Charlie snapped the picture.

"Now *this* is a party." Charlie smiled and Sofia finally burst out laughing.

I giggled. "I'm going to refill on the lemonade."

"Hey, I can use some more too," Charlie called out.

"I got it." As I walked through the thick crowd towards the refreshment table, I passed by the teachers.

"Camper Gwen!" Mrs. Copperpot came over to me while adjusting her glasses.

"Calliope," I corrected, thinking how awful it felt to be confused for Gwendolyn. I wondered how the older woman didn't suffer from overheating with that thick velvet dress on.

"Oh right dear, sorry. This is Mrs. Bijou, the gymnastics activities director."

Mrs. Bijou smiled graciously and corrected Mrs. Copperpot, "The sewing and arts director."

"Hello."

"I'm hoping that you've signed up for sewing and art class," sparkling white pearls shone bright from around Mrs. Bijou's necklace. While all of the other teachers wore a Camp Eerie shirt and shorts, these two ladies clearly did not get the memo. Mrs. Bijou dressed in a fancy blue dress adorned with white pearls and sequins and her hair was held up by a few red feathers. She obviously sewed the dress herself.

"Can't wait," I answered with a tight smile.

"Go off and enjoy your birthday party dearie," Mrs. Copperpot sang and as I walked away I heard her say, "Camper Calliope is *very* patriotic…"

It wasn't my birthday, but at least she remembered my name. I filled two cups with pink lemonade and when I turned around to walk back a hand reached out and grabbed one of the cups right out of my hands. "Hey-!"

"Shh, just keep walking."

I felt myself being pushed to walk and glanced at who was pushing me. He was a boy! And he was drinking the lemonade I'd just poured. "But that's-"

"Just keep walking." He led me to a window and looked down at me. "Is she still looking at me?" He closed his eyes tightly.

"Who?" I looked behind this rude, mystery camper and realized right away what was going on and who he was talking about. Sheila was staring fire at his back. I thought I literally saw steam coming from her nose and ears. The feathers from her pink boa were falling all over the floor. "Yes," I answered.

"Just laugh," his bright blue eyes shot into my boring brown ones, "really loud."

I laughed so loud that a few heads turned in our direction

"Please stop now," he begged.

I stopped right away. "Sorry."

"Is she gone now?"

I peeked behind him and saw in time as Sheila huffed and stormed to the other side of the room. "Yes."

He sighed with relief. "Thanks, I owe you one."

"Nah, consider yourself debt free," I smiled and saw him glance at the dimple in my cheek.

He smiled back at me. "I'm Brandon." His hair was pushed over the front of his forehead. He had a ton of really nice blond/brownish hair.

"Great hair."

"Huh?"

I felt my heart stop. And I don't mean like 'ha, ha, my heart stopped!' I mean I literally couldn't feel it. My face went completely numb. Okay, did I really just say that out loud? Had to cover up fast. "Calliope. My name is Calliope."

"Hey, that's a great name."

"Callie." Someone sang.

I turned to see the smug smiles of Charlie, Saliesha and Sofia. "We're gonna start walking to the lake to see the fireworks. Care to join us? That is, if you don't wanna walk down there by yourself." Charlie couldn't take the smug smile off of her face. I had a pretty good idea of how to wipe it off.

"Uh, right!" I looked back at Brandon. "I've got to go, my camp is having fireworks. I mean, you're at the same camp so you would know, *duh,* because if you weren't really a camper here it would be *really* awkward, not that it isn't awkward right now in this moment. I'm pretty much hoping the floor would open and swallow me, but then that would be even more embarrassing."

I heard a few coughs from the girls. I couldn't even bare to look at Brandon just then so I looked at his sneakers. "So right, I've got to go."

"Hey, thanks again." I looked up and saw him smiling at me. I was pretty breathless for a moment. "Hope to see you again."

"Same here." I turned and walked out of the rec center as fast as my feet could take me.

The laughter from the girls tore through the rare chill of the night.

*****

"I am telling you Saliesha, I saw her."

Sheila's dramatic sigh was heard from the back of the group. "There *is* no Camp Eerie ghost. I truly wish they would stop telling the new kids this outlandish lie."

"I can't believe I'm saying this, but I agree with Sheila." Charlie sighed.

I thought I'd enjoy the fireworks that night, but it was ruined when I thought about my family. Seeing the colorful bursts of light shoot through the air, I could just see them at the beach back home.

My mom and dad, as usual, would be holding each other. Adele would be giggling with Jelly Bean and I would be lying on the wet sand as I watched the show. We'd all clean up, head home and laugh about everything that happened that day. Then my mom and dad would carry us to our beds because we'd fall asleep on the sofas. I was missing it all.

"But I *did* see her." Sofia insisted.

"Yeah, my *backside* knows you did," Saliesha complained as she reminded Sofia of when she dropped her onto the ground.

"Well Sofia, indulge us. What was she wearing?" Charlie teased and jumped over a tree root. The sounds of crickets and other wood creatures filled the air.

"Probably something so completely devoid of all fashion taste that the other ghosts couldn't stand to be near her. That's also probably why she was by herself," Sheila explained.

"That answers it," Charlie announced. "The ghost was raiding Sheila's closet."

I covered my mouth to stop the giggles bubbling in my throat.

"Har har, you've got your laugh for the day. You must feel incredibly significant to the world now," Sheila stated haughtily.

"I do not have to explain anything to you all. If you do not believe me; fine." Sofia defended. "You will see for yourselves." Sofia crossed her arms and quickly walked ahead of the group. Saliesha looked and me, and Charlie shrugged.

When we made it to the scary looking bunk (which I tried to ignore was even scarier in the dark!) Charlie stated, "I am going to crash into my bed and pass out."

"Amen sister," Saliesha yawned as she climbed up the porch steps. When Sofia flicked the lights on we were greeted by bright orange sticky notes all over the bunk.

"What on *earth*?" Sheila asked in horror and she read a note. "'Dear Sheila, we were bored so we decided to take a walk. Love, Your Shoes.'*?*" She looked up in disgust and demanded, "*What* is the meaning of *this*?"

Charlie read another note aloud. "'Dear Charlie, we blankets and pillows were bored so we took a walk to the lake. We hear canoe rides are fun.'" She raised her brows and looked up, "Oh boy."

Saliesha read another one. "'Dear Saliesha, we got tired of waiting here all alone so we decided to take a swim. Love, Your Luggage.'?!" She looked around and waved her finger with an attitude. "Oh *no* they *did*n't!"

We looked around and found more of our things missing. All with sticky notes detailing of their "walk" to the lake and in a canoe. "You know what this means right?" Charlie asked us.

"We've been pranked," I replied in shock.

"By none other than our wonderful camp counselors," Sheila exploded in anger.

Saliesha sighed. "Let's go get them." She started walking back outside, Sofia followed, not speaking to anyone.

"I can*not* live without my facial creams. If they got wet, *someone* is going to pay *literally* and *figuratively*." Sheila stormed out into the dark night.

"Well," Charlie added and smiled at me. "Welcome to Camp Eerie!"

Chapter 4

I Think You're Onto Something

Note to Self: Never wear vintage shorts when falling down a hill.

THE BUGLE played a loud rendition of Reveille, signaling everyone to wake up. When Mary and Madison walked in and were told about the prank that was pulled on all of us, they looked innocently shocked…a little too innocently shocked in my opinion. We all just grumbled, too exhausted to fight. It had taken all six of us a little more than an hour to find, retrieve and lug back all of our belongings. Charlie and I were soaking wet since we were voted to go swim for the canoe…in the middle of the dark lake.

I washed up, saw the Flag Raising, ate breakfast and did my chore in the bunk house. I played tennis and met a few more friendly campers in the process. I had never really been so active back home and realized how much I'd been missing out. It was only the second day here, yet I felt that I'd already made myself at home. I tried not to get too comfortable though, in case something bad happened. But I really couldn't think of anything going wrong. I'd never been so optimistic either.

My ponytail swung back and forth behind my head as I went to show Mrs. Bijou the disaster I made with my sewing. We'd all been working on aprons for an hour and I honestly didn't give it any proper attention. My mind had been on food and what I'd do later in the day. All of the other campers turned in their aprons and ran as fast as they could to lunch. I turned in mine and started to leave when Mrs. Bijou's hand grabbed my arm. "Camper Calliope, may I have a word?"

I sniffed and gave her a smile. "Yes Mrs. Bijou?"

"I have been working at this camp for more than twenty years." I scanned Mrs. Bijou's prim and proper face and continued to listen.

"And in that twenty years I have never come across a face I did not recognize." She began to neatly fold all of the aprons as she spoke. "And you bear a striking resemblance to a camper I knew…" she trailed off. I stood there awkwardly, not sure whether I should say something or not. "And never in my years have I received a *sloppier* apron." She held up my so-called apron.

"Well…" I began. "What's wrong with it?" I asked brightly.

"Camper Calliope, I know my aprons and I am pretty sure that *this* here resembles a hat."

I big my bottom lip and shrugged. "To-may-to, to-mah-to."

"Excuse me?"

"Well, *you* see a hat and *I* see an apron," I explained cheerfully.

She shook her head. "No, no. I-" Mrs. Bijou put her hand up and stopped what appeared to be an incoming lecture due to the sound of my stomach growling. "I'm sorry…"

"Goodness me, go and eat." She put the offending garment down, looked back up and gave a hopeful smile. "Hopefully we can try it again another time."

"Yes Mrs. Bijou." And with that, I turned and ran for the dining hall.

I spotted Charlie and Saliesha at the lunch table. Sofia was nowhere to be seen. I joined them, wasting no time devouring my turkey and cheese sandwich. I never really liked turkey, but after a morning filled with activity, the stomach pretty much wants everything. "Wow, take it easy Callie, I'm not certified for CPR yet," Charlie grinned and her mouth turned into a smug smile. Her thick chestnut-colored hair was up in a sloppy ponytail and her jeans had holes in them. I wondered how she still looked so pretty.

"I'm stark raving famished!" I muttered between quick bites.

"You'd think they never fed us here," Saliesha added as she watched me with fascination.

"Well, we have to get our energy up anyway, we have hiking after lunch," Charlie explained.

My mouth was full of food, but I still tried to talk. "We 'ave a ak-shi-vi-jee to-ge-der?"

"Yeah we do, finally."

"The fact that you knew exactly what she said amazes me," Saliesha laughed.

I swallowed a big lump of food and asked Saliesha, "Where's Sofia?"

"She's still pretty upset about yesterday. She-"

"Upset about what?" Sofia asked as she sat down with her tray of food.

Saliesha gave her a wary smile, "Nothing."

"Are you gonna eat that?" I pointed at Saliesha's cup of applesauce.

"She's worse than me and that's saying a lot," Charlie shook her head as Saliesha giggled and handed me the applesauce. "We have to find a way to get back at Mary and Madison."

"I know! I can't believe they got us on the *first* day!" Saliesha exclaimed.

"So didn't see that coming," I added. I've been pranked by Adele more times than I cared to admit. How I didn't see this one coming is beyond me.

"That was the point. We wouldn't think they'd prank us on the first day. That's why it was so genius," Charlie explained and threw a fist into her other hand.

"I did not know they were allowed to prank us in that way," Sofia said.

"That's the beauty of camp life I guess and we were played for fools," Saliesha shook her head.

"Well, we're getting them back. When they least expect it. It's gonna be epic." Charlie pursed her lips and nodded.

"They will be expecting retaliation. You do realize that right?" Again, I know this from experience.

"Well, we'll need some help getting what we need." Charlie decided.

"What is going through that mind of yours? You look down right scheming." Saliesha couldn't help but say.

"Oh you'll see."

There was suddenly a loud bang from the door hitting the wall as it opened, followed by the sparkle of the one and only Sheila. "*WHERE* is the bulletin board? A star is ready to be re*born*!" Sheila wore the same pink feather boa from the welcome party the night before.

Her pink camp T-shirt and jeans had been bedazzled with hundreds of sequins and her flaming red hair seemed higher than the day before. Lane followed behind, pushing up her glasses repeatedly since she never held her head high. Everyone in the dining hall stared as Sheila and Lane walked up to the bulletin board. The board was full of sign-up sheets for various activities such as the talent show, an art contest and, not to be forgotten, the camp play.

"Laney! Pen." Sheila lifted her hand and without a glance at her friend, snatched a glittery pen from her hand.

"Scalpel please," Charlie muttered and we giggled.

Like an autograph and taking up the entire page, Sheila signed her full name to audition for the camp play. "I don't even know *why* I have to audition. I *always* get the lead role." She turned with a grand flourish and gazed upon everyone in the dining hall as if she were the queen observing the work of her peasants. Chin high, she made a big *harrumph!* and said haughtily, "Let's go Laney. We shall eat our lunch in the private dining hall."

"She means the bathroom," Charlie muttered and the girls giggled.

"Why dosh Jay-nee fa-wo?" I asked with a mouth full of food.

Saliesha looked at Charlie for translation, but she shook her head, "Now that, I didn't get."

I swallowed and asked again. "Why does Laney follow Sheila around like that?"

"Because Sheila needs someone to make her confidence high. Lane is an easy target," Charlie shrugged and took a sip from her carton of milk.

"It's a real shame cause I think Lane is a real nice girl," Saliesha added.

"We should not be gossiping," Sofia said quietly.

We stopped talking and ate the rest of our food quietly.

*****

As Charlie and I followed the other campers on the hike, we updated each other on our mornings. Once we were deep in the forest, we heard someone clear a throat with exaggeration. Charlie turned her head and halfway there she snapped it back ahead, "*Oh no.*"

"Ha-*hum*," the clearing of the throat became even louder than before.

"Callie, do not turn around, I beg you." I couldn't help but turn around after she said not to! Huge mistake. I groaned, but stopped before the person in question could hear. I should have turned before seeing red in my peripheral vision.

"Cal*lio*pe and Charlotte, how devastatingly wonderful it is to see the both of you."

"Likewise," Charlie replied and muttered to me, "at least the *devastating* part." She cleared her throat, "So no feather boa for hiking?"

"No, but I'll need it tonight to block my sensitive ears from Sofia's *ghastly* tales of that missing girl."

"I agree," Charlie nodded.

"Come on guys, behind every tall tale there is some truth to it." I skipped over a tree root as I reasoned with them.

Charlie gave a disbelieving laugh, "Right. I'll believe it when I see it."

"That is not always true Charlotte," Sheila shook her red hair. "For example, I have so much sparkle, it's ubiquitous," she twirled her hand around in the air. "You can just feel it, but you cannot *see* it, however."

I'm sure I looked amused as I nodded slowly. "Sheila is right…on the seeing it to believe it part…"

Charlie gave up and shrugged, "Sure."

"The point I'm trying make," I continued, "is that I think one of us should get to the bottom of how this story started circulated."

"Like I've said before," Charlie rolled her dark blue eyes up to the sky, "they're just rumors to scare campers like us. Like *you*. Looks like it's working."

"Not a chance!" I jumped over a tree root.

Just then, there was a scream and we turned to see Sheila sprawled on the dirt ground. "I tripped over this *horrendous* tree root!" Sheila made an extra show of getting up from the ground and wiped her pink shorts, "I fervently hope this hike is worth wearing these unearthly sneakers. I'm not used to wearing such unpleasant footwear."

Charlie opened her mouth to say something snarky, I was sure of it, so I covered her mouth with my hand. With her famous *harrumph!* Sheila stuck her chin into the air and continued walking on the trail.

Half an hour later, we were in one of the deepest parts of the forest. The trail bent sideways and circle ways and was thin, then wide and then twisted. Charlie and me hung in the back of the group, talking and admiring all of the sights in the brooding and mysterious forest. Two girls; one blonde and one brunette (but with the same face) walked next to us. Our instructor, Mr. Mendel, pointed out different flowers, plants and creatures that lived in the forest; to which an appalled and shocked squeal came flowing from Sheila.

The two girls laughed and the blonde one said aloud, "She has to win for the funniest camper here."

The brunette one added, "Definitely."

Charlie heard and said happily, "I couldn't agree with you more."

The two similar faces looked over her and the blonde one laughed. "See? We have a voter already."

"Let's get the petition going then."

"Hey, what's your name?" The blonde one asked Charlie.

"I'm Charlie and this is Callie."

"The blonde girl smiled. "I'm Carrie and this is my twin sister Liz."

We looked at them curiously. "Twins?" We asked at the same time. Carrie had long, straight blonde hair, light blue eyes and a small black beauty mark next to her right eye.

Liz had long wavy black hair, light brown eyes and her beauty mark was next to her left eye. The only similarity to prove they were twins was the shape of their face. They had the same nose, mouth and even the same thick eyebrows.

Knowing what we were thinking, Carrie laughed out loud. "It's called 'fraternal twins'."

"We're just really glad our parents didn't make our names rhyme."

"Like Macy and Stacy."

"Starla and Darla."

"You know; names like that," Carrie said and looked like she shivered at the thought.

Charlie nodded. "Yeah that's not cool. That's definitely something to be glad about."

A few minutes later we were shown a nice spot in the middle of the forest with a spectacular view of half the camp down below.

"Alright everyone, you're free to roam around or rest. We'll meet back up on this spot in fifteen minutes," Mr. Mendel announced and started showing a few campers some rare bird nests.

Being so high, I closed my eyes and enjoyed the light breeze that hit my face. It was a welcome feeling since the day was so hot and muggy. I leaned my head against a tree and smiled as I looked out at the view. In the distance, I saw the humongous camp lake, complete with rowers and sail boats.

I thought I heard something on the hill below and looked down to see a figure running so quickly through the trail, it was almost...*ghostly*. And all I could think about was Sofia and the ghost that she saw. My eyes grew wide in shock and just then, Charlie touched my shoulder.

I didn't know it was her at first and my first instinct was to jump and holler. My foot slid off the side of the hill and I went tumbling down, but not before grabbing onto Charlie's shirt to help me stay up. It didn't work. So Charlie came down the hill with me.

Sheila was right behind and Charlie grabbed onto her shirt and ended up pulling *her* down the hill as well. I felt like I was rolling down forever before finally landing on some hard, dirty ground. I groaned and pulled some leaves out of my mouth. What was worse, I had a few scrapes on my knees. They burned!

Charlie's back was sprawled on the dirty ground and she groaned. "You okay Cal?"

I was touched to know that Charlie was truly concerned, but I winced at the soreness I felt on my legs and arms. "I'm fine. You?"

"I'm not gonna lie, I've been better."

I looked around and saw the offending little rock that caused the nasty scrape on my knee. I got up, walked to it and kicked it over. "This rock did most of the damage." I grunted as it rolled away.

"My vintage shorts!" Sheila wailed, gripping her beloved shorts in horror. Her face turned the color of her hair.

"Nothing lasts forever Sheila." Charlie dusted her own shorts and blew some hair out of her face.

Staring at the spot where the rock once was, I noticed something red sticking up from the ground. Without saying another word, I bent down and started to dig.

"What on earth are you doing?" Charlie bent down beside me.

"There's something under the dirt." I grunted as I tried to dig out the hard dirt.

"Sheila would catch a fit if she saw your nails right now," Charlie smirked and crossed her arms.

"Actually," Sheila bragged as she finally got up. She shook the leaves out of her big hair as she walked towards us, "In some countries, dirt is very good for exfoliation, most specifically for the nail beds."

Charlie ignored Sheila and looked down at the ground. "You're right. I see it too." She began to help me dig.

"You know, Mr. Mendel is probably looking for us." Sheila continued to dust every speck of dirt off of her clothes. "And besides, we fell down a tiny little hill," she justified with her nose in the air, "it won't do to look as though we've fallen into a treacherous abyss." She looked down at her grass stained pink shorts and let out a whimper.

Charlie and I finally got to the bottom and lifted out a small red box. It looked very old, like it had been buried in the ground for a number of years. There were patterns of faded gold leaves all over with a gold opening snap. I wondered how long it was buried in the dirt.

"Seriously Callie, what are you waiting for? Open it." Charlie was excited with curiosity while I stared at it, dumbfounded.

"Oh, right." I furrowed my eyebrows as I carefully opened the old box.

"You both are taking a *mighty* long time," Sheila huffed. "What did you find anyway?" She stomped over and looked on, pretending she wasn't interested.

The first thing I pulled out was a flatted purple-pinkish wild flower. I handed it to Charlie and pulled out a faded picture. It looked like a girl with wild brown hair, but her face had faded with time and some water damage. Charlie put her head next to mine. "She's wearing camp clothes."

I looked hard, wracking my brain for answers. "It looks like an eighties hairstyle maybe."

Sheila bent down. "Let me see that," she snatched the picture from my hand and held it up to her face. "Her hair doesn't look all that great."

"It's better than yours," Charlie muttered.

"What was that?" Sheila asked with a face that knew Charlie was being snarky again.

I snatched the picture back and flipped it around. "Nineteen-eighty...the rest is faded." I looked into the box, "Look at this; a note." I handed the box to Charlie and opened the tiny piece of torn paper. "'The other half of my heart is here.'" I looked up and then hesitated before asking, "Do you think this has anything to do with the missing girl?"

Charlie and Sheila both groaned, "Cal, not you. Of all the people to get pulled into that story-not you." Charlie stood up and crossed her arms.

I decided at that moment not to tell them about the probable ghost I saw running through that very trail.

"I am SO done!" Sheila sniffed. "My *feet* are swollen from this *horrid* hike. I'm all dirty from playing Secret Spy with you two," she sniffed again and her eyes watered; her voice broke, "*And my vintage shorts-*"

"Ohhh!" Charlie groaned. "Listening to this is worse than falling."

Sheila continued on as if she didn't hear her. "Now you've found some *ugly* old box that means absolutely nothing-" she gasped...but this was a different gasp. Her hands shot up in delight and her eyes literally sparkled. She looked by my feet and we followed her gaze. "That is the most *magical*, most *beautiful*, most *dazzling*, most *divine* bracelet I have ever been so fortunate enough to see in my entire life!" She picked up the gold charm bracelet and gazed at it with wonder.

"It must have fallen from the box." I reached out to grab the bracelet and Sheila pulled it away from me. She held it against her heart protectively.

"I saw it *first*! You can keep that ugly old box, but the bracelet is *mine*."

I shook my head, fuming now. "I'm trying to find out who it belongs to-"

"Why?! It's probably been in the ground for *thousands* of years!" Charlie rolled her eyes.

"Nobody wants it anymore! After all, it was buried in the dirt!" Sheila continued.

"Let her have the bracelet Callie," Charlie begged just to get Sheila off of our backs.

I pinched my face, trying to decide to agree, but Sheila chimed in. "It's not up to *her* to *let* me have it." She started back up the hill and then dramatically turned back around. "Have fun with your silly 'ghost' investigation." She did what she did well and that was to stick her nose up in the air.

Just then, we heard Mr. Mendel's voice. "Hey, you girls okay?"

"Yes," me and Charlie called out.

She tripped. "I may need a rope to help pull me up Mr. Mendel!"

Charlie put the picture back into the box and turned to go up the hill, "You coming Callie?"

I looked up at Sheila, who was already wearing the bracelet, "Yeah." I stared at the letter as I walked and noticed an inscription at the very bottom, near a tear, 'C & F. I made a mental note, tucked the paper into my pocket and climbed up the hill.

I didn't talk to Charlie for the remainder of the hike or when we went to the bunk for a quick snack and a change of clothes for swimming. For one, I was really thinking about the box and all of the things inside of it. I wondered if it really *did* have something to do with the missing girl. I thought about the figure running through the trail. Was it really a ghost or just my imagination? Was Sofia right after all? Would Charlie turn on me and start poking fun with the other girls?

I didn't even realize that I was already at the lake. Charlie came next to me. "Callie, are you angry with me about the box thing?"

The instructor was a very athletic looking woman I remembered seeing on the camp bus that first day. She spoke loudly as we gathered next to the lake. "Good afternoon campers," she looked around, her blonde ponytail whipped behind her cap. "I'm Ms. Davies, your swimming instructor. We're going to have a great summer and you'll learn a lot of new things. First things first, let me go over some safety rules…"

I whispered back to Charlie, "Isn't it the other way around?"

Charlie crossed her arms and gave me a face. "What are you talking about?"

"...now, why don't you all take off your shoes and dig your feet into the grass so we can do some stretches..."

I kicked off my sandals. "Oh come on Charlie, now you and the other girls will make fun of me just like you laughed at Sofia."

Rolling her eyes to the sky, Charlie replied, "I would never laugh behind your back."

"Reach your hands up to the sky," Ms. Davies continued. She smiled brightly and I saw a mouthful of gleaming white teeth. I'd never seen teeth so white before.

"Besides," Charlie continued, "you were laughing at Sofia too, remember?"

Ouch. She had a point there.

"Now reach down low to the ground..."

I looked uneasy as I copied the teacher. "You're right."

Charlie gave a breathy laugh. "Cal, you have to start learning how to trust me. I'm your friend."

"...now lightly jog in place."

I looked at Charlie with wonder. "My mother calls me Cal."

"See?" Charlie smiled. "I'm practically like family already."

"That was a great warm up everyone. We'll be doing this before every swim..."

"And listen, if you think there's something to this box and the," she sighed, "*missing girl*, I'll help you every step of the way. We made a pinky deal after all."

I knew Charlie was sincere. And that felt really good.

"...always have to be attentive to your surroundings. And never swim by the lake alone during free time. You always need a partner with you just in case."

"You mean just in case of the creature that's at the bottom of the lake." A shy-looking blonde girl spoke out. I noticed that she was standing next to Gwendolyn Merchant, the girl who tried to make me look silly in front of Mrs. Copperpot.

Ms. Davies just gave a sparkling laugh and pointed at the shy girl. "Now that is a new one, my dear." She clapped once and continued on, stopping the discussion of the lake creature. "Now we're going to do a little 'trust' practice. What's your name?"

"Gwen." She answered brightly.

"Come on over here Camper Gwen." As soon as Gwen approached her, Ms. Davies told her to turn around. "Now fall backwards with the trust that I'm going to catch you."

"Not a problem Ms. Davies." Arms stretched high in the air gracefully; Gwen lightly fell back without a worry in the world. Of course Ms. Davies caught her and gently pushed her back into a standing position.

"Wonderful. Gwen had complete trust in me. And that's what you all need when we're out there swimming, that your partner is going to help if you need it. "Now," she clapped once, "you'll be teaming up in pairs and practicing the 'trust fall'." I looked over at Charlie right away and Ms. Davies spoke again. "I'll randomly pair you off."

I groaned. There was just no way I could do this exercise. Trust was hard for me. I knew that was what Charlie asked for…but could I really just leave all my doubts aside and put all my faith in my new friend? Now I had to do this with a strange camper.

"What's your name?"

I looked up at Ms. Davies, swallowed and answered. "Callie."

"Camper Callie, you'll be teamed up with Camper Gwen." She pushed Gwen over towards me. I groaned. "Is there a problem?" Up close, I noticed how perfectly tanned and smooth Ms. Davies' face was.

I shook my head, "Not at all." She nodded and moved on to the next camper. I folded my arms and slowly walked closer to Gwen. Dreading every second.

"Hello Miss Liberty," Gwen smirked.

"Nice nickname. I might ask my friends to start using it."

She frowned and rolled her eyes because she didn't get me angry. "Let's just get through this."

"Alright, everyone's got a partner now. Decide who goes first and do the fall," Ms. Davies announced.

"I'll fall first," Gwen offered with a haughty tone of voice.

I stood there and quickly looked across the river to where Sofia said she saw the strange figure. I didn't see anything and deep inside I was glad that I didn't. But it still didn't explain…

"Yoo-hoo," snapped Gwen.

"Huh?" I was really that distracted.

Gwen sighed really loud. "Pay attention."

"Oh yeah, right."

Gwen shook her head and her hair swung in the air as she turned around. I counted to three and caught Gwen firmly. Gwen straightened back up and flipped her hair over her shoulders. "I almost didn't believe that you'd catch me." I just couldn't believe that Gwen actually trusted I'd catch her. Not that I would have made her fall on purpose, even though that would have been hilarious. "Okay, your turn. Let's get this over with so I can go swimming," Gwen sniffed. I stood with my back to Gwen and took a deep breath as she counted, "One…two…three."

I didn't move.

"Calliope, you're so weird. Come on. Everyone's practically done. Ready? One, two three."

I didn't move…again.

She sucked her teeth and slapped her hips angrily. "Ms. Davies! I need a new partn-AHH!"

Everyone started to scream and I quickly turned around and saw campers running away. I spotted what looked like a few campers running out of the lake dressed as swamp monsters. It was pure chaos. Ms. Davies started running after them, blowing her whistle all the while. I turned when I heard Charlie laughing really hard. I'd never seen her face so red before. "Did you…see…that?" She gasped between belly laughs.

"Barely!" I replied and saw Gwen with her hand to her heart and a disapproving look on her face.

"I mean…the look on…everyone's *faces*!" Charlie fell to her knees.

I was astonished and couldn't help but admire Charlie in that moment. Here I was, unable to trust anyone, over thinking every move I made. And there Charlie was, belly laughing without a care in the world.

Charlie found the strength to get up and walked on the small dock leading out onto the water. I followed, thinking all the while. She wiped the last tears from her eyes and said, "Ms. Davies will catch up to them in no time I'm sure. They probably hid under here until they thought the time was right," she laughed again, "Classic prank. Love it."

I looked down at the wooden boards and noticed some letters scratched into it. I bent down to take a closer look.

"Cal, what is it?" She bent down beside me.

"The letters I found in that old note. Here they are again, C and F." I looked up at Charlie with wonder.

"Wow," Charlie said with fascination. "I think you're onto something."

I looked back down and said softly, "Me too."

Chapter 5

That's Going to be Hard to Top

Note to Self: Juggle fruit whenever you can. Looks like fun!

FOR THE next week I buried myself in camp activities. I played softball, tennis, went canoeing and kayaking. I even continued to sew that perfect apron, though it really started to look like a hat. It had taken us an entire week to come up with a prank for Madison and Mary. We knew it was a long time, but we wanted the element of surprise on our side and it was really funny to see Madison's cautious pretty face and Mary always looking over her shoulder.

After many meetings, we decided that a week after the incident was the perfect moment. That Monday, we all got up right before the morning bugle rang. We each chose a hidden spot to hide before Mary and Madison walked in. As we waited, there were some chuckles, giggles and shushing.

When Mary opened the door, she opened her mouth to greet us but before she could say anything, Charlie jumped out and attacked them both with silly string. The two counselors shouted, totally surprised. Me and Saliesha came from the other side and shot more silly string.

They turned to leave the bunk, but Sheila and Sofia were on the porch waiting for them and shot even more. Just as Madison and Mary ran down the stairs, Lane popped out from behind the big tree and got them. We all stood on the porch and watched them retreat. Then cheered and jumped up and down.

"We are *sooo* in trouble," I laughed.

"But it was *sooo* worth it," Charlie gloated.

"It completely covered them," Sheila bragged. "*I* got them good."

"We all did," Saliesha corrected.

"Good job Lane!" I called out to her.

Lane lifted her can of silly string and blew on the tip.

"We better watch our backs," Saliesha shared cautiously.
Sofia agreed. "We are in for it now."

*****

I sat in the dining hall eating breakfast later that morning while Charlie, Saliesha and Sofia were at the bulletin board signing up for an activity or two since they were starting up that week. I thought eating was more important than signing up for something. The truth was that I didn't join anything back home so why should I start now? A few minutes later the girls came back to the table grinning and giggling. "What's so funny?"

"Charlie just signed up for the camp play," Saliesha answered as she sat and started eating from her waiting tray.

"Is this just to get under Sheila's skin?" I asked with a smirk on my face.

"Dude, totally!" Charlie laughed. "It's awesome. The play this year is about some beautiful princess and a prince. It has witches, magical forest creatures and I'll be trying out for the lead role."

Sofia smiled. "We hear that Sheila gets the lead every year."

"And my girl Charlie here is gonna try and change that," Saliesha high-fived Charlie.

"I know I don't have a chance, but it's gonna be fun trying," Charlie said with a smirk.

"What did you two sign up for?"

"The camps annual obstacle course race at the end of summer," Saliesha answered as she tucked some of her chin length hair behind her ear. "Sofia and I will be partners. We're going to show a thing or two to the competition this year."

"Do you know Gwen? She is in a few of our activities," Sofia asked me.

I groaned. I couldn't help it, "All too well."

Sofia just smiled shyly. "Well, she won last year. And people say that she and her partner Miranda were unstoppable."

"Yeah I've heard of Miranda. She's always getting into trouble." Charlie added.

Saliesha swallowed some of her toast and pointed at the bulletin board with her thumb. "Their names are already on the sign-up sheet."

"Well the obstacle course sounds like fun." I didn't realize what was coming out of my mouth really, something made me say it. I lifted my empty tray and said firmly, "I think I'll do it."

"Yeah, but who's gonna be your partner?" Saliesha asked, waving her fork in the air.

We all looked at Charlie, who just swallowed a bit of her apple. "Don't look at me. All my energy is going into this play."

I sighed. "Charlie, you sound like Sheila now. But don't worry," I started walking away from the table, "I'll figure it out."

"Something tells me that this is not going to end up well," I heard Sofia say nervously as I placed put my trash away near the table.

"Nah," I heard Charlie say, "I know Callie by now. When she sets her mind to do something, she does it." She took a huge bite of her apple and it was a wonder anyone could understand what she said next, "Just *how* she does it is what scares me."

I stopped listening to them and walked calmly towards the sign-up sheet. Before I could second-guess myself, I signed my name neatly on the sheet for the obstacle course race.

"Hi Callie," came two voices.

I smiled brightly, "Hi Carrie, hi Liz." They waved and kept walking by and I smiled because I was sure that I could do this race. I had friends now…I had people saying hi to me in passing…things were a whole lot different from home.

I smiled to myself, gave a thumbs-up to the girls at the table and went outside to get to my next activity early. Or really, to get out of the dining hall because if I sat there and stared at the sheet, I'd probably be tempted to change my mind and erase my name.

The sun was bright and it gave me high spirits. As I walked down the hill, I spotted Brandon running across the field. He didn't see me, but I certainly saw him. I realized that I hadn't talked or seen him since the welcome party. I noticed that a piece of paper fell out of his pocket, but he just kept running.

I took a deep breath and ran towards the paper. I called out to him when I grabbed it, but he didn't hear me so I ran after him. I was glad that I was an okay runner since Brandon was obviously a gold medalist. He ran so fast that when I blinked I wasn't sure if he ran into the library or the main office. I caught my breath for a second and decided to go into the library.

I was shot with a refreshing blast of cold air and sighed in delight. It was quiet and mostly empty since the majority of the campers were still in the dining hall. I looked around the spacious library but didn't spot him at all.

"Hi Callie."

I felt my ponytail hit the side of my face as I turned to see Lane behind the counter. "Hi Lane," I smiled. I hadn't seen Lane too often unless she was behind Sheila. As a matter of fact, "Where's Sheila?"

Lane smiled and shrugged, adjusting glasses that were too big for her face, "Most likely the theater. She's over there a lot." She pushed her silver glasses up the bridge of her nose.

"What about you? Do you have any interest in the theater?" I asked and leaned my elbows on the counter. Lane was pretty short, so as I leaned I realized we were at eye level.

"Well," Lane's cheeks turned a little rosy, "I kind of do."

"Then you should most definitely audition for the play. I didn't see your name on the sign-up sheet."

She shook her short dark blonde hair. "I don't think so. Sheila would be upset."

"Why on earth would she be? Did you want to go for the lead or something?"

"Oh no," Lane chuckled. "There's a good witch in the play and I was thinking of…well, auditioning for *that* part. It's minor, but she gets her own song."

"You should go for it. You'd make a great witch!" I froze. Really? Why do I say these things? "I didn't mean it that way."

Lane giggled. "I know."

"You could probably curl your hair," I pointed at her stringy hair. "Maybe wear contacts and give the glasses a rest just for the stage."

Lane gave a secret smile and stuttered, "I…I don't know." She shook her head. "I don't think so."

I felt the corners of my mouth twitch up and down. "I'll tell you what I didn't know. I *didn't* know you volunteered at the library." She really *was* the one bunk mate I didn't know too much about.

"It's a nice getaway. "Lane said quietly. And without saying anything else, I knew she was talking about Sheila. "So what can I help you with?" She asked sweetly.

I suddenly remembered why I bolted into the library in the first place. I looked down at the paper in my hand, but dropped it. When I bent down to pick it up from the burgundy carpet, I noticed the scibbles... *C & F??*

I nearly dropped the paper again. My eyes widened in shock. I wasn't sure if I was reading this right.

"Callie, you okay?"

Before I could respond to Lane, I heard another voice. This time it sounded deeper. "Hi Lane. Calliope? Is that you?"

I took in a breath and looked at the gray sneakers that were eye level with my face. I looked up and saw the amused face of none other than Brandon. I shot up quickly, but too quickly in fact. The back of my head hit under the counter. Lane flew around the counter to me and Brandon made an oh-boy-that-hurt kind of face.

And oh boy, that kind of hurt!

"Are you alright?" Lane asked in concern.

Brandon looked concern as well. It was so embarrassing to see all of these concerned faces! "Callie?" He tried to check my face for any signs of distress.

"I'm fine!" I breathed, smiled brightly and touched the back of my head. It was only a tiny bit sore...okay so it was *majorly* sore, but I ignored it.

"I don't expect you to remember me, but we talked for a minute the first day of camp?"

"Um...Brandon right?" I played if off like I didn't really remember his name. I didn't want him to think that *I've* been thinking about him all week. Which I haven't, but still, who could forget what happened? "Or was it Brian?" Maybe that was too far.

He smiled brightly. "Yeah, it's Brandon." In the light of the library, I noticed that his hair had a hard time deciding if it wanted to be light brown or blond. His blue eyes had all of the colors of the ocean.

"Checking out that book?" Lane asked as she grabbed the small blue book from him and walked back behind the counter.

"Uh...yeah," he scratched the back of his head.

I couldn't help but notice that the book was a short history about the camp. As Lane checked out the book I explained, "I was chasing you down actually."

His bright blue eyes (sorry, can't stop talking about how blue his eyes are!) flew to my face in surprise. "Really?"

"Yeah," I held out the small piece of paper. "You dropped this by the hill."

"Oh." He said in another breath of surprise and grabbed the paper, quickly stuffing it into his pocket. "Thanks," he smiled.

I was itching to ask him about the note and the book. Could he truly be searching for the same answers as I was?

"Here you go," Lane said with a chirpy smile, handing him back the book.

"Thanks Lane," he said in a friendly voice and then turned to me. "Well, I've gotta run. I was supposed to be at soccer five minutes ago."

"Mr. Mendel isn't too harsh about tardiness."

Brandon laughed. "Now way, I've got Ms. Davies. I'm already looking at twenty push-ups." He started his way towards the door. "Bye."

"See ya."

"Oh," he turned back around, "and you don't want to take any chances with that bruise on the back of your head. Maybe you should see Nurse Wilkins and get some ice on it."

"Yep," I nodded. He left the library and I wanted to melt right where I stood. Lane gave me a knowing look. "What?" I felt my face turning an embarrassing shade of pink.

"I didn't say anything." Lane began to whistle and left the counter to go organize a cart full of misplaced books.

*****

Walking into the outdoor theater a few days later; I realized what things friends do for each other. Me, Saliesha and Sofia had promised Charlie that we would support her while she auditioned for the camp play.

"Hey Charlie, what's in the backpack?" Saliesha asked with amused interest.

"Nothing important," Charlie said as if she didn't really care.

"Good luck Charlie," I whispered.

"What is it that you say here? Oh yes, break a leg," Sofia smiled.

"In fact, break both," Saliesha added and we giggled.

"Har, *har*." Charlie walked to a seat in the front row with the other hopefuls.

I settled in my seat and noticed how nice the view was. We were outside. The stage was spacious and open and the lake was right behind it. We sat on silver bleachers that went up very high and formed a 'U' around the stage. Campers signed in with the directors and sat down, looking pretty excited as they were about to perform on stage.

"I cannot believe Charlie is doing this." Saliesha shook her head in disbelief. Her heart shaped lips smirked in wonder.

Sofia raised her slender eyebrows. "Remember, it is all to rattle a few of Sheila's feathers."

"Speaking of feathers," Saliesha pointed out, "Sheila's feather boas are shedding all over the bunk house!" She sucked her teeth with an attitude. "Man, this morning I woke up with a rainbow of feathers on my face. Now please tell me how does that even *happen*?" She waved her hand in the air.

"That's nothing compared to her vocal warm ups this morning," I added thoughtfully.

Sofia sighed because she didn't like to gossip and Saliesha rolled her eyes. "Girl, *please* don't remind me."

That morning, Sheila woke up before the sun came out and started singing in the bathroom. As a matter of fact, I wouldn't actually call it singing. She kept rolling her tongue and making all kinds of noises claiming that it helped her vocal chords. Charlie had shouted that Sheila should let the rooster keep his job.

"I wonder how long this is gonna take," Saliesha complained as she put her sunglasses on.

"Don't whine," I stated firmly. "We're supporting our friend." I actually felt really good saying that bit.

"Callie," Saliesha rolled her eyes, "the actors are down there," she teased.

Sofia giggled and I smirked at Saliesha. "I'm serious."

"So am I," Saliesha said and this time I couldn't hold in my laughter.

A few minutes later Sheila made her grand entrance, minus Lane. She sat right in the front row, wearing sparkly red sunglasses even though it was a cloudy day. A short and friendly Mr. Niles and a tall and outgoing Mrs. Niles made their introduction to the auditions and made a speech about the rules and what they were looking for. Sheila raised her hand and insisted that she be able to audition first, saying that her act would be a tough one to follow. I was surprised that she actually sang pretty well. However her overdramatic hand and head movements were really exaggerated.

After she proudly sat down, Mrs. Niles called out, "Carolina and Elizabeth Anthony."

Standing side by side, stiff and straight, hands by their sides, Carrie and Liza nervously recited a poem.

Carrie started. "Roses are red."

Liz took a deep, nervous breath and said, "Violets are blue."

"Camp Eerie rocks."

With surprising enthusiasm, "And we'll show you why!"

"Hit it!" Carrie pointed to a girl sitting by a stereo. She hit the play button and the song "It Takes Two" by Rob Base came on. The crowd started clapping and cheering as Liz started twirling a baton while keeping rhythm with the hip hop eighties song. She did an effortless front flip and then placed the baton carefully in Carrie's mouth.

They both started doing the same choreography. The crowd clapped along and watched in surprise as Liz lit a long match and set both ends of the baton in fire…while it was still in Carrie's mouth!

All of our jaws hit the ground. Mr. and Mrs. Niles sat nervously in the front row; Mrs. Niles clutching her neck in nervous shock. As Carrie danced with a fiery baton in her mouth, Liz did a few flips and suddenly pulled out another baton.

Carrie took the baton out of her mouth as Liz twirled over to her and when she made it to Carrie; they lifted their arms high in the air. Carrie's fiery baton lit Liz's baton and a loud blaze of fire lit up. Everyone in the audience, me included, was blown away! We all looked on with open admiration.

They both twirled away from each other, posed briefly and just as the music ended, they looked at each other, went to the back of the stage and back flipped into the water, extinguishing the flames on their batons. The entire stadium erupted into a loud applause, whistles and whoops.

"That's going to be hard to top!" I exclaimed to Saliesha as we clapped.

"You said it girl!"

My comment proved true. Everyone else seemed plain compared to the fiery musical stylings of Carrie and Liz. After what felt like an hour, it was finally Charlie's turn. We applauded with extra enthusiasm as Charlie awkwardly walked onto the stage. She bent her one knee and crossed her arms. From the front row, Sheila just stared at Charlie with amused disbelief, thinking Charlie wouldn't go far. But I had a feeling that Charlie would surprise them.

And surprise she did.

"Okay," Mr. Niles looked down at the sign in sheet and said, "Camper Charlotte. Which musical selection are you going to perform for us?" He smiled expectantly at her.

She grabbed her blue backpack and took out three oranges and a ripe banana. A snort came from the audience and she glanced at Sheila. She just covered her mouth and peeped, "*Do* excuse me."

Charlie ignored her and said, "I uh, I guess I'll sing 'Patty-cake'?" Most of the campers laughed in amusement, but she didn't look like she cared.

Mrs. Niles touched her long and skinny throat in horror. Cracking a weary smile, she nodded encouragingly and said, "Go on dear."

"I'm also going to hop on one foot." Charlie lifted the fruit and then began to juggle them all while singing her nursery rhyme and hopping on one foot. She bowed at the end and everyone applauded...everyone minus Sheila, that is. Charlie winked at a shocked Mrs. Niles and walked back to her seat with her head held high.

As the girls and I let out extra cheers for her, Sheila stood up and abruptly spoke very loud. "Well that was positively charming!" She looked at Charlie and all of the campers who auditioned that morning. "However, I think we all know to whom the coveted lead role of the dazzling princess will go."

"Ho-ho-hold on there Camper Sheila!" Mr. Niles said enthusiastically. "We've got one more audition."

Sheila's jaw dropped. "How can that possibly be? I've visited the sign-up sheet every day and Charlotte was the last name added," she pointed her sparkly nails at Charlie.

"Actually we've got a late sign up." Mr. Niles explained and Mrs. Niles nodded happily.

"Well that certainly isn't fair," Sheila crossed her arms and plopped back down on her seat. "It wouldn't hurt I guess. I mean, how good could this person actually be?"

Mr. Niles looked at the sign-up sheet and looked around the bleachers. "Lane Wesley?"

Saliesha, Sofia and I gasped, looking around for Lane. "Oh no she didn't," Saliesha said in amazement.

But nothing beat the gasp that came from Sheila as she sat there with her jaw hanging down to her feet. Everyone waited a few seconds and finally spotted a nervous Lane making her way onto the stage. Her hair was curled up, she didn't wear her silver glasses and she was dressed in a jean skirt with a camp T-shirt tucked inside. "Is that Lane?" Sofia asked in disbelief.

Charlie turned back to find me and gave me a shocked look. I shrugged in return.

"She looks...good," Saliesha added in surprise.

I smiled down at the stage. "She always looked good." As Lane continued to make her way onto the stage, I clapped, "Go Laney!" Charlie joined me and clapped as well.

Mrs. Niles smiled charmingly at Lane. "So Camper Lane, you're auditioning for the lead role, I understand."

A strangled gasp of outrage came from Sheila's general direction.

When Lane nodded, Mrs. Niles asked, "What are you going to sing for us?"

Lane clasped her hands together nervously in front of her and squeaked, "A love balled...written by me-me." Lane avoided Sheila's gaze. Everyone felt the heat coming from Sheila.

"Oh!" Mrs. Niles said in delight. "Go on then."

Lane cleared her throat and started off a little shaky, but then her voice became stronger and higher and by the time she was finished, the audience exploded into applause and we all gave her a standing ovation.

"Wonderful!" Mr. and Mrs. Niles praised. "Absolutely wonderful!"

Lane smiled triumphantly and walked off of the stage.

"We'll announce the cast tonight at the camp fire!" Mr. Niles proclaimed over the steady chatter of the excited campers.

Everyone stood up to leave and I noticed a group of people praising Lane's vocals. The majority of the campers surrounded Carrie and Liz.

I saw Sheila loom over Lane.

"Don't think that shaky performance actually gives you any inkling of hope at getting the lead role."

"Sorry to disappoint Sheila," Lane said in a haughty voice that sounded nothing like her usual self. "Maybe you'll be lucky and I'll get the other lead role of the witch."

Sheila raised her red eyebrow unnaturally high. "You'd better hope so. They say art imitates life."

"Isn't it life imitates art?" Charlie asked as she approached the girls, biting into her banana. The girls and I finally got closer as Charlie continued. "Actually Sheila," she said with her mouth full, "I think she's a shoo-in for the lead." She swallowed and said to Lane, "You were great out there."

"Thanks," Lane chirped in almost the same conceited attitude as Sheila.

Saliesha and Sofia looked a bit confused at Lane's attitude but congratulated her anyway. I gave Lane a hug. "I agree with everyone else, you were awesome."

"I didn't know you could write songs girl that was good. I already want the CD." Saliesha slid her sunglasses to the top of her hair.

"And your hair is gorgeous. You should wear it like this more often," Sofia added, her wide green eyes looked sincere.

"Thank you." Lane said matter-of-factly.

Sheila stood there with her arms crossed and rolled her eyes. "What*ever*." She teased her wild red curls and yawned. "Well I'm going to go and catch up on my much needed beauty rest by the peaceful surroundings of the lake. I need to conserve all of my delicate energy when I celebrate tonight." She looked at all of us. "You know, when I get the lead role." She gave one last hurt look at Lane, huffed and walked away with her nose stuck in the air; the smell of peppermint trailing behind her.

"I was just so good," Lane bragged breezily and glanced at Charlie, "Your act was okay."

Charlie chuckled. "Well I was good if I say so myself." She looked at us, hinting to agree and a second later we blew up with 'Yeahs' and 'Of course!'.

"Well, we have to get to hiking," Saliesha said, pulling Sofia along.

"Will I see you at Mrs. Copperpot's?" Sofia asked me. I wasn't looking forward to another 'Getting-to-know-you' session and seeing Gwen, but I was doomed.

"Yep," I answered. Saliesha and Sofia looked once more at Lane and then left.

"Well then I'm going to be late to volunteer in the boring old library," Lane looked at me and said, "Toodles," before strutting off.

"Tootles?" Charlie and I asked at the same time.

Charlie pulled her backpack over her shoulder and polished off her banana. "Off to cooking?"

I groaned. "Don't remind me. I made a cake explode in the oven. I mean, how can you possibly make a cake *explode*?"

Charlie laughed. "I'll walk you there. I have basketball and it's on the way."

We started walking away from the theater and onto a hill and I decided to share something with her. "Hey, did I ever tell you that I bumped into Brandon the other day?"

"Brandon *who*?" Charlie started to peel an orange as I realized that I had been thinking about him so much, it already felt like I told her all about him.

"Um…" now I was nervous. "Remember back at the welcome party?"

"Oh wait." Charlie stopped walking and her face changed. I was in trouble now. "I remember him." Her eyes were accusing as she pointed at me. "You have a crush on him don't you?"

"*What?*" I really wasn't expecting her to say that. And then I felt my face turn as red as Sheila's hair. "How did you know?"

"You just told me."

"That's not fair!" I pushed her arm and looked down at the floor. "That's not important anyway," I looked back at her. "There's something else going on with him-"

"No, no wait." Charlie interrupted me. "Back up, reverse and start from the beginning. Since when did you have a crush? Does he have a crush on you?" She gasped and her eyes grew, "You guys are dating aren't you? You secretive little girl!"

"Stop!" I couldn't help but shout! I took a deep breath. "No. It's nothing like that. I've only said two words to him. But you're not listening to me. He's investigating the C and F initials too."

Charlie just smirked. I hope that meant that she would drop the whole 'I-have-a-crush-on-Brandon' part of the conversation. "So now you two are detectives together?"

I hate it when I'm wrong.

"No. He doesn't know that I'm searching for answers too."

Charlie threw the orange peel into a passing trash can. "So how do you know about what he's doing?"

I told her all about finding the note and the book he checked out about the camp's history. Charlie finished her orange as she listened. "What would he want with a book about the camps history?"

"Well," I pushed some hair behind my ear and took a breath. "I've been thinking that maybe he wants to find out the names of campers…locations…things that match up with whatever he's found."

"Based on two initials there is really no way you can find out who they are." She added, "There's an ocean of info you have to find and narrow down and you can't fit an ocean into a cup."

"I know you're saying it's impossible, but there are ways. I can look at the places I've found the initials, narrow down who stayed where…" I stopped talking when Charlie started shaking her head.

"Maybe you should team up with Brandon. If there is more than one person really searching for answers, you're bound to find something. What? I don't know…but something."

"You're right, but I'm not sure." My face felt hot again.

Charlie hit my arm playfully as we walked down the hill. "You're thinking about this way too much. Just *let* things happen. The answers will come when you're not looking."

I sighed, but smiled. "Why do I have the feeling that you're right?"

"Because I just *am*. Besides, you have to put more energy into finding a partner for the obstacle relay."

I groaned. "Would it be possible if you…"

"I've already told you Cal, I'm off limits. You'll find someone good I'm sure of it." She shook her head as they neared the cabin where I would meet with the cooking teacher and bake another disaster.

My mind turned into knots as I approached the door. "You're right…I guess."

Chapter 6

As Long As It's Only One Time

Note to Self: You can find out a lot of things in the girls bathroom.

BY THE end of the day, I felt hopeless. I'd asked a few other campers if they would team up with me for the race, but they had all signed up for something else. The only thought that crossed my mind was that I had to beat Gwen. I just had to. I didn't know why it was so important, but it was. At the dining hall, all of the campers were buzzing about the results of the auditions.

Charlie made her first claim to fame when word spread about her unique audition. She was surrounded by a group of campers asking about it and telling her good luck. Saliesha and Sofia were deep in conversation about the first relay practice coming up, so I basically ate my dinner by myself, which wasn't too bad because I had a lot to think about.

However, the temporary peace ended when I felt someone looming behind me. I quickly turned around and found the main subject of my thoughts standing right in front of me. "Gwen," I said politely. "Can I help you with something?"

She wore her hair down with a pretty thin red headband holding it away from her face. "Not really," she smiled at me, but I didn't really feel the kindness coming from the smile. "I just wanted to say that I noticed your name on the sign-up sheet for the annual obstacle course race."

"O...kay."

"I also wanted to say that you don't stand a chance against me and Miranda."

"Oh how nice," I stood up to face her. "You came all this way just to tell me that I don't stand a chance." I talked to her the way I did to my little sister...with as much sarcasm as I could muster. "That says a lot." I smiled brightly.

Gwen giggled, "No, not really. Since you're new to the camp this year, I just wanted you to know how hard this obstacle is going to be. I don't want you to practice so much for no reason." She shrugged innocently.

"Oh," I said with false innocence, "Well let me just say this one time: You don't have to worry about me. I think I'll do just fine."

"Yes, you're right." Gwen nodded, "*Especially* since you don't have a partner yet."

"Gwen, I think you should spend a little less time worrying about my lack of a partner and more time prepping yourself for your toughest competitor yet." I looked right into Gwen's surprised eyes.

"Hey, is everything alright Cal?" I heard Charlie's question, tinted with aggression.

Gwen answered Charlie with a fake smile, "Never better." She looked at me one more time and then walked back to her own table at the other end of the dining hall.

"She ruffles my feathers," I said heatedly as I sat back down.

"Well don't you sound like Sheila," Charlie said smugly.

"Well that's probably not a bad thing anymore."

Sofia and Saliesha turned quickly and I realized that I snapped. Talk about embarrassing. I felt my face heat up when I realized how they were staring at me...with straight disbelief. I got up quickly and turned around, never wanting to leave a place faster in my entire life.

"We should go after her," I heard Sofia say.

"No, that Gwen girl has her pretty upset, that's all it is, I'm not taking it personal. She just needs space that's all. We'll see how she is at the camp fire tonight." I heard Charlie say as I walked a little faster.

I didn't mean to snap at the only best friend I'd ever had. I was going to apologize at the first chance I got. I just couldn't believe how easily Gwen angered me! And the girl didn't even do much besides smirk and say a few words...but it didn't mean those words weren't hurtful.

The sun was setting and the sky was streaked purple, pink and gold. I stopped in my tracks and took a moment to look at the beauty of it. I knew that the sky never looked exactly the same every time the sun set. Even the rare rainbow I saw once in a while looked the same. But the sunset...nah, the sunset sky was never the same. Taking a deep breath, I thought about going back inside of the dining hall, but was too embarrassed, so I decided to go into the ladies room in the library. It would be virtually empty and I needed the quiet to compose myself for a minute.

Going inside of the library, I felt the cool blast of the air conditioner. It was such a humid day and the air was a nice feeling. When I got inside the restroom, I walked to the mirror and looked at myself. A porcupine's hair was neater than mine! I searched for a comb in my backpack and as soon as I pulled it out and pressed it into my hair, I heard sniffling coming from one of the two stalls.

My hand froze since I thought I was the only one inside the restroom. I decided to ignore it and continued to comb out my wild brown ponytail. I heard more sniffling followed by the sniffler blowing into a napkin very loudly. Tying my ponytail up again, I decided to hurry up and get out of there.

Suddenly, the stall door swung open and none other than Sheila herself came sweeping out of the stall. I noticed that her eyes were rimmed red. Sheila stopped short when she saw me and held her nose high in the air like she did so well.

"Hello Calliope," she gracefully went to the sink to wash her hands.

"Hi Sheila," I put the comb back into my pack. "Are...are you okay?"

Sheila cleared her throat and sounded like she had a stuffy nose. "Never better, thank you very much. Although I'm sure you enjoyed Lane's grand production today at the theater."

I looked at Sheila through the mirror, noticing that her nose was as red as her hair. "Well yeah...didn't you?"

"Hah!" Sheila turned off the water and dried her hands. "I daresay it wasn't even close to what a real solo should be. It lacked the sparkle of a stage performer."

"Why would you say that about your friend?" I knew I was getting angry again.

"*Friend?*" Sheila snorted. "I don't think Lane is any sort of person I should ever be unfortunate enough to spend my precious time with."

I thought that Lane *did* act a little differently that day, but shrugged it off. "You know Sheila; I always ignored your vanity. Because even though it's obnoxious, it's good that you have so much self-esteem. But the way you're standing here and criticizing the only person who's followed you around with open admiration shows just how much self-esteem you don't have." I didn't have to look in the mirror to know my face was red and blotchy.

"You sure have a good amount to say without knowing the entire truth of the situation."

"What situation? That Lane was good today and you're so jealous of her that you can't stand to see her happy?"

"I will admit that I was especially jealous of Lane today," her words tumbled on top of each other as they rushed out. "But that is the extent of it."

"Sounds like more to me."

"Lane called me fat!" Sheila exclaimed with tears in her eyes.

I stared at Sheila for a moment as the word 'fat' echoed in the restroom in the following silence. Sheila Penelope Ann Van Housen was a lot of things. She was pretentious, loud, over-bearing and very sparkly; but one thing she wasn't was a liar. She had no time for lying in her world.

I finally whispered, "You're not fat."

"Well it took you a while to tell me that!" She wailed, taking out a star-patterned handkerchief from her pocket and dotting under her eyes.

"That's only because I'm shocked Lane would say something like that to you."

"I mean I know that I am delicately big-boned. It runs in my family. But fat?" Her voice broke at her last two words. Her feelings were truly hurt. And that's when I decided that I wouldn't let anything Gwen say bother me because there were worse things one could say to another and those words ran deeper than ever.

"Were you two arguing? Maybe she just said it out of anger. I know I do-"

"Ha." Sheila sniffed. "You say what you really mean when you're truly angry with someone."

"Well what happened?"

"I approached her a little while earlier and asked her why she auditioned. Like I said, I was truly jealous that she signed up without even telling me. But she must have known that I would approach her. She was on the defensive from the start. She went on some silly rant expressing feelings she must have been holding for ages." Sheila sighed. "It doesn't matter now, does it? The words were said and they can't be taken back." She cleared her throat as she put her handkerchief away.

"But you two were friends…you can forgive each other-"

"Forgive? Hah! That is the most hilarious thing my ears have ever picked up. It's too late. My poor heart has hardened against her. And it's very obvious that she will now get the coveted lead role." She shook her hair out and looked in the mirror as she pulled out a bright pink compact to pat her red cheeks with some blush. "I have cried all I am going to cry," she said as fresh tears brimmed in her light brown eyes. "I'm going to walk out of here with my head held high like the lady that I am."

"Well then, good for you Sheila." And I meant that.

She threw her compact into her sparkly yellow bag and began to walk out of the restroom, "Oh, by the by," she turned around to face me. "You remember that magnificent bracelet I found in that ugly old box?"

"You mean the bracelet *I* found and *you* took?"

"To-may-to, to-mah-to. *Any*how, I've ended up giving it to a camper named Brandon. I think you spoke to him once before? Who wouldn't know who he is? He's simply divine. In any case, I have someone who tracks down what he does-"

"You what?"

"Disregard that last sentence. *Any*who, I've found out that he's *also* poking his *perfect* nose about those hilarious initials.. Even though I can't stand it, you two obviously have something in common. In any event, I hand delivered that bracelet and vaguely mentioned your name."

My ears perked up. "You mentioned my name?"

"I said '*vaguely*'."

I nodded and acted like it wasn't so important. "Oh, okay."

"Just thought you'd like to know." With a sweep of her uncivilized red curls, Sheila and her sparkles left, leaving me with a new look on Gwen and the thought that Brandon could actually know I was investigating the same thing as him.

*****

All of the stars were twinkling brightly in the deep black sky. The moon was large and floated serenely over the camp. Mrs. and Mrs. Niles stood proudly with lists in their hands. Every camper who had auditioned for the play and all of their friends…and anyone interested in the play…gathered by the two hundred year old tree. The bonfire was roaring on the other side. I slowly walked up to Saliesha, Sofia and Charlie. We kind of left on bad terms.

"Hi," I knew I sounded nervous, but I couldn't help it.

"Don't even worry about it Cal," Charlie waved her hand and pulled me into the group. "We just hope you feel better."

Charlie was just awesome. "Yeah, I feel much better."

"Good."

Lane stood on one side of the crowd and Sheila stood on the other, trying not to look as if she'd cried at all that day. Only I could tell though. Lane was still dressed in her fancy new style that just didn't quite seem like her.

"Lane!" I called her over. She flicked her eyes over at us.

"Good luck!" Charlie called while I gave two thumbs up.

Lane lifted her chin and rolled her eyes. "I really don't need it but thanks anyway…I guess."

Charlie and I looked at each other. I'm sure my face looked as confused as hers. "Oh…kay," Charlie said slowly.

"She's probably just really nervous." I could feel the nervous energy and excitement of the crowd. The smell of burning wood and food naturally made me even more excited.

"Sure," Charlie said dryly.

"We'll announce the top lead roles first and then hang up the complete list of the cast and crew," Mr. Niles announced.

Mrs. Niles' skinny hands held up the clip-board in front of her. "The role of the friendly and caring Queen Gracious will go to…Rachel Mathis!"

I turned in surprise as the gum-smacker from the bus excitedly stepped forward to collect the script from Mrs. Niles. She jumped up and down and ran back to her excited group of friends.

Mr. Niles spoke in a deep, sinister voice as he said, "The role of the mean-hearted, wicked Queen Minacious goes to…Sheila Van Housen!"

There was a slight pause in the crowd and a few minor gasps, but some new campers began clapping loud and soon everyone clapped. "Sheila, come and get your script!" exclaimed an enthusiastic Mrs. Niles.

Sheila snapped out of her trance, cleared her throat, lifted her nose into the air and sashayed towards Mrs. Niles to grab her script. She avoided all eye contact and said nothing as she went back to her spot in the crowd.

"The cunning and tricky witches will be," Mr. Niles looked right at Carrie and Liz, "Carolina and Elizabeth Anthony!"

The two girls jumped up and down excitedly while everyone cheered them on. They jumped all the way to the drama teachers and grabbed their scripts.

"No more need for fire ladies," Mrs. Niles said with a weary, but excited voice, reminding them of their audition.

"Prince Handsomely Charming will go to Edward John!" A large portion of the crowd whooped and cheered in delight as the handsome blond camper went to get his script.

"I'm probably gonna get a role like the Witch's Assistant or something and I really, really don't mind," Charlie whispered to me.

"We'll be cheering for your one-line from the audience, don't you worry," I encouraged and patted her shoulder.

Charlie smirked. "Hey, I'll have more time now so I'll be able to be your partner for the obstacle race."

"Really?" I practically glowed in delight. "Oh thanks Charlie!"

"Shh!" A few campers shushed us.

"Sorry," we giggled.

"Now. For the lead role of the beautiful and loving Princess Dulcet…" Everyone held their breath as Mrs. Niles gripped everyone in suspense.

All day, everyone spoke of Lane getting the much desired role. They all expected Mr. Niles to shout her name. She had sung beautifully. Even Sheila knew that Lane's name would be called. That's why it was a shocker when…

"Charlotte Mackenna!"

"What?" Charlie asked in disbelief.

"What?!" Sheila squealed in outrage.

An audible gasp could be heard throughout the crowd, but it was followed by a resounding round of applause, mostly from me, Saliesha and Sofia. "Go Charlie!"

"Get it girl!"

I pushed Charlie forward because she was pretty much frozen in shock. "Go!"

Charlie didn't smile, she was too stunned. Somehow she managed to walk up to Mrs. Niles and grab a script.

"Congratulations Charlie!" Mrs. Niles exclaimed.

"Why me?" Charlie squeaked.

"Because, Camper Charlotte, we saw something in you that the other girls didn't have," Mr. Niles explained as he placed his clipboard under his arm and shook her hand firmly.

"That je nais se pas!" Mrs. Niles explained.

"Your juggling act was very original!"

"Oh..." Charlie nodded and numbly walked back to us while we jumped up and down.

"A-*hum*!" Mrs. Niles cleared her throat loudly to get everyone's attention. "Rehearsals begin tomorrow evening. On the back of your scripts you'll find the dates and times of every rehearsal leading up to the big show." The two directors turned around and started to staple the rest of their papers onto the old tree. A few minutes later they turned around and announced, "There you'll find the rest of the roles, the understudies and the crew. Please be on time! And again," Mrs. Niles stared at Charlie, "Congratulations!"

All of the campers ran to the tree once the directors left, including Saliesha and Sofia. Campers kept congratulating Charlie as they passed her.

"I guess I'm sorry Callie. I won't be able to partner up with you now for the obstacle course."

"Hey, it's okay. I think this is a pretty good excuse."

Sofia and Saliesha ran back towards us. "Guess what role Lane got?"

"What?" Me and Charlie asked at the same time.

"The Witch's Assistant."

"Ouch." Charlie winced.

I thought briefly about something my mom told me once...that pride comes before the fall. I never really understood its meaning or met anyone who experienced it, until Lane. No more was said when Sheila approached us.

"Well Charlotte, you've managed to somehow steal my lead role. You must be very proud of yourself."

"I didn't steal anything Sheila; you just weren't as good as me," Charlie said with an imitation of Sheila's nose stuck in the air. I tried hard not to giggle.

"Oh please spare me. I hardly merit juggling bananas and oranges 'better than' moi." Sheila placed her hand over her heart, one pinky sticking up.

"You forgot to add singing," Sofia added.

"Oh and didn't she hop on one foot too?" Saliesha asked.

Sheila rolled her eyes. "This is going to be a debacle of a play. Well, all except *my* role, that is."

"Whatever you say Sheila," Charlie smiled brightly. "Excuse me while I look through the script and start memorizing my lines as the Princess." We followed her as she passed by Sheila. We all flipped our hair over our shoulders 'Sheila-Style'. She let out a strangled snort and proudly walked in the opposite direction.

We giggled as we walked towards the fire.

"I can't believe you're gonna play a princess," Saliesha shook her head. "I can't even imagine you wearing a dress."

"Hey, I may like to skateboard, play football and hockey, but I don't mind acting like a girl once in a while." She looked down at the script, "As long as it's only *one* time."

We all laughed and she added. "Now all we need to do is find Callie a partner for the obstacle course."

I jumped over a few tree roots. "It's useless. I might as well drop out."

"Never!" Charlie shouted. She rolled up her script and held it up to her mouth like a microphone.

"What are you doing?!"

Charlie hopped onto a log. "Hear ye! Hear ye! Camper Calliope Thornton needs a partner for the annual obstacle course race! Any takers?"

I noticed that the campers started looking at us with confused amusement. I took the rolled up script from Charlie and swatted her arm with it. She snatched it back and we all sat on the log as Mr. Mendel, Brandon and another boy camper began playing their guitars.

"Let me check out this script," Charlie opened it up.

Saliesha passed out some sticks and Sofia passed out the marshmallows and I absently took them as I glanced at Brandon. Saliesha and Sofia started chatting and my imagination started to take me far away. I was in a fifties-style lounge singing on the stage with a tall microphone. I had that wonderful wavy blonde hair and bright blue eyes. Everyone was captivated by my voice and Brandon was on the other side of the stage playing the piano.

"Earth to Calliope…"

"Huh?"

"Your marshmallow is on fire," Charlie said calmly.

"What?!" I shrieked and jumped up when I saw the black goo on my stick.

As the girls giggled, a girl with wavy strawberry-blonde hair approached us. A single braid went down the side of her face. "Are you Calliope?"

I set the burnt marshmallow down and nodded, "Yeah."

"I'm Quinn."

I couldn't help but admire her hair. Compared to my boring brown hair, it was way better. "I know you; we've been in a few activities together."

"Yes and you're Mrs. Copperpot's granddaughter," Saliesha pointed out.

Quinn nodded and smiled. "I hear from Charlotte that you're still in need of a partner," she stated in her English accent.

I looked at Charlie and she only smiled as she waved her script in 'hello'.

I turned back to Quinn. "Yeah, I do."

"My friend Daisy and I signed up for the race too, but she changed her mind last minute. Interested in partnering up?"

"I'd love to!"

"Great! I'll see you at practice tomorrow."

"Yeah cool, thanks!"

Quinn left and I rolled my eyes at Charlie. "Thanks Charlie."

She rolled up the script one more time and said through it, "You're welcome!"

We all erupted into laughter.

Chapter 7

I Look Forward To Our Next Meeting

Note to Self: Rain can be fun.

THE FOLLOWING afternoon I stood in front of a great big obstacle course on a large open grassy field. Ms. Davies was currently checking off campers' names from the sign-up sheet.

Arms crossed in front of her, Gwen came over to me with a smug look on her face; Miranda at her hip. "Still no partner? I don't think Ms. Davies will appreciate *that*. I think you're going to have to drop out of the race." Her shiny black hair was held away from her face with a purple headband. I briefly wondered how many headbands Gwen owned.

"My partner should be here any moment, thanks for being so concerned," I said pleasantly. There was no way I'd let Gwen get the best of me.

She looked around and then smirked at Miranda. "I don't see anybody."

It was really hard to smile, so I felt my teeth grind. "Don't worry about it."

"Well I would worry about it if I were you," Miranda added. Her wavy black hair billowed around her shoulders.

"Then it's a good thing you're not me," I bit back.

"Alright Camp Eerie Campers! Line up with your partners!" Ms. Davies called out.

I felt my ponytail hit my face as my head swung back and forth. Quinn had to show up…she *would* show up wouldn't she? She was a Copperpot. They looked reliable enough…

Saliesha and Sofia walked over to me. "You okay girl?" Saliesha asked as she scratched her dark arm. The mosquitoes had been out in full force lately.

"Yeah," I kept looking around and mind started spinning.

My spinning thoughts were interrupted when Ms. Davies' perfectly tanned-self came over to me. "Hey Camper Calliope, Gwen tells me that you don't have a partner. Is everything okay?"

I looked at Ms. Davies' pretty green eyes. "I…" my mouth moved up and down like a fish begging for water. I glanced behind her and saw Gwen and Miranda smirking; very satisfied.

"Hey! Calliope!"

We all turned around and watched as Quinn ran towards us. Her strawberry blonde hair was up in a ponytail, a single braid swept up with the mass of hair.

"I'm so terribly sorry that I'm late," she gasped out of breath as she stopped in front of me. She placed her hands on her knees for a second and stood straight up. "It won't happen again. Did I miss anything?"

Ms. Davies' sparkling white teeth made an appearance. "Don't worry about it Camper Quinn." She went to the front of the group.

I couldn't help but glance over at Gwen and saw the look of wrath on her face. I smiled gratefully at Quinn. "I was getting scared for a minute."

Quinn smiled back. "My bunk-mate got lost on the way to the library and I had to show her the way."

"I don't care if you're late, I'm just glad that you're here." I didn't have to look at Gwen to feel the laser beams at my back.

"Okay," Ms. Davies raspy voice caught everyone's attention. "This obstacle was designed for each team to go through together. There are a total of six teams. Each team will be assigned a time to come and practice. You can practice at that time every day or one day a week or every two weeks leading up to the race." Ms. Davies continued on with a few safety rules and guidelines and then pointed at Gwen and Miranda.

"…our two winners from last year, campers Gwen and Miranda." Everyone clapped and the two girls bowed. Ms. Davies continued. "Practice hard. I know for a fact that these two are out to take the title again."

She handed each team a packet with all of the safety rules she just explained and the practice schedule. I pulled out the paper from the folder. "Four to five pm." I looked up at Quinn. "Should we meet twice a week?"

"I think we should meet every single day," Quinn stated firmly. Her accent seemed stronger. "We have to make good use of all of our time given."

I was sure she saw my eyes twinkle in delight. I had a great partner. "I like how you think." We planned to meet the next day to start practicing.

"This is Easel and Rebecca," Ms. Davies pointed to two camp counselors who looked competitive. "They'll be running through the course to show you every stage of the race."

After they finished, Ms. Davies dismissed us and each team walked in different directions as we schemed a plan of attack. Gwen looked at me and I felt the challenge in her gaze. I turned the other way.

The challenge was on.

*****

"Rain. Not fun."

I looked out of the bunk window and could barely see outside. It came down in torrents and hit the window heavily. Thunder boomed furiously. There was no way I could meet Quinn for practice now. I turned around and saw Charlie and Sheila buried in their scripts. Lane was staring at herself in the mirror, uncharacteristically powdering her nose. Saliesha was drawing in her notebook and Sofia was intently reading her mail.

Mary had delivered our mail early that morning after breakfast. I decided to open mine. I was anxious to hear from my mom and dad; I missed them so much. I even missed my little sister Adele. If I missed my little sister, I *knew* there had to be a hole in the universe somewhere. The little tyrant was probably having a field day in my room.

I sat on my bed, letting my back lay against the pillow as I opened the white envelope. There were two letters inside; one from mom and dad asking all about my time at camp and telling me how much they missed me. The second letter was from Adele.

Her handwriting wasn't that good, but I got the gist of the letter, especially since it was really short. 'Callie, I miss you.' which was probably true. 'I can't wait to show you my new video game.' Which I *also* knew was true. If I actually wanted to play it though, that was a different story. The letter ended with, 'I'm not going through your things; which I knew wasn't true.

I knew for a fact that Adele was going through every bit of my room; section by section. It was pointless to get a lock on my door because Jelly Bean would have that thing opened in a heartbeat. I happily noticed that Adele didn't mention anything about the traps I set. I smirked; Adele would never admit any sort of defeat.

Smiling because the letters made me feel good, I flipped open my notebook and started writing back to my family. The first one let my parents know that I was actually having a good time...that I'd actually made some friends and described them all. I even described Gwen and told them what happened the first time we met in Mrs. Copperpot's class.

I told my parents a lot...except for the investigation about the missing girl. I didn't want my parents to think I went crazy. I had a hard time facing that myself.

I also wrote back to Adele, telling her that I missed her too, that I couldn't wait to see what game she bought and also telling her to stay out of my room and that I wasn't joking around. I sealed the letters and placed them in the mailbox next to the door.

"Hey Cal," Charlie called out from the top bunk.

"Yeah," I walked over to her.

"I need you to be the prince for me. I have to practice out loud and memorize these lines.

I shrugged. "Sure."

Charlie handed me a script and I climbed up to sit across from her. Sheila was on the top of her bunk on the opposite wall, bedazzling her costume for the play. "Have you ever even *acted* before?" Her bracelets made sounds as she waved her hand back and forth.

Charlie looked at her happily. "I played a tree in my first grade school play."

Sheila made a snort of disgust and placed the back of her hand against her forehead and tilted her head back as if she were going to faint. "This is a mockery to the art of performing."

"Too bad Mr. and Mrs. Niles don't think so." Charlie said tongue-in-cheek.

Sheila placed her hands over her heart. "Alas, that is positively devastating."

Charlie rolled her eyes and looked at me. "Can we practice now?"

"Gladly," I tried to ignore the drama queen on the other side of the room.

"Calliope," Sheila gracefully jumped down from the bunk bed. "I implore you to allow me to be the prince just this one time. I have *much* training to do."

We looked down at Sheila's big red hair, which had little butterfly clips scattered throughout.

"Training?" Charlie asked in disbelief and then laughed, "I don't want training from you. I don't need it!"

"*Fine*," Sheila scoffed and folded her arms in front of her. "Go ahead Callie; I'd love to see how you'll play the prince."

"Fine!" Charlie answered instead and looked at me. "Go ahead Callie, start with the moment the prince meets the princess."

I pursed my lips and glanced at Sheila and Charlie, then took a deep breath and read in monotone, "Are my eyes tricking me or have I seen a real angel?"

Charlie tried to bat her long lashes and said in a high-pitched voice, "You haven't been deceived. I am Princess Dulcet...beauty of all the lands-"

"Cut! Cut! Cut!" Sheila's face turned really red. "Charlie, you sound like a scary clown and Callie, you sound like a zombie!"

"How many zombies have you met?" Charlie muttered.

I sighed. "Well I'm not *really* a prince. She just needs to memorize her lines! And how do you know what a scary clown sounds like anyway?"

Sheila imitated Charlie's acting voice, "Hi boys and girls! I'm Sloopy the Clown!"

Silence.

Charlie made a face filled with disgust. "You made your point. That was bad."

Sheila laughed sardonically and nodded her head. "See what I mean?" She looked at me, "Please start again and this time," she looked at Charlie, "watch me." She cleared her throat as I started again.

I tried to put a little more feeling into it. "Are my eyes tricking me or have I seen a real angel?"

"You haven't been deceived!" Sheila shouted. Sofia and Saliesha jumped in fright.

Standing straighter and smiling wide, Sheila batted her lashes perfectly. "I am Princess Dulcet…" she waved her hand around, "…beauty of all the lands!"

Clapping rang out from Saliesha and Sofia. They cheered and whistled.

"Thank you!" Sheila bowed. "Oh you are too kind," she said graciously.

Charlie's mouth hung open in wonder. "Huh."

"And that," she swept hair behind her shoulders, "is how one acts in the art of performing."

I nodded impressively, "Hats off to you Sheila." I turned to Charlie, "You have a lot of work to do."

Sheila piped up again. "I don't mind coaching you Charlotte." She placed a sparkly nail by her mouth. "I do have two songs to rehearse and a big part to memorize, as you know I *am* playing Queen Minacious. However, I can extend some of my time to you since you obviously have much to work on." She smiled proudly at Charlie, "What do you say? Would you mind being my protégé?"

Charlie looked at me and I nodded encouragingly. She shrugged and finally said, "I guess it wouldn't hurt."

Sheila clapped. "Then it's done! Move over Calliope, Charlotte and I have much work to do."

As I moved to get down, Charlie gripped my arm. "I think I just sold my soul."

"The pain will probably last for a little while, then you'll get used to it and it'll probably turn into more of a numbing feeling." I patted her on the shoulder.

Charlie took a skeptical deep breath and smiled at Sheila as she climbed up Charlie's bunk. She settled in and looked around. "Your sheets are so drab. You need some more sparkle." She said in obvious distaste. Charlie looked down at me in a What-Have-I-Done face and Saliesha and Sofia giggled.

"I think I'll run out to the library," I told Saliesha and Sofia.

"Are you crazy girl? We nearly drowned out there just to eat breakfast." Saliesha wrapped herself into a warm gray shawl.

"The rain will only get harder," Sofia said softly.

"I have to go there too," we heard Lane say.

She was missing her glasses again and her face was drowning in heavy makeup.

I didn't know what to think about Lane any longer. Especially after she had called Sheila names. But my mom had always tried to teach me not to be judgmental; that everyone had a reason for doing what they do.

"I guess we can try to go together," I replied.

We grabbed the tent-like umbrella and raced out of the bunk house and down the long, muddy road. There really was no time to talk as we ran. A few minutes later we went barreling into the quiet library. As I shook myself off and closed the umbrella, I looked around. The air conditioner was pumping and it gave me a slight chill. The lights were on and everything was quiet save for the sound of rain pounding on the windows and roof.

"I don't think you'll have much volunteering to do today," I told Lane.

She squinted because it was obviously hard for her to see without her glasses. "This is my last day volunteering," she shook off her rain jacket. "I'm going to quit."

"But you love the library."

"*Geeks* love the library," she muttered, or at least I thought that was what she muttered.

"Lane?" I grabbed her arm before she hurried away. I let go when she turned back around to face me. "Why did you call Sheila fat?"

She looked caught off guard and straightened up. "I really don't want to talk about this." She adjusted her clothes and played with her hair. I couldn't help but shake my head. This wasn't the Lane I once knew.

"There's barely anyone here," I explained and pointed to the empty work tables. "And I just want to know. I really don't like seeing Sheila and you not speaking. You two were supposed to be friends."

"I didn't mean to call her names. It just came out wrong…out of anger. And she didn't even give me time to explain. You know how Sheila is. Once she's upset there's no calming her down." Lane pushed some blonde hair behind her ear and I was surprised to see her face turn pink; at least I thought it changed color; I really couldn't tell with all the makeup.

"It seems that you two need to sit down and talk."

"I don't think so. I've changed."

I let out an impatient breath. "People change all the time, but it doesn't mean two friends couldn't learn to accept the changes. There's a chance you two can be friends again."

She shook her head. "I don't think so." Looking around, "I'll see you later."

I watched her walk away and felt helpless. The tension between Lane and Sheila was terrible and it just had to change. But there was only so much I could do. And as far as her looks…I had a feeling *that* was all my fault. I was the one who told her to change up her look, but I didn't think she'd do it every day. Total backfire.

Putting that situation in a different part of my mind, I brought forward the investigation. I brought along the box I found in the ground that day with Charlie and Sheila and put it on top of a table. I sat down, opened it up and stared at it. "There has to be something here…" I glanced at the picture of the girl with the blotted out face. I leaned back on my chair, lifting it off the front two legs, knowing it was a bad habit I couldn't stop.

"Callie?"

I looked up, saw Brandon and fell backwards in surprise, hitting my head on the floor. He hurried to help me up and my face turned tomato red in embarrassment, "Hi Brandon."

"Are you okay?" He asked as he helped me straighten my chair.

I was mortified. I wanted the floor to open a hole and swallow me! Although that might be even more humiliating. I quickly checked the floor just in case. "I'm fine. Thanks."

"Didn't mean to scare you," he sat down on the opposite side of the table and placed his own books in front of him.

"It's okay, really. *Please* just forget about it." I touched the back of my head and felt the lump. I tried to ignore it.

"I've been meaning to talk to you."

"Really?" I squeaked.

"Yeah," he folded his hands and looked at me square in the eyes. His eyes were so blue. It was so brilliant. The sparkle, the pure clarity. Blue was now my favorite color.

"Blue what?"

"Huh?" I smiled at him curiously.

"You said 'blue eyes' and then stopped."

Hole. Floor. Now.

"I meant...what did you want to talk to me about?" I was *really* bad at talking.

"Sheila mentioned something about you wanting to know about the camp tale...about the missing girl?"

"Well...I'm not really talking about it much."

"I've found a few things about it...but I don't think the girl is actually missing."

I sat up straighter. "Really?"

He shook his head. "Have you ever heard the actual story? It's changed a few times since I've been to camp."

"How many times have you come to camp?"

He sat back. "This is my third year."

"Three years? Wow. So have you been thinking about this story all this time?"

"No. Just this year actually. I mean I've noticed the initials here and there but didn't really think anything of it."

"So what got you thinking about it now?"

Brandon smiled bashfully and looked down at his hands and then up again. And he had a dimple on his cheek. Seriously? This just wasn't fair. "I kind of overheard you talking about it...so I got interested."

I didn't know what to say. "Oh..." Okay, anything would have been better than 'oh'!

He pulled something out of his pocket and I saw the gold charm bracelet from the box. "Sheila told me you found this on the hiking trail...something about a box?"

I slid the box over to him. "You mean this box?"

"Wow," he grabbed it and looked at me. "May I?"

I nodded with excitement as he opened it and pulled out the flattened flower. Laying it aside, he skimmed the note curiously and then he stared at the faded picture. "'The other half of my heart is here.'" He scrunched his brows together as he thought aloud. "Obviously the heart is the girl in this picture; whoever she is."

I nodded. "So I'm trying to figure out if she's C or F."

"Well that's easy," he picked up the flower and twirled it. "F is for flower because that's the other half of his heart, so she's the F."

"Why didn't I think of that?" I asked in disbelief.

"Because," he pointed the flower at me, "you've been *over*thinking it."

I nodded again. "You're right." I pointed at the picture, "So what do you think of that?"

He picked it up and stared at the blurred face. "I don't know. One things for sure though," he looked at me, "this all has a sad tone to it. Like a final goodbye or something."

"And then she went missing?"

"Let's take the 'missing' out of the equation and look at the facts. C and F were obviously boyfriend and girlfriend. F is the girlfriend. The handwriting on the note doesn't look so girly, so C plainly wrote that and placed it in the box."

"Do you think F even knows about the box then?"

He shook his head. "I don't think she does."

I sat thoughtfully for a moment as I imagined the little love story we found.

"It's too bad her face is blotted out, maybe one of the camp teachers would have remembered her."

I remembered something. "Mrs. Bijou. She told me that she doesn't forget a face and she's been here over twenty years."

Brandon turned the picture towards me. "Do you think she'd remember the hair?"

I grabbed the picture and stared hard. The girl was sitting on a log by a tree. The picture was faded, but I was pretty sure that water was in the background. "It wouldn't hurt to ask, would it?"

"You have to let me know what she says. I think if an older lady says she never forgets a face then it's probably true. I live with my grandma and she never forgets a face. Every time we're at the market or anywhere, she always knows somebody."

"You live with your grandma?" He looked back at me in silence for a moment. Oh wow, I've done it now. How do I always do these things? "I'm sorry, I didn't mean to pry."

"No, it's okay." He smiled. Dimple. *Sigh*. "I was just thinking about her." He started putting the stuff back into the box as he spoke. "My parents died when I was young...around two years old."

"I'm sorry."

He closed the box and looked at me. "It's okay. I barely remember them; I just know them through pictures." He didn't get emotional as he spoke. I guessed he had spent enough years being sad. "By my mom's mother took me in and made me really happy. My grandma's the best."

"Good," I smiled at him.

"You're with your parents I take it?" He asked.

"Complete with an annoying little sister!" I couldn't have been more sarcastic if I tried.

He laughed. "It can't be that bad."

I thought about it and realized that it really wasn't that bad.

"Just never take them for granted," he said, a little more serious now. "Be thankful for them Callie. You never know when a drunk driver will strike."

I realized that he was telling me how they died and my heart got a little bigger. "I am."

We stared at each other for a few seconds and then I broke the spell. "So you almost forgot," I reminded him and leaned on my elbows. "What's the story on the missing girl?"

Brandon sat back and moved some hair away from his forehead. "Well the first story I heard was about this thirteen year old girl named Symphony."

"Symphony? Couldn't you tell the story was a fake just by that name?"

"Believe it or not, I've met a person with that name." At my disbelieving look, he nodded and continued on with the story. "It was her first year here at camp and she always got lost. Her bunk-mates never helped her and she was so quiet that the counselors even forgot about her. One night after a bonfire, she walked down the long, dark path alone…no one ever saw her again. They say her ghost still wanders the forest, looking for the way back to the bunks and she writes the initials C and F to remind everyone of her presence. Come and Find me."

Shivers ran through me. "H-how did the story change?"

He shook his head and in a dismissive tone explained, "That she never even made it to the bonfire that night. She had gotten lost *on the way* because her bunk-mates played a prank on her. Now her ghost haunts campers in revenge. Anyone who walks alone in the night would be sure to see her."

I felt my eyes grow really large. "And," I swallowed, "the third story?"

He leaned on his elbows and spoke in a scary voice. "That this camp was built on an old burial ground and the ghosts come alive at night, walking the forests. That's why our curfew is at ten o'clock."

I counted three whole seconds of silence.

Brandon couldn't help but laugh. "Sorry Cal, but where's Charlie's camera when you need it? You should see your face right now."

I blushed and shook my head. "I *so* don't believe any of that nonsense."

"Please don't. They only spread it to new campers to scare them. It's just a tease, that's all."

I nodded, "Right, of course."

He watched me dubiously.

So I have homework to do," I cleared my throat, desperate to change the subject. I grabbed the box. "I'll go see Mrs. Bijou tomorrow and ask her about the picture."

"Great," he stood up. "As soon as she tells you anything let me know. Then we can move on to the next phase of our investigation."

I couldn't believe it had turned from 'my' investigation to 'our' investigation. Especially when that 'our' meant me and Brandon. And how did he know that Charlie liked to snap pictures? I tried to stop a goofy smile from forming on my face. Really, I've been embarrassed enough. "And what is the next phase exactly?"

He winked at me and picked up his books. "We'll know when it comes. It was nice talking to you Callie."

"I look forward to the next meeting."

He chuckled and went outside to brave the storm. Meanwhile I had to brave the storm happening in my heart.

Chapter 8

This Could Be Bad

Note to Self: Fireflies are beautiful.

THE BIG band music cracked into the air and I was surrounded by a group of people. Everyone congratulated me for my stellar dance moves at the party. I spotted Brandon in the distance. He looked handsome in his dark blue suit and hair slicked back with mousse. He smiled with that dimple and walked in my direction. I blushed as he got closer. Suddenly a hand touched his arm and he turned to someone else.

It was me…but the blonde version of myself; the *better* version with the wavy blonde hair and blue eyes. I turned around and faced a mirror. No! It was plain old Callie! Brown hair. Brown eyes. Frumpy clothes. I turned back around to the glamorous me who was surrounded by admirers. Suddenly there was an earthquake and I was thrown to the floor! I looked up at glamorous Callie and heard her shout, "Wake up!"

I was shaken really hard. "What? What?" I could barely open my eyes.

"Wake up! Wake up!" Madison pleaded. "It's time for the raising of the flag and you'll be late for attendance!"

I didn't even have time to look around. We all scrambled to our feet and were shuffled out of the bunk house.

"Whodunit?!" Sheila shouted, half asleep.

"We'll get into trouble if you guys are late!" Madison shouted as she pushed Saliesha and Sofia outside.

Mary sang hurriedly, "Let's move your fab-tastic selves faster now!"

"Huh?" Charlie mumbled as she was pushed outside, barefoot.

Sheila complained, still half asleep, "But I set the timer! I can't go out so quickly! *Look at me*! I need to brush my teeth and exfoliate my face! I need to do my hair!"

"*Can* it! I mean," Mary gave a nervous laugh, "It's alright Camper Sheila you'll be able to freshen up later. Come on!"

None of us wanted Madison or Mary to get into trouble, so in the confusion we ran as fast as we could and saw the rest of the camp gathered around the pole.

"Oh my goodness!" Sofia shouted. "For a minute I thought this was a prank but it is true. We all woke up late!"

"You're very observant Sofia," Charlie huffed sarcastically.

As we lined up, we noticed the other campers staring at us and laughing.

"Do I have something on my face?" Sheila asked in horror. It was the first time we got a good look at each other.

"You do!" I squealed.

"What?!" Sheila touched her face and looked at her hand and saw…blue…and *purple*! She screamed as she touched her hair which stuck up at all ends with hairspray.

"Your hair is painted pink!" Charlie said to Saliesha.

"Nah ah!" Saliesha grunted in denial and touched her hair. "Yours is yellow!"

Charlie squeaked and told me I had heavy makeup all over my face.

"Starting a new trend Bunk Thirteen?" All six of us looked at Mrs. Reeves who was highly amused.

Mary jumped out in front of us. "Over here!" she sang and snapped a picture with Charlie's camera.

"I want aliens to appear and zap me up right now!" Sheila screeched.

"You guys make up all the colors of the rainbow," Madison said smugly. The entire camp broke into laughter and all six of us girls ran back to our bunk screaming in horror.

*****

"Now when you pronounce the word 'allow', you should open your mouth like an 'o' like this," Sheila demonstrated for Charlie as we sat in the dining hall for breakfast.

It had taken us extra time to scrub off the makeup on our faces and hair. We learned that our 'trusting' camp counselors set up our clocks the night before and made us oversleep and while we slept they painted our faces with the heavy, colorful makeup.

We decided *never* to bring up the mornings embarrassing events.

"You should also push one shoulder down and half way close your eyelids like this," Sheila showed her.

Charlie, meanwhile, stared at her as if she had a foot attached to her face. I placed my tray on the table as I joined the girls and looked at the display Sheila made of herself.

Saliesha and Sofia giggled as they watched my disbelieving face.

"Then," Sheila continued, "as you continue the 'ow' sound, you should roll the shoulder up and back like this…"

"Wait, wait, wait," Charlie closed her eyes and shook her head, then gawked at Sheila, "Dude, am I soul-train dancing or am I just saying the word 'allow'?"

Saliesha and Sofia giggled harder.

Sheila looked offended. "Number one, don't ever refer to me as a 'dude' and two, you wanted me to teach you how to act and *this* is how you act. *This* is how the Princess would say the word 'allow." And she demonstrated it again.

I couldn't help but laugh with Saliesha and Sofia.

Sheila's neck snapped in my direction. "I wouldn't expect any of you to understand the world of drama."

I held my laugh by holding my mouth shut, but my face was turning red from holding it in.

Sheila snorted in disgust and grabbed her back pack as she furiously stood up. "We'll continue later Charlotte. I cannot work under these conditions." And she swept away from the table.

I couldn't help it. As soon as Sheila left the dining hall I exploded in laughter. "I'm sorry Charlie," I gasped. "I just feel bad for you."

Charlie shrugged. "I think I'm confused about acting now more than ever."

"Why do you have to do it the way Sheila wants?" Sofia asked, her long black hair swept in front of one shoulder.

Charlie shrugged again. "I don't know, I guess because she's the one with the acting experience."

I looked at Charlie. "Mr. and Mrs. Niles chose you because you were original. You were yourself. If they wanted someone who acted like Sheila did then I think they would have given her the part."

Saliesha nodded somberly, "Callie's right girl."

Sofia agreed. "Just be yourself."

Charlie pondered for a moment and said, "You're all right. It shouldn't be that hard to be myself." She looked towards the area where we got our food and said, "I'll be right back."

Carrie and Liz walked to our table.

"Nice look today!" Liz exclaimed brightly.

"We think you'll start a new trend," Carrie laughed.

"Maybe you guys can give us a few tips."

Sofia and I turned pink.

Saliesha sucked her teeth. "Just let us know what time we can come over to make you both nice-looking for the dance. Pink and orange hair probably looks better on you than us." She explained with attitude.

"Oh come on!" Liz laughed. "We're only messing with you guys."

"You were kind of asking for it." Carrie continued, moving some blonde hair away from her face.

"Getting pranked isn't the worst part. The worst part is that you were pranked by your own counselors," Liz said in amazement.

"So tell us you didn't get a prank pulled on you yet," Saliesha said dryly.

Liz and Carrie looked at Saliesha as if she just announced she once lived on Jupiter, "Of course not!"

I didn't believe it. "How did you *not* get a prank pulled on you yet? I've been hearing of other bunks getting victimized by their counselors."

Liz said matter-of-factly, "We sleep in shifts."

"What are you talking about?" Saliesha asked.

Carrie explained, "The best pranks happen in the middle of the night. Sleep in shifts and you'll be ready to catch the pranksters better."

I exchanged looks with Saliesha and Sofia.

"And if you ever need help getting them back, you can ask us anytime." Carrie offered.

"Remember that the best pranks are the ones where you don't get caught."

"Thanks…I guess," I said with uncertainty.

Carrie and Liz giggled and walked away, leaving us lost in our own thoughts. One minute later Saliesha broke the silence. "So who's excited to see their parents on the last day of camp?"

"That eager to see them huh?"

Sofia looked at Saliesha with her big caring green eyes and answered me, "She is very homesick."

"It's nothing really." Saliesha said as she looked down at the table, her chin propped in her hand. "It's just I miss my crazy brothers," she looked up at me, "I have four. Two are older and two are younger and they all make me crazy." Tears welled up in her eyes as she thought of them. Sofia patted her shoulders sympathetically.

"Why didn't they come to camp?" I asked.

"Well Michael Jr. is actually going to be an intern at my dad's law office this summer. Jamal wanted to stay with his friends. Devon had to go to summer school and Buster is still too young."

"I know how you feel," Sofia said softly. "I am very far away from my home."

Saliesha looked curiously at Sofia and sniffed. "You know girl, I never asked you where you were from."

Sofia stared at her and said nervously, "Um…I did not mention it. But this is not about me," she rushed, "this is about you."

"Well then," I leaned forward on the table and asked Saliesha, "What do we need to do to make you feel better?"

"Happy un-birthday everyone!"

We turned around and saw Charlie carrying a tray of sliced birthday cake. She handed each of us one before setting one down for herself. We all looked at Saliesha, "Happy un-birthday Saliesha!"

She laughed gratefully, sniffing back tears. "I forgot about that."

"Happy un-birthday to you…happy un-birthday to you…" we sang and afterwards applauded.

"No un-birthday celebration is complete without one thing," I remarked.

"Presents?" Saliesha asked hopefully.

"Nope," I leaned forward, swiped some vanilla icing on my finger and smeared it on Saliesha's nose. She screamed in shock and the girls laughed.

"Well it's *your* un-birthday too!" Saliesha laughed, quickly grabbed icing and smeared it on my face before I had time to back away.

Charlie howled with laughter and that's when I reached over and got her square in the face. Soon, each of us had cake on our faces. I was sure that we were the noisiest table.

Sheila came back inside the dining hall, not noticing what was going on since her nose was so high up in the air. She simply announced, "I forgot my notebook…" her voice fell when she saw all of us with cake everywhere. We stopped and stared at Sheila…and evil grins cracked on our faces. "Ohhh no. No! No! I *just* conditioned my *hair*!"

Charlie raised her icing covered hand and stood up.

"*Nooo!*" Sheila ran outside squealing as all four of us got up and ran after her.

It took a few wipes of the paper towels to get the cake out of my hair, but I managed to look presentable before going in to see Mrs. Bijou. Throughout the activity, I kept glancing nervously at the fancy looking teacher…she almost reminded me of a grown-up version of Sheila. At the end of the class, I realized that I sewed together a scarf instead of an elaborately decorated shawl. As the campers filed out, I approached Mrs. Bijou at the front of the classroom.

"Mrs. Bijou, can I speak to you for a moment?"

Her brown-grayish head came up from her basket of fabrics and her older mouth formed a warm smile. "Yes darling?" She glanced at the scarf in my hand. "That's a charming…sock."

I shook my head.

She patted my hand sympathetically. "We have much to work on." She gracefully placed a pencil behind her ear. "Some people have the talent and some just do not."

"Oh, I didn't want to talk about the shawl or scarf or…whatever this is. I actually wanted to ask you something completely off topic."

She nodded her head in understanding, "Of course darling. *We can talk about boys if you want*," she whispered.

Shocking much! I shook my head right away. "No, I didn't want to talk about boys. I wanted to talk about-"

"Girly problems?" She raised a perfectly arched brow and winked.

"Ah…no." I cleared my throat. "You had mentioned before that you never forget a face." I pulled the old box out of my backpack and opened it, taking out the faded picture.

She looked curiously at me as she took the picture and pulled up the glasses that hung around her neck on a pearly necklace to study it. "Well…it would help if there was a face to remember."

I bit down on my lip. "I know, but it faded through time. It was buried in the ground. I was kind of hoping you might remember the girl by her hair." I watched her frown as she stared at the picture and I added, "I'm thinking her name might begin with an F?"

She looked as if she was thinking really hard. I thought that maybe the more information she had, maybe the memory would click. "She might have been a couple with a boy camper…maybe they were a really popular couple. Around twenty years ago?"

"You know," she tapped her chin thoughtfully. "I think I do recall a cute little couple roaming around the camp, but her name didn't start with an F…if I can recall." She handed me the picture. "She was so beautiful and he was a charmer."

"Do you remember their names?" I asked hopefully.

She took in a deep breath. "Sorry. I'm only good with faces, not names."

"Well thanks for your help."

"Anytime. And if you ever *do* have to speak about boys and things," she patted my hand again, "I'm here."

I'm gone. "Uh…thanks."

That night at the camp fire, I told Charlie all about Mrs. Bijou and the picture.

"Well that's a bummer," Charlie replied as she roasted some marshmallows in the fire.

"Tell me about it. I just need a good picture of the girl. But it seems impossible. She would have been a big help. That reminds me," I took out the scarf I made and handed it to her. "Happy un-birthday."

Charlie raised her thick brows in surprise and took the red cloth, "Just what I always wanted," she squinted and then smiled, "a bandanna."

"No, it's a scarf."

She raised her brows again.

"It was supposed to be a shawl…well, Mrs. Bijou thought it was a sock."

"Whatever it is, I love it. Thanks."

"So no lessons with Sheila tonight?" I asked with a smirk.

"Let's just say we mutually parted ways." She blew her marshmallow carefully before taking a bite.

"I'm sure she's miffed about it."

"Actually she looked relieved. Not to mention she told me that I was a 'hopeless trainee'."

We both giggled and looked over as Sofia and Saliesha walked in our direction. Charlie noticed a boy camp counselor, probably four or five years older than us, staring openly at Sofia. "Who is the cutie checking out our Sofia?"

"I don't know, but I notice that he does stare at her a lot."

Charlie shook her head. "There's just something about him, something different. It's like he really knows her or something."

I wondered about that for a minute. Just then, Sofia and Saliesha reached us. "Hey girls," I called out.

Sofia lifted her shoulders and asked me, "Where were you?"

"What do you mean?"

"We just saw Quinn and she said you didn't show up for practice."

My heart dropped to the bottom of my feet. No, my heart actually jumped up into my throat. Either direction was wrong! "I can't believe I forgot!"

"Quinn seemed pretty upset," Saliesha added as she watched me hide my face in my hands.

"But we told her that if you missed this then something *must* have happened," Sofia said sympathetically.

"Oh no, oh no, oh no," I smacked my forehead. "I need to go and find her."

I appreciated that Charlie looked concerned. "Do you want me to come with?"

"That's okay. I have to do this myself." I nodded and went off in search for Quinn. I couldn't believe that I had actually forgotten about the practice. I was even looking forward to it! Had I become too obsessed with the initials? Maybe I *was* thinking about it too much.

One thing was for sure; I wasn't thinking about where I was walking because I suddenly tripped on a tree root and slipped down the hill...backwards. I yelped and tried to hold onto something, but the only thing I could grab were fistfuls of mud. Landing with a *thump*, I groaned and tried to sit up. I heard voices coming from somewhere and I called out, "I'm oka-*blech*!" For future references, I noted that dirt and grass taste horrible together. I also noted that I could never see Brandon without being in horrible, embarrassing pain.

Charlie walked over with him and helped me up. "You sure?"

I was glad for the dirt smudges on my face because I knew it covered up my red splotches. "Hey Brandon. We always seem to meet this way." I started to pick grass from my rumpled hair with Charlie's help.

He actually smiled. "It's actually pretty lovely."

"That's Callie," Charlie pointed at my dirty clothes and messy hair, "very...lovely."

I rolled my eyes. "I was trying to look for Quinn. I must have not been paying attention where I was walking." I started to wipe my shorts.

"Well that's obvious," Charlie snickered and crossed her arms. "I figured I should follow you anyway."

"Stop acting like I'm accident prone," I glanced at Brandon and gave him a warning look, "Not a word."

He laughed. "What? I didn't say anything."

At the top of the hill, the campers started to sing worship songs and laughed with each other by the roaring fire.

I stared ahead of me at the dark forest and got a chill, "Why don't we go back up to the camp fire."

 With witnesses.

"Yeah and I was looking for you," Brandon caught my attention. "I wanted to find out if Mrs. Bijou said anything."

"Okay, but I really need to talk to Quinn first."

"Let's go," Charlie shrugged.

As we turned to climb back up the hill, something in the dark forest caught my eye. "What was that?"

Brandon and Charlie turned to me. "What?"

I took a deep breath. "I'm not sure, but something in the forest caught the light of the fire…"

Charlie looked puzzled as she turned to look into the forest. "I see it too."

It was some kind of light flickering on and off.

"That's pretty creepy," Brandon said with his hands in his pockets.

"It's only a light, not so creepy," Charlie looked at me. "Cal, let's go back to the fire."

I couldn't just leave. Maybe it was the actual ghost of the girl…like the one I saw that day during the hike. Maybe I could talk to it. Maybe I was going crazy. What did crazy people do in a situation like this?

I bolted into the forest.

"Callie! Wait!"

"This could be bad."

I knew they were behind me, but then I remembered how fast of a runner Brandon was and within a few seconds he was right next to me. "Callie! Hold on!"

"Okay you two! Wait up for me!" Charlie huffed.

I couldn't see the light any longer and I called over to Brandon in the dark forest, "Do you see it? Do you see anything?"

"Yeah," he slowed down. "More lights."

We ran through the trail and ended up at the lake…surrounded by hundreds of fireflies.

"Wow," Charlie said after she caught her breath. "This is pretty cool…"

Everywhere I turned there were fireflies; all of them lit up the night sky with the moon. It looked like a painting.

Brandon looked around and then smiled as Charlie started skipping through the pretty bugs. I caught one and let it crawl in my hands. "Sheila would be catching a panic attack right about now."

"A lot of girls would be scared around these things," he caught one and then let it go. "We're so busy with the camp fire we don't ever see this stuff."

"Some must have trailed towards the fire," Charlie said as she tried to catch some more.

"You okay Callie?"

I turned to Brandon and smiled weakly. "I just feel like a fool."

"Don't say that," he moved some hair away from his face and walked towards a tree that sat comfortably in front of the water.

I followed him and folded my arms, "For some reason I…"

He leaned back against the tree, planted one foot behind him and said, "You thought it was the ghost, didn't you?"

Busted.

Brandon chuckled at my guilty face. "There are no such things as ghosts, Callie."

"You sound like my mom."

"Hey, I don't think that's so bad," he replied. "You're probably thinking too much about the initials and the picture and everything."

"You're right again. Are you ever wrong?"

He leaned his head against the tree and looked down at me, "Are you ever boring?"

I looked down before he noticed how pink my face turned.

"Hold it right there!" Charlie called out.

We turned to her and saw her shocked expression. I hope she didn't see a ghost.

"What's wrong?"

Charlie held her hands out in front and walked slowly towards us. "Cal…you look just like that girl in the picture."

I giggled. "What do you mean?"

Brandon pushed away from the tree and walked towards Charlie; then he looked at me. I saw the change in his face the moment he realized something. "The picture…this is where F took the picture."

I got up quickly and turned around to face the water. There was a log, a tree…and water. "You're right! This is where F took the picture!"

"How cool is that?" Charlie sat on the log. She looked up at us, "We just solved a piece of the puzzle. Happy un-birthday!"

I walked up to the tree and looked around for initials.

"This place was probably really important to C and F." Charlie noted as she looked up into the massive tree branches.

I looked at Charlie. "Oh, remember that we found their initials on the wooden dock out by the water," I pointed to where I found them that day. "But why wouldn't he want to bury the box here?"

"So many people come in and out of the lake," Brandon pointed out. "He probably didn't want anyone to find it."

"That's true," Charlie agreed and looked at me. "I mean look where you found it; way out in the middle of the forest, off the edge of the hiking trail."

"Hey I never asked how you got off the trail in the first place," Brandon's blue eyes faced me.

"Um…well…"

Charlie stepped in. "Let's just say if you've seen her fall once, you've seen it a thousand times-*ow*!"

I elbowed Charlie on the side. Really, she deserved it. "I thought I saw something running through the woods. It was probably a deer or something." I was *never* going to admit that it was ghostly! "Charlie distracted me and I got scared and slipped."

"Sure, blame the sane one," Charlie said dryly.

"Wait a sec, what day was it on again? And what time?"

I thought back and told him and he nodded. "Hey, I think I was jogging around that time through the deep parts of the forest. You probably saw me and the guys."

So it wasn't a ghost. I should have been happy about this. Why wasn't I?

I had to change the subject fast before they realized my mind was drifting. "So do you think more things are buried there? Maybe he left things buried all over camp."

"That sounds like way too much effort for a boy," Charlie said dryly.

Brandon crossed his arms and huffed, "Hey!"

"No offense," Charlie giggled and playfully hit his arm. "I think you're looking into it way too much Cal."

"Okay, okay," I put my hands up in surrender and looked around, "but it's obvious that this place means something important to them."

"Maybe this is where they met?" Charlie suggested.

"Maybe one of them was in the swim club," Brandon guessed.

I pointed at him. "Hey! That would narrow down the search tons!"

"I guess Mrs. Bijou wasn't too helpful with the picture?" he asked.

I shook my head. "She meant it when she said she's only good with faces. She *did* say that there was a couple a long while ago who were inseparable."

"What were their names?" Charlie asked.

"She doesn't remember," I rolled my eyes reminding them, "faces."

"Right," Charlie drawled out.

"I suppose we'll be hitting the library tomorrow?" Brandon asked me.

Nodding, I began to walk back to the bonfire. "We've got a lot of work to do."

"Don't worry Cal," Charlie put her arm around my shoulder. "I'm sure you'll find lots of answers tomorrow. Things will get better."

"I really hope so."

Things only got worse.

Chapter 9

It's Funny How Things Work Out

Note to Self: Be yourself!

I FOUND Quinn and begged for forgiveness. Quinn wasn't too angry and told me that we'd just try again the next day. We practiced faithfully for rest of that week.

Unfortunately, practicing for the race and all of my other camp activities made it impossible to investigate the initials, so I didn't find the time to meet up at the library with Brandon.

At the end of the week, we were taking our sweet time cleaning up the bunk. Sheila's responsibility was the bathroom and well, no one really wanted bathroom duty. Madison and Mary sauntered into the bunk like they owned the place and then demanded to know why we were taking so long to clean.

"Oh Madison!" Sheila called from the bathroom, "A moment of your time sil vous plait!"

Madison's mass of black curly hair bounced as she walked into the now peppermint scented bathroom. "You did a good job in here Sheila." She pointed at spot on the toilet. "You missed a spot."

Sheila scrunched her face up. "Charmed, really I am. However, I'm having a serious problem with my blow dryer. My curls are begging to be dried and it's taken me all morning since the dryer isn't working and how could I possibly finish cleaning if I didn't diffuse my hair? I think it's the outlet."

"My dryer will not turn on either," Sofia complained and pointed at her own dryer.

"Yeah and if her dryer won't work, then my fan won't work tonight," Charlie added to the list of complaints.

"You guys might think it's funny," Saliesha reasoned. "But it's *not* fun sleeping in sweat," she bobbled her head as she spot.

"Since this bunk is older than the others," Madison had a smug know-it-all attitude, "some things won't work as well."

Mary nodded, her French braid not moving an inch. "Don't worry campers. We've heard about this bunk, we'll have it all fixed in a flashity-flash!"

"I highly doubt it," Sheila announced and handed Madison her dryer as Sofia handed Mary hers.

Mary sang. "I'm sure it just needs to be plugged and re-plugged, then turned on at the same time."

They both re-plugged the dryers. Madison looked at Sheila and pointed the dryer at her own hair. "Watch this and learn."

Mary stared right down the barrel of the dryer.

Madison called out to Mary, "On the count of three. One, two, three-"

Baby powder flew out of the dryer and exploded all over Madison's pretty curls. She shouted and closed her eyes from the particles of powder. Mary shouted at the same time when baby powder shot into her entire face and hair.

There was another explosion as well; this time it was laughter by all six of us girls in the bunk.

*****

At the beginning of the following week, it was Backwards Day at camp. That morning, Charlie dressed, eager to get to the dining hall. She roughly brushed her hair and talked in a rush. "We get to have dessert first!" She beamed with delight. "Then pizza and soda with fries!"

"Or the alternative," Sofia said as she braided her long black hair over the front of her shoulder, "a spinach salad and a tuna sandwich."

Charlie rolled her eyes and tied up her thick brown hair sloppily. "Either way," she wagged her thick brown eyebrows, "we're eating good this morning."

"Good morning campers!" Mary came barreling into the little cabin. We all groaned as she danced while passing out schedules. "Or rather, good evening!" she giggled.

"Where's Madison?" Sheila asked, disappointed. We had come to admire Madison and wanted to be around her as much as we could.

"She had to help set up the bonfire for this morning," Mary sang.

Even Sheila took the schedule with an exasperated face…and it took a lot to exasperate Sheila. I should know; she taught me the word 'exasperate'.

"After a delicious dinner, we'll be having our fantastic bonfire!" She handed a schedule to an excited Charlie and looked at me with over-excited gray eyes. "Camper Calliope, you have to wear your clothes backwards! That's right ladies; the Camp Eerie lettering should be on your back!"

She laughed and handed a schedule to Saliesha, who asked sarcastically, "So what? We have to wear our shoes on opposite feet too?" She giggled and nudged Sofia.

Mary looked straight at Saliesha and sang, "Of course! Start switching those tootsies!"

Saliesha's mouth, all mouths for that matter, dropped to the floor. Mary cackled with a burst of laughter, "I'm just kidding!" She settled down. "But you *do* have to walk to the dining hall backwards."

Some of us snickered; most of us sighed.

"Have an awe-so-riffic day!" She chirped and flew out of the cabin.

"Someone seriously needs to stop allowing her sugar," Sheila stated as she adjusted her sparkly purple hair band. She hopped off of her bed. "Charlotte, I'll see you at the rehearsals today after the bonfire…I *hope* you memorized some of your lines. You're new to this so just know that Mr. and Mrs. Niles expect everyone to know their lines by now.

"Of course, *I'm* always the only one to actually accomplish this," she placed her hand over her heart and pranced outside.

I tied my shoe laces and asked Charlie with a knowing look, "Is she a little bitter about something?"

"She's still miffed that I'm playing the lead," she answered as she placed a slim camera in her pocket.

Saliesha whistled and I said in a scary voice, "The plot thickens."

Charlie grabbed a pillow and threw it at me. "Cut it out."

We giggled but stopped when Lane came out of the bathroom. Wearing high heels wasn't something I thought was comfortable in the woods. Not only did Lane wear high heels, but her clothes were tighter and shorter, her hair was up in a fancy do' and she wore heavy makeup.

"Lane?" Saliesha asked in disbelief.

I straightened and stood next to Charlie as we gawked at her.

"Wait," Charlie reasoned, "it's backwards day...this is for backwards day right?"

Lane took in a deep breath and raised her chin up. She sounded completely different. "As you know, I got a really small part in the play," she glanced at Charlie with menace and clicked her heels on the wood floor as she grabbed her backpack. "Mr. and Mrs. Niles will notice me more..." she sounded a little hesitant to reveal that bit of information.

I thought she was trying too hard not to be herself.

Saliesha and Sofia looked at each other with disapproval and then Saliesha announced, "We've gotta get to the dining hall. Come on Sofia."

The two girls quickly left the cabin, leaving me and Charlie looking at Lane's high shorts and tightened camp shirt. Charlie covered a cough and turned to me, "I don't wanna miss dessert so let's go." She tugged on my arm.

"One second," I looked at Charlie's unbelieving face. "I'll catch up."

She sighed, "Okay," And ran out to catch up with the other girls. When she reached the door she stopped, turned around and started running backwards.

Lane angrily threw books into her backpack as I approached her. "What is it Callie?" she asked shortly, avoiding eye contact.

"Lane, this is not you."

She turned to me sharply. "Why are you judging me?"

"I'm not judging you. I'm the only one brave enough to tell you the truth." I sighed with frustration. "It's obvious to everyone that you've changed...and not in a good way."

She swung her backpack over her arm. "Yeah well mind your business-*no*!" She gasped and flew to the floor to find the contact that popped out of her eyes.

I went down to help her. "I'm trying to tell you this as a friend. I miss you...*you*. The way you were, the way you really are."

Lane found her contact and rushed to the bathroom.

I followed. "I can't help but feel that this is my fault. When I told you to change your hair, I didn't mean to change all the way. Maybe you should talk to Madison. You see how beautiful she is and she doesn't have to wear tight clothes for us to see it-"

Lane slammed the door and shouted, "Leave me alone!"

It was the first time in my life I ever talked to a door. "You know, I don't have experience having friends, but I'll tell you this; I don't like my new friend acting like someone she's not when everyone likes her the way she is."

Silence.

Then more silence.

I stared at the wooden door. Experience was needed in these situations and I had none, but Madison had to know about this. Lane was a sweet person. Maybe she *did* change inside…it was obvious that Lane was tired of following Sheila everywhere, but I didn't think it was a reason for her to change her entire personality.

It was all too much to handle on my own. I took a deep breath and turned to leave. Going outside into the humid day, I was shocked to find Charlie standing by the big scary tree. "Aren't you excited for dessert?"

Charlie pursed her lips and leaned her head towards the tree, her dark blue eyes glancing, "You ever notice this?"

"What?" I walked up to where she pointed, narrowed my eyes and then opened them in shock. There, etched into the bark of the giant tree were the initials; the same C and F. It was very small, but clear. "*What*?" I looked at Charlie, then back to the tree. "This means…no…it can't be…"

"That's right," Charlie crossed her arms triumphantly. "This used to be F's bunk. Wow I am *so* good," she bragged and started to river dance. "I'm on *fire!*" She licked her thumb, placed it on her side and made a sizzling noise.

I was astonished. "What are the odds that I'm staying in the same bunk she did?"

She stopped dancing and wiggled her fingers towards me, "Very spooky."

This meant very good things for the investigation.

*****

After a very interesting breakfast...or dinner, all of the campers made their way to the bonfire...the daytime bonfire.

"This day just started and it's already too weird for me," I commented as I caught up with the girls.

"Why? Breakfast was awesome!" Charlie exclaimed.

"Tell that to my poor stomach," Saliesha groaned. "I know now why my mom always wants me to save dessert for *last*." She rolled her eyes.

"Cake in the morning is definitely a bit too harsh on the stomach," Sofia agreed.

"Eh," Charlie waved them off, "you guys complain too much."

"Hey Callie," Brandon came over with a friend.

Sofia and Saliesha gave me knowing looks and giggled as they walked ahead of us. I stuck my tongue out at them and then turned to Brandon. "Hi."

"This is Edward," he turned to Charlie, "you guys know each other."

"Yep, hey." Charlie said stiffly.

Edward had landed the role of prince in the play and was pretty popular at camp. His hair was a very blond and he had really bright green eyes. "Hey," he smiled.

I nodded, "Nice to meet you."

"Are we still meeting up at the library later?" Brandon asked me, his hands in his pockets as he rolled on his feet back and forth.

"Yeah," I brightened up, "you'll never believe what we found. Well, more Charlie than anyone."

"She's been solving this case more than we have," he commented and smiled at Charlie. She was still frozen and nodded awkwardly. If my guess was right, he looked a little disappointed that she didn't have a witty come back.

"Come on, I'll tell you about it." I started walking towards the large group of campers that started singing and roasting marshmallows under the bright sun.

Charlie walked like a mummy alongside Edward.

"What's wrong with her?" Brandon whispered to me.

"I think she might have a little crush on Edward." I giggled and Brandon laughed. As we got closer to the bonfire, I noticed the handsome junior counselor staring at Sofia again. "Who is that?"

"That's Brom, our bunk counselor."

I didn't even realize that I asked who he was out loud! I had to pay more attention to my mouth.

"He's really strong," Brandon marveled. "He could play every sport like a pro."

Since it was out in the open, I figured to ask about him. "Where is he from?" noting his white skin and black hair. I could even see the gray color of his eyes from the distance.

Brandon shrugged absently. "Some country in Europe I guess. He didn't really say, but I'm guessing Spain or something."

I thought about that as we made it to the fire.

Half an hour later, Brandon was filled in about the initials on the tree and Charlie was laughing and being herself again. As a matter of fact, she was surrounded by a crowd of campers as she told a scary story; which ended up being a funny scary story. Edward looked hooked on every word she said.

I sat on a log next to Brandon. "It didn't take her that long to loosen up."

Brandon looked at Charlie. "She's great. She doesn't seem to be a girl who has a problem being herself."

I was going to open my mouth to agree, but stopped when I looked at how Brandon watched Charlie.

I looked at Charlie and then back to Brandon.

And my heart stopped.

Brandon liked Charlie.

Brandon liked *Charlie* and not *me*. My stomach became an expert acrobat as it flipped and spun into knots. Brandon had never really showed me that he liked me…not really. We only ever talked about the investigation…never really anything else. Well, except that time he said Charlie should take a picture of me and he hadn't really met Charlie yet. So he was watching her?

That one time he told me about his grandmother, but that really wasn't much. I considered him a friend and maybe he did the same. I looked at him as he became enthralled in Charlie's story.

It was *obvious* that I was considered just a friend. I looked back at the closest friend I'd ever had. When did Charlie become the object of every guy's affection? What did Charlie have that I didn't? We were both pretty…I stopped myself. I was joking.

Charlie was drop dead gorgeous with all of that thick brown hair and deep blue eyes. She even made freckles look good. Maybe if I was a blonde…

Just then Charlie ended her story with an exaggerated shout that had even the counselors howling with laughter…and that's when it became clear to me; it was Charlie's personality. She was friendly of course, but she was so down to earth.

She didn't take everything too seriously and wasn't scared to poke fun at herself. Not to mention she loved getting dirty in sports and most definitely wasn't scared to eat in front of everyone. Her face was basically inside of her ice cream bowl at the dining hall.

As my heart slowed down to a normal human beat, I understood why Brandon would adore Charlie.

It was just hard to cope with.

Charlie walked over to us and quickly snapped a picture. "Gotcha," she laughed. "Cal hates getting a picture taken by surprise."

"Who does?" Brandon joked. "Right Callie?" he nudged me.

I couldn't swallow because a gigantic frog decided to make a home in my throat. Coughing lightly, I nodded and tried to smile, "Yeah I can't stand it."

Edward joined us and looked at Charlie. "We have to get over to rehearsal now. You mind if I walked you there?"

I quickly glanced at Brandon and if he was jealous, he really didn't show it.

"Uh, yeah, sure," Charlie replied.

Edward's blond head bobbed up and down as he offered to take her backpack. Charlie declined because she liked holding her own things. "Cal, don't forget to try and fit in practice with Quinn and I'll see you at lunch."

She looked at Brandon, then Edward and back to me. "It's funny how even though it's backwards day, lunch is still in the middle."

"It's funny how things work out," I said softly; talking about my new revelation more than anything else. "Have fun."

As they walked away, Brandon turned to me and smiled. "So I'll catch you later?"

"Yeah, definitely."

He nodded and started to walk away backwards. "Catch you later!"

"Callie," Quinn came over to me as soon as Brandon turned back around.

"Hey Quinn," she had her pretty wavy blonde hair down with a French braid down one side.

"I've just talked to Ms. Davies. Saliesha and Sofia are practicing *first* since they're usually *last* which means we're *second*."

My brain tried to register that sentence and then I smiled. I definitely couldn't wait for practice since it would distract me from Brandon and Charlie and that entire dilemma. "Great."

"Also, Ms. Davies gave me this form we have to sign for being in the race. I've signed my part," she showed me the paper. "You just have to sign there and turn it in at the main office."

I nodded. "I'll do that right now."

"I'll meet you in an hour," she said in a stern English accent.

"I promise I won't forget."

I walked over a few hills towards the main office. It was located next to the library, the nurse and all of the art cabins surrounding a cute courtyard. I went inside of the screen door and loved feeling the blast of cold air. It was always a relief from the humidity outside.

A nice acoustic song played in the background. An older, chubby girl with curly brown hair and friendly smile came over from behind the counter, "Hello."

"Hi," I furrowed my brows, "Do you mind if I ask who's singing?"

"Are you kidding me? That's the new single from Zipporah."

"I love Zipporah!" Seriously, Zipporah was a great singer I adored. Her songs were full of encouragement and love. She was the only singer I loved besides my swing music. Nothing beat swing in my book. "She came out with a new CD?"

"Yes!" The girl said with excitement, "Just last week. Where have you been?!"

I was silent for a moment and answered, "Here."

"Oh that's right." She pursed her lips and asked, "What's that for?" She pointed at my paper.

"The obstacle course form from Ms. Davies."

"Oh," she looked around, "there's a folder for that. I'll be right back." She left the room and went to the back area. I leaned my elbows on the counter and tapped my feet as I looked around, seeing a lot of camp pictures in frames.

They looked identical to the ones in the brochure my mom gave me. I saw a great view of the lake and a beautiful picture of the scary tree path. I turned around to see the pictures behind me and froze.

Lane was sitting in the small row of chairs by the back door, avoiding eye contact with me. Pink, blue and black makeup smeared all over her face from tears. Her bright red lipstick was smudged around the side of her mouth. She was a mess.

She held her stomach as if in pain and leaned over, her red high heels still on.

"Lane?" I quickly kneeled down beside her. "Lane, are you okay?" She didn't reply and the screen door swung open.

Madison walked in with a somber look on her face, "Hey Callie."

I stood up and went to her. "What happened to Lane?"

Madison put her hand on my shoulder. "We'll have to talk later. Now isn't really the time."

The door opened again and I recognized the camp directors, Mr. and Mrs. Reeves, as they walked in.

"Hello Camper Calliope," Mrs. Reeves smiled gently. Her blonde hair was tightened into a bun.

"Hello," I said shyly.

The chubby teenage girl came out from the back, talking loudly, "I found the folder! Whoo hoo!" She stopped when she saw the small crowd in the main office. She quickly walked to the counter, grabbed the paper and said in a business-like tone of voice, "Thank you."

"You're welcome." I turned to see Mr. and Mrs. Reeves lead Lane to their office, Madison following.

It left a bad feeling in the pit of my stomach. I knew she was getting in trouble for what she was wearing. I went back outside into the humid weather and tried to shake off the bad feelings. I needed to concentrate for practice.

This day wasn't going very well.

Chapter 10

What's The Catch?

Note to Self: Practice doesn't make perfect, but trying does.

AN HOUR later I was at the obstacle course ready to practice. Quinn seemed relieved that I was there and sooner than later we both got started. I grabbed the baseball bat that lay on the ground and placed it upside down. I put my forehead on the end and began to spin around five times.

One, two, three, four, five! Getting up, I ran back towards Quinn to tap her hand, but the sky was falling and I fell down with it! I tried to get up again and this time collided with Quinn. We fell down to the ground and I couldn't hold in my laughter.

Quinn was not laughing. She immediately ran towards the tires and jogged through them. I quickly grabbed an oversized set of scuba flippers and waited at the end of the tires. I stuck my sneakers into the large opening and waddled to a large broom. Quinn sat on the bristle part and I struggled as I pulled the stick, dragging her across the field; which was hard to do quickly in scuba flippers.

We made it to a long table and Quinn grabbed a candy bar, opened it, tore it in two and split it with me. Together, we hurried to finish eating it. After nearly swallowing it whole, we opened our mouths to show each other we were done and I threw off the flippers.

Next to the table on the ground lay two potato sacks. We jumped into each one and hopped all the way back across the field to a high wooden wall. Quinn made it first and grabbed the thick rope. She made it to the top quickly. "Come on Callie!"

I struggled with the rope; I just couldn't lift myself, it was so hard.

"Plant your feet on the wall!" Quinn shouted. She sounded even more intimidating with her accent.

Letting out a short, frustrated scream, I blew the sweaty hair that stuck on my face and started climbing. Quinn glanced at her stop watch and shouted, "Come *on* Callie!"

"I...can...*do it*!" I gasped as I tried.

"You have to grab my hand! I'll pull you up!"

"I can do it myself! I know I can!"

"But this is a team effort Callie!"

I ground out through my teeth. I looked up and saw Quinn's wavy hair disappear over the wall. I had to do this on my own!

It was just too hard. So instead of going over the wall, I jumped down and ran around it. I called out to Quinn who waited impatiently, "I'll keep working on it, I promise!"

She rolled her eyes. "Let's just keep moving."

We fell onto our backs, head to head, reached up over our heads and grabbed each other's hands. Like a rolling pin, we began to roll all the way down to the finish line. My head was spinning by the time we got there.

Quinn let go of me and checked the stop watch. "Ugh!" She exclaimed in disgust. "That took almost five whole minutes! *Horrible*! We're *never* going to win with time like that!" She sat up and groaned, placing her hands on her face.

"That was...harder than...it looked..." I tried to catch my breath.

"We were absolutely dreadful on time."

"We're doomed." I sat up. "There's no way we can do that in less than five minutes."

Quinn stood up and placed her hands on her hips. "We've got loads of time to practice. We'll get better. We *have* to."

"Or we're doomed."

"We just need a system." Quinn bit down on her lip as she thought.

I couldn't help but add, "Well for one, you shouldn't waste time calling out to me. I can climb the wall just fine on my own."

She was already shaking her head. "You need to be right behind me. I shouldn't *have* to slow down. This is a team effort. You have to trust me-"

"I heard that last year Gwen didn't help Miranda up the wall...it's too hard but-"

"Then you'll have to focus on that wall until you get it down right." She stated, cutting me off.

Quinn sounded exactly like her grandmother; very stern and no-nonsense.

"I had no idea you were so competitive."

"I'm not competitive. I just like to win." Quinn nodded, "Right then. We'll meet back tomorrow?" She asked, yet it sounded more like a direct order.

"Yep," I agreed with no enthusiasm. We only had a few weeks before the big race and had to come in at the fastest time.

It was going to take a ton of work to get there, but I kept my chin up, knowing that even if we didn't come in first place, we at least gave it our all.

*****

I entered the library wearily. It had been an emotional day and I couldn't face Brandon. Not now when I *knew* he liked Charlie. I had just washed my face and some hair stuck to the sides of my cheeks. I knew I looked a mess.

Brandon was piling books on a table. "Hi," I said with a small smile. I thought I saw his eyes light up, but that was most likely my imagination and the trick of the light.

"Hey Callie."

I plopped down on the cool chair. "What do you have there?"

He shrugged and sat opposite me. "I figure something here can help us."

I glanced at the pile and said uneasily, "This is just more history on the camp."

He ran a hand through his hair. "I know. What we need are records and we aren't allowed access to that."

I slumped in the chair and heard familiar giggling. I looked behind Brandon and spotted the twins, Carrie and Liz, coming towards us. They both wore jean overalls.

"Hi Callie," Carrie said cheerily, her blonde hair was swept to the right of her head in a ponytail.

"Hi Brandon," Liz sang, her brown hair swept to the left of her head.

"Hi," Brandon and I said at the same time.

Carrie looked at the books on the table. "What are you guys up to?"

"Nothing you can help us with," Brandon said as he sat back against his chair and put his hands behind his head.

"Unless you can grant us access to information on campers from twenty years ago," I said playfully.

"We can do that," Liz said.

"You *can*?" I was not expecting that.

"Yeah," Carrie smiled. "We *happen* to be in charge of the camps yearbook committee."

"We can get together a whole pile of them if you want," Liz sat down next to me.

"Really?" I could barely keep down my excitement.

Carrie sat down next to Brandon. "What year do you need?"

Brandon and I looked at each other. Brandon answered, "All of the nineteen-eighties."

Liz let out a low whistle.

"That's asking too much Bran," I shook my head.

"No," Liz put her hand up. "It'll be pie; it'll just take a few weeks to get together."

"Yeah, they're not exactly piled up in order," Carrie explained.

"What's the catch?" I sang like Mary.

Carrie smiled proudly and looked at her sister. "We choose friends very well Elizabeth."

"That we *do* Carolina."

Carrie glanced at Brandon and me and leaned forward, wagging her blonde brows, "We want an *entire* tray of the chef's famous mini chocolate cakes."

I couldn't help but snort. "And how are we supposed to get *that*?"

"Yeah, the chef doesn't make those unless it's someone's birthday or if someone won a contest or something," Brandon added.

"You're both smart. You'll figure it out." Liz stood up, Carrie following her lead.

"You can get it to us whenever you can," Carrie added.

Liz leaned on the table with her knuckles. "As long as it's *before* we leave camp."

"Do we have a deal?" Carrie asked, putting her hand out to Brandon.

Me and Brandon looked at each other once more before saying at the same time, "Yes."

I made it to the lake, threw my backpack on the ground and ran up to Charlie, who was standing in a group listening to Ms. Davies.

"You'll never believe what I have to tell you," I whispered urgently.

"You'll never believe what *I* have to tell *you*," Charlie whispered excitedly.

"Okay ladies, no time for socializing. It's time for business." Ms. Davies cut in. "We'll be going through the trust exercise one more time before swimming with your partner…the same ones you had on the first day. Go and stand next to that person." Charlie and I huddled together and Ms. Davies walked by laughing, "Nice try ladies. I believe you were with Camper Gwen," she said, peeking out from under her cap. "And I'll forgive your tardiness just this once."

"Right," I said weakly and grudgingly walked towards Gwen.

"Okay campers! Get to it!"

Gwen snickered, "Late again huh? I hear you've made a habit of being late to things." She wore an orange, thin headband, her black straight hair falling like silk behind her.

"I applaud you for having great hearing," I tried to muster Charlie's dry voice.

It must have worked because she rolled her eyes. "Just catch me."

I pinched my lips, wishing that I could just drop her, but of course my good side won and caught her as she gracefully fell backwards.

After getting up, she said, "So are you going to fall this time? Last time you didn't even budge" Her voice was really snippy.

And I didn't like snippy voices.

I didn't have a retort for that anyway because I didn't know if I'd fall either. I turned back to Gwen and closed my eyes.

And didn't move.

Gwen sighed. "Not again. Ms. Davies!" She raised her hand and called out.

Ms. Davies ran over. "Yes Camper Gwen."

"Callie refuses to let me catch her." Gwen crossed her arms.

I still didn't turn around. I felt Ms. Davies come up beside me. "Camper Callie, what's wrong?"

I looked over at her and tried to speak very low. "I don't know why I freeze up every time." I shook my head. "I just can't do it."

"Listen Callie, I can't force you to trust Gwen, that's something you have to do on your own. However, there will come a time in your life where you'll probably need Gwen to pull you up.

"It may not be in any other activity, but here at least, as your swimming partner, you need to find trust that she'll help you if something happened." She patted me on the shoulder. "Let's move on to the water. Maybe a few exercises will help you out."

I took a deep breath and turned around to the disapproving face of Gwen. "Just don't say anything," I practically begged her. "Just don't."

Chapter 11

I Love That I Can Laugh At Myself

Note to Self: The inside matters more than the outside. Really, it does!

AFTER A TIRING swimming session, I was ready to pass out on my bed and sleep for twenty-four hours. The day had been too much at once. Charlie caught up to me as we walked back towards the bunk. We had to clean it up and head to dinner…or really breakfast.

"You look beat," Charlie observed.

"Thank you Captain Obvious," I said smartly.

"Ha. Ha." Charlie said dryly and began to glow. "So I have to tell you something big, huge, ginormous!"

"That reminds me," I brightened again, "the initials. We are so close to finding out who they are!"

"Okay then, you go first."

I took the rest of the walk to tell her about our new deal with the twins. Charlie loved it. "Those are my kind of girls," she bragged.

By the time we got back to the bunk, Madison was there on the porch wearing a warm smile. "Hey girls, we're just waiting for Sheila. We're going to have a bunk meeting."

"Oh," Charlie replied.

"Okay."

When I walked in, I spotted Saliesha and Sofia sitting in some chairs brought into the center of the cabin. The chairs were placed in a large circle and Charlie and me sat down as well. Lane sat on the other side of the circle. She was quiet, yes, but the other thing was that she was wearing her regular clothes, complete with glasses.

A few moments later, Sheila came into the room laughing with Madison."…I'll definitely have to try that hair tip some time. We do have the same hair type, you know," Sheila faced the room, "oh."

She spotted Lane and lifted her chin in the air. "I'm assuming I have to sit down next to *her*."

I noticed the two empty seats on either side of Lane. "I can move," I volunteered.

"That's okay Callie," Madison looked at Sheila, "I think it's best that you sit down next to her. And her name is *Lane*."

Sheila *humphed!* and sat down. Mary walked in and sat down in the circle with Madison.

We all stared at Madison as she spoke. "We have to talk about something important. Instead of cleaning the bunk, we've decided to have this little meeting."

"Well I can't complain about that," Charlie cheered.

Saliesha and Sofia giggled and I sat up straight with interest. When Madison crossed her legs, I noticed that her white canvas sneakers weren't so clean, but when she wore them it looked like they came right off the runway.

"Who can tell me what self-esteem is?" Madison asked.

We all looked at each other and Sofia cleared her throat, "How you feel about yourself."

Mary nodded encouragingly and Madison replied, "That's right Sofia." As she spoke, Mary got up and passed around little red notebooks. "I want you each to write down something you love about yourselves; only one thing."

I stared at the blank paper and quickly scribbled something down. After a minute, Madison started, "Saliesha, what do you love most about yourself?"

"I love my braces," she gave a big, shiny smile.

Madison nodded. "That's great. Why?"

"Because nobody else has the smile that I do," she said with pride.

Madison turned to Charlie; who was sitting on the chair with one foot planted on the seat. "What do you love about yourself?"

I smiled faintly as I looked at Charlie. I had thought about this earlier in the day. She had so many great qualities; it was hard to choose just one.

Charlie scratched the back of her head with the pencil and leaned her elbow on her knee. "I love that I can laugh at myself."

"Wonderful. I love that about you too." Madison looked at all of us. "It's always important to remind yourselves what you like about *you*. Callie, you're next."

I tried to block the image of blonde Callie and thought about the number one compliment I got growing up. "I love my smile, I guess. Mom and dad always wonder where I got my dimple from."

Sheila cleared her throat. "It's so hard to pick just one thing about myself that I love." At everyone's dry faces, Sheila continued quickly, "I *love* my hair."

Lane spoke so softly that none of us heard barely a word. "I love my nose."

Madison spoke next. "I love my eyelashes."

Mary went, "I love my fab-tastic eyes."

Sofia smiled. "I love my feet." We giggled and Sofia defended, "I am serious! Not too many people are fond of their toes."

Madison continued, "I'm sure there are negative things that live in your mind too. Charlie, what *don't* you like about yourself?"

Charlie's cheeks flushed a little, "My hair."

I looked at the mass of thick chestnut brown hair. "Are you crazy? I love your hair. I've always wanted that shade of brown. Mine is way too mousy."

Charlie looked confused. "Really? But Cal, your hair is not mousy."

"Stop right there," Madison spoke. "You see that? Charlie has this perception of herself that isn't true. The way you think about yourself might not be what everyone else sees. Callie, give me a negative."

I shook my ankles nervously. "Um…I guess my eyes. They're not like my mom's."

"Is your mom someone you admire?" Mary asked with genuine interest.

I nodded and felt warm inside talking about my mom. "She's really beautiful. I always thought I'd look more like her, but my little sister is her twin. I'm more like my dad; not that he's ugly or anything because my dad is pretty handsome, but I wish I looked like my mom. My hair is horrible. I wish it was like yours too."

Wow. I did not mean to reveal so much, but there it was.

Madison frowned. "Why mine?"

"I don't know; maybe because it has a good bounce and a perfect curl."

Sheila spoke up. "Calliope, then you *must* be envious of *my* hair as well since it has the same bounce. My fire-engine red curls only *accentuate* the bounciness."

I couldn't help but roll my eyes.

Sheila continued. "If I must choose a negative about myself, it would be that I'm *too* pretty for words."

We all groaned and for the next five minutes Madison spoke to us about self-esteem.

"I know you're all hungry from the long day so I'll wrap this up. Mary and I decided that every Friday night before lights out, we'll meet and have a talk about anything that's bothering you."

We all looked at her with interest.

"And I want to leave you with these parting words...there has never been anyone like you and there never will be. Beauty comes from the inside and that, my friends, is what we have to spruce up."

Mary chimed in, "This is going to be fun-tabulous!"

"Now everyone hold hands."

Sheila didn't hold Lane's hand. Madison frowned. "Sheila..." she warned.

"Oh all right," Sheila grumbled and grabbed Lane's hand.

Madison gave a short prayer and it gave me some encouragement. I looked up at her and thought that I had the best counselor in the entire camp.

Minutes later, we headed towards the dining hall. Charlie was practically running out of there because breakfast was her favorite part of the day.

"Callie," Lane called out as I walked off of the creaky porch. Charlie's stomach growled. "Cal, I'll meet you there okay?"

"Yeah," I replied.

"Beat you there!" Saliesha teased.

"Dude, you're so wrong."

Saliesha bolted down the path and Sofia laughed as Charlie tried to grab Saliesha's arm.

I walked beside Lane as we headed there. "What's up?"

"I just wanted to say," she paused and pushed her glasses up the bridge of her nose. "I'm sorry."

I looked over at her and stopped. "Lane, I can't help feeling that this was my fault. I told you to change your hair and-"

"Callie this has nothing to do with you. You said what anyone would when we're about to go on stage. You only gave me tips about the audition." She continued, "I let myself get carried away. I tried to become popular by dressing less…I guess it was my way of getting attention." She looked at the ground. "I got the wrong attention *and* a call home to my parents."

"Lane, you don't have to apologize to me."

"Yes, I do. You told me that my friends liked me the way I am…the *real* me. I also kind of slammed a door in your face," she said the last with regret.

"It's okay Lane. I forgive you."

"Can we just forget it ever happened?"

I shook my head. "No. We'll remind ourselves of this if we ever come into this type of situation again. We'll know we learned our lesson."

"How do you know so much?"

I looked at the sunset sky and then back to her. "My mom teaches me a lot."

"You have a great mom."

"Thanks." I hugged her and felt her squeeze me back.

When we pulled away, Lane blew a long breath and laughed, "I am so relieved I don't have to squeeze into those heels anymore," she pointed at her blue and white sneakers.

"Well now we can both run to the dining hall before Charlie eats all the bacon and eggs."

We ran and laughed all the way there.

Chapter 12

She's A What?!

Note to Self: Wear your hair down more often...

IT WAS officially one month and one week since I arrived at Camp Eerie. We had done un-birthday day, backwards day, even a clown day. And if I thought clown day was weird, I was in for a huge surprise. As we finished up our chores in the morning, Madison and Mary swept in.

"It's Be Your Bunk-Mate Day!" Madison sang. Yes...Madison sang just like Mary! I was horrified...and by the looks on everyone else's face I know we were *all* horrified.

We knew this meant something really bad.

"Um," Sheila was the first to speak "Could you please clarify?"

Madison's beautiful black curls were tied up in a Mary-like French braid. She wore a loose fitting pink camp shirt and dowdy knee-length jean shorts...everything Mary would wear.

"I don't know if I *want* her to clarify," Saliesha said, taking off her sunglasses and placing them on her head.

Nothing was as shocking as the sight of Mary. Her usually tied up blonde hair was out and free; lying nicely around her shoulders. She wore a nice fitting dark blue camp shirt with short beige khaki shorts. She was dressed just like Madison!

Charlie nudged me. "We don't have to worry; I think you dress normal, it won't be hard to dress like you."

I closed my eyes in relief. "You're right. This'll be fun."

Madison sang in a voice we all thought only Mary could do, "I don't think so Camper Charlie!"

Mary's voice was unrecognizable. "Maddy, give the girls the low down."

Madison broke character, "I don't say that, I don't say 'the low down'."

"Well it sounds cool-tastic so I'm going to say it," Mary argued in a voice we recognized.

Madison ignored her and exclaimed loudly, "We said 'bunk mates'. Not necessarily the girl you a *share* a bunk bed with!"

We all held our breaths.

Madison looked down at her paper. "Camper Saliesha! You'll be Camper Lane today!" She handed Saliesha a pair of see-through glasses.

Saliesha took off her sunglasses and handed them to Lane. Saliesha looked terrified, but said nothing. Well, she couldn't exactly say anything while frozen in shock.

Mary continued, "Camper Sofia, you will be switching with Camper Callie."

"Yes!" Sofia and me said at the same time and laughed.

Charlie was already shaking her head, "Oh no..." she muttered. "Oh no, *Oh* no, oh...*no*..."

Sheila crossed her arms tightly against her and stared at Charlie with a look of dread.

"Camper Charlie!" Madison squeaked.

"Oh *no*," Charlie continued.

"You'll be having an awe-so-riffic time-"

"*Oh* no."

"...dressed as-"

"..."

"Camper Sheila!"

Charlie gripped my arm. "Help me."

I looked at her with sympathy and whispered. "Sorry."

"Now here's the best part," came Mary's voice. "It's also a competition."

All of our heads snapped to her with renewed interest.

"Nothing's wrong with a little healthy competition now is there?!" Madison exclaimed.

"All of the teachers and camp counselors will be observing you today," Mary explained. "The person from each bunk who does the best impersonation gets a surprise tonight at the bonfire." She placed her thumbs in her pockets, Madison-style.

"Is this surprise say...edible?" Charlie asked.

Madison cheered. "You can posi-lutely say that.

"Sheila, hand over those butterfly clips."

Sheila put her hands protectively on her hair and declared, "Over my *cold* and *lifeless* body!"

"You have to be ready to walk into the dining hall like your bunk mate. So read their schedules and get going," Mary *winked*.

"And have a wonder-fabulous, mag-tastic, marvel-ful, extra-ficient day!" Madison bent over to catch her breath. "How do you do that Mary?" She asked in her own voice.

"Well, I don't say wonder-fabulous," Mary frowned.

Madison looked at her in doubt. "You say mag-tastic, but you don't say wonder-fabulous?"

Mary shook her head.

"O…kie dokes…"

"I say *that*!" Mary exclaimed in her own voice.

Madison shook her head and then nudged her. "You say the next bit. I won't be able to breathe."

Mary winked again. "Also ladies, tonight before the bonfire you have to stop by the rec center and cast your votes for this year's yearbook."

"Toodles!" Madison sang with renewed energy.

They left the bunk, leaving all of us in silence.

"Guess we'd better get a move on," Saliesha finally said as she approached Lane.

Lane smiled. "I really like this one shirt you wore before…"

Sofia and I walked to our closet spaces and pulled out our best outfits.

Charlie roughly grabbed a hockey jersey and a pair of jean shorts and walked over to Sheila. "You'll have to throw all that hair into a ponytail."

Sheila looked a bit disgusted. "But your ponytail is always messy. I can't do this. It's atrocious on so many levels," she said miserably.

"Look," Charlie reasoned, "I know this is not gonna be fun, but I think we both come out winning."

Sheila's light brown eyes focused on Charlie, "How so?" She sniffed haughtily.

"Well, *I'll* win the food and you'll get to play the princess today at rehearsals." Charlie wagged her brows.

When Sheila realized this, her eyes lit up and she snatched the clothes from Charlie. "I'll show those directors a thing or two!" She walked over to the small closet she shared with Lane and pulled out her best outfit. "If you're going to portray me, you're going to do it right!"

"Wait just a minute," Charlie put her hands up, "I don't need to look crazy here; I just need to resemble you a *little*."

"Do you want to win the prize or not? Which, need I remind you, *just* might be the chef's famous chocolate mini cakes?"

Charlie pinched her lips and nodded in regret.

"Boa time!" She shoved her favorite pink feather boa in Charlie's face.

I changed into a simple pair of dark green shorts and a white Camp Eerie t-shirt. Sofia came out in a pink t-shirt and jean shorts. "I will tie my hair into a pony-tail. That is all I ever see you do to your hair," she said quietly.

"I guess I'll have to wear my hair down."

"I'll do my favorite side braid on you."

I sat on a chair while Sofia gently braided my hair. When she was done, the braid went down my front shoulder and ended by my stomach. "There, fit for a princess," Sofia remarked.

"Thanks," I smiled and looked at myself in the mirror. "I guess this isn't bad." Actually it was great! For the first time in a very long time, I didn't get angry at my reflection. "Let me see your schedule."

Lane tried her best Saliesha imitation. "We're headin' out!"

"We are right behind," Sofia called out.

I tied my sneakers. "One sec. I want to see how Charlie's doing." I knocked on the bathroom door since Sheila locked herself and Charlie in there. "You okay Charlie?"

"Don't leave me!" Charlie called out in desperation.

"Okay, I'll wait." I looked at Sofia, "She's going to need me." I knocked on the bathroom door. "Keep in mind that we're going to be late for breakfast!"

Charlie's whining voice came through, "Sheiilllaa!"

"One minute!" Sheila shouted.

One minute turned into several minutes in which Sofia and I heard growls, groans, cries and for a split-second it sounded like laughter.

The door swung open and Sheila swept out.

A messy ponytail, a hockey jersey, shorts and black sneakers completed Sheila's look. She was unrecognizable! She lifted her chin, "*Not a word.* Now. Presenting, Sheila number two."

"Oh cut the dramatics," Charlie mumbled as she walked out of the bathroom angrily.

Sofia and I held our giggles, "Oh my…"

Sheila had curled Charlie's thick brown hair with a curling iron and topped it with a big purple headband. She wore a bright pink shirt with that matching bright pink feather boa wrapped around her neck. Her jean shorts were covered in glittery sparkles and her beloved high-top sneakers were bedazzled with rhinestones and sequins.

Sheila even powdered Charlie's face with a little bit of pink blush just to make her pale face rosier, according to Sheila.

"Don't. Say. A word," Charlie ordered through her teeth.

Sheila sighed, "Likewise. This goes against everything I believe in." She touched her cheeks and muttered, "What will Brandon think of me?"

Charlie gasped. "Callie, I totally forgot to tell you something."

"Not now Charlotte!" Sheila looked at her with envy, "I want to get this morning over with as soon as possible. The faster I can play the princess, the better." She grabbed Charlie's hand and started to drag her out of the bunk.

Charlie turned to me and mouthed, 'It's about Brandon.'

I wondered what was going on. Brandon? Did Charlie find out that Brandon liked her?

"Earth to Callie," Sofia waved in front of her face.

I refocused. "Right, sorry."

That's when we heard Charlie and Sheila scream and barrel back inside of the bunk house.

Sheila went behind me and gripped my shoulders.

"What's going on?" I was so worried and looked over at Charlie's rosy face, "You're not running from a bug are you?"

Charlie was downright terrified. "We saw someone-"

We all screamed when a boy's face came into view at the window.

Sofia calmed down when she took a good look. Touching her heart she said, "No worries everyone. It is only the junior counselor for the boys bunk."

"What on earth is *he* doing here?! Boys are *not* allowed here!" Sheila yelled.

Sofia looked exasperated and walked out onto the front porch, we all followed. I saw the handsome Brom standing in front of the steps. "I am sorry for scaring you all," he said in a deep voice.

Sofia groaned and ranted in Spanish.

I never heard Sofia rant before. She hardly ever talked over a whisper!

"Hey, do you know Spanish?" I muttered to Charlie.

"A little actually. It's kind of rusty." Charlie narrowed her eyes as we watched the two argue back and forth. "She's asking him why he's here…something about a cover being blown? He said he needed to know where she was today since everything was switched…"

"Are you sure you know Spanish?"

"*Shh*! She said that she told her father that she's safe here and she doesn't need a sitter and he said that it's not for her to decide and she smells like cheese…"

"*What?!*" I whispered.

"I think I got confused in that last part."

Saliesha's panicked voice came through the trees. "We saw him run this way!" She and Lane were pulling a worried Madison along. "Dang if I was right!" Saliesha exclaimed.

Madison's gray eyes grew wide as she neared the porch and spotted Brom. "What are you doing here?"

Brom crossed his arms and rolled his eyes to the sky, "Being uncommonly sloppy."

"I'd say," Madison crossed her arms and looked at our confused faces. She looked back at Brom, "Sofia has switched schedules with Callie today," she pointed at me.

Brom's handsome face moved to me and then back to Madison, "That is all I needed to know."

"Hurry back before someone else sees you," Madison actually gave him a smile. He smiled back and headed into the woods instead of taking the path.

"I demand to know what is going on!" Sheila declared.

"Yeah, I'm confused," Saliesha raised her hand.

Madison nodded and pushed us back inside of the bunk. "We've got a lot of explaining to do."

*****

"She's a what?!" Saliesha exclaimed in amazed disbelief.

"Lady Sofia Helena de Venustos la Luna, Princess of El Guapo," I said the name over again.

"And I though Sheila's name was the longest I've ever heard," Charlie said dryly; Sheila rolled her eyes.

"Don't say it too loud," Saliesha reminded us as we walked towards the dining hall, "Madison said it's a secret and only Mr. and Mrs. Reeves know."

"Well," Sofia spoke softly, "I do not want everyone to know that I am royalty."

"Darling, *I* am royalty and *everyone* knows it," Sheila said haughtily with her nose in the air.

"She's not talking about make-pretend," Charlie said smartly. "We're not in pre-school anymore."

Sheila snorted and stomped off ahead of everyone else.

Saliesha whistled. "I think someone is jealous."

"This is so cool," I said to Sofia…because it *was* really cool.

"Curious to know why you came across the world to come to this camp," Charlie said as she pushed the boa away from her face.

Sofia had a faraway look on her face and she answered, "You must understand that I come from a very magical world." Charlie and me looked at each other and our eyes got a bit bigger. Sofia continued, "I wanted to experience something different before I went back to Academy in the fall."

"Well you sure enough picked the right place," Saliesha nodded.

"You go to an actual princess academy?" Sheila turned around and asked in pleasant surprise. She went next to Sofia. "What's the name? I'm going to call my father and ask if he enrolled me there. I've sent out dozens of resumes. I'm very selective when it comes to princess academy."

"Girl, princess academy is for *real* princesses only. Besides, they'd kick you out the moment you walked in," Saliesha giggled.

"Yeah, *you* in princess academy? I'd like to see that," Charlie added.

"And you will!" Sheila *humphed*.

We all giggled.

I had uncovered a cool fact today. Little did I know that I was about to uncover something bigger than Sofia being a princess.

*****

I easily survived all of Sofia's normal activities. And to pretend to be Sofia wasn't hard. All I had to do was smile politely and speak softly. I happily went to lunch and took an extra helping of the fruit cups. Not something Sofia would do, but I was just too hungry!

"This has been the hardest morning of my *life*!" Big surprise; as I walked over to the table, Sheila was wailing dramatically.

"I've been having an alright time," Saliesha said as she ate some carrots. "Lane, you spend *way* too much time in that library."

Lane just smiled and played with her applesauce.

"Where's Charlie?" I asked as I wobbled my tray impatiently.

Sheila stared at me with an attitude. "Don't you know that I *never* eat lunch in here? She's outside on a cozy little bench."

"So she's by herself?" I asked defensively.

"I said it's cozy for a reason."

I couldn't help but roll my eyes. "I'll be outside with Charlie."

"Me too" Sofia agreed and picked up her tray. Saliesha and Lane followed.

"Well look at me! Now *I'm* by myself!" Sheila whined.

Saliesha looked back. "You like a cozy lunch, don't you?"

Lane adjusted Saliesha's sunglasses on top of her head and said, "You're welcome to join us."

Sheila looked shocked because number one, Lane spoke to her and number two, she was invited. "Well of course!" She picked up her tray and bumbled after us. "I'm just ridiculously glad that this is for one day."

I walked outside with the girls and looked for Charlie. I spotted her finishing an apple at the bottom of the hill by a tree.

"Hey, isn't that Brandon?" Lane asked.

"Brandon?! Where? Oh *dear*, hide me! He absolutely *cannot* see me dressed this way!" Sheila lifted her lunch tray in front of her face.

It was Brandon for sure. And he was walking towards Charlie. He smiled and she smiled back.

"Oh well I don't think we should interrupt," Saliesha said smartly.

I didn't like what she said! Brandon looked like he was telling her something really important. Charlie laughed and nodded, then shook her head, then nodded again.

Really, what was she talking about to have to nod so much!

"Looks like they're talking about something very important..."

I didn't know who said that last comment, but it really didn't matter since the frog in my throat turned into a big fat hippo.

Charlie and Brandon looked cute together...

"Well I do not want to stand here forever you guys," Sofia said.

"Oh, right, sorry," I croaked and I was thankful the girls didn't seem to notice.

We all started down the hill, my eyes never leaving the camps newest couple. They'd probably end up in this year's camp yearbook.

"What's up Camper Sheila!" Saliesha exclaimed and she and Sofia sat on the bench next to her, pushing Brandon off.

"Hey ladies," he said and put his hands into the pockets of his shorts.

"We did not want you to eat by yourself," Sofia explained.

Sheila and Lane sat on the small bench on the opposite side of the small path. "It was all *my* idea to come and join you," Sheila bragged.

"I somehow doubt that Sheila," Charlie muttered and Brandon laughed.

I knew I was going to have to see an eye doctor when I got home because I rolled my eyes again and felt my throat go as dry as the desert.

"Hey Cal," Brandon looked at me.

"Hi Brandon," I had no idea how that hippo let me talk.

"No, he's Edward today," Charlie pointed at him.

"Can't you tell? I spiked up my hair," he modeled his head and the girls giggled.

I didn't find anything amusing. It just wasn't in me right then. "So...you'll both be playing the prince and princess today at rehearsals?" I couldn't help but point out. I probably sounded a bit jealous, but I couldn't help myself! Charlie and Brandon are going to be staring into each other's eyes.

"Did you forget already Cal? Sheila's taking my part today," Charlie narrowed her eyes at me curiously.

I was busted for sure now. Charlie knew me better than anyone.

Sheila stared at Brandon with admiration and love in her eyes, "I can't wait."

Brandon scratched the back of his head and cleared his throat, "Right, well, I gotta go."

The girls said bye and Brandon walked up to me. I really *could* see all the colors of the ocean in his eyes. "Hey Cal, you look really pretty today. Nice hair."

I was so taken by surprise; I almost forgot to say anything at all! My mouth moved up and down for a few seconds before answering…"Thanks."

He smiled. "See ya later."

"Later." I was so confused! I looked at Charlie to see if she got jealous or looked like she wanted to pound me, but I only saw her signature smug smile.

"*Ohhh*Oohhh," all of the girls sang.

I opened my mouth, almost forgetting that I was still holding my lunch tray. "What?"

"I think I know who Callie should ask to the end of the year dance," Saliesha sang before biting into her hot dog.

"What are you talking about?" I sat on the grass pretzel-style.

"I'm loath to admit this, but it's obvious to the entire camp," Sheila looked right at me.

"I'm getting annoyed, what are you talking about?"

"How can she be that blind?" Saliesha asked Charlie.

"Beats me; Cal, what's the deal?"

"Can someone please tell me what's going on?"

They couldn't have made it clearer when they all sang at the same time, "Brandon likes you."

I dropped the tray. "No way! He likes Charlie!" I pointed at her.

"*What*?!" Charlie squealed, nearly choking on her own spit. "Who told you *that*?!"

"No one had to *tell* me that. I can just see it by the way he looks at you."

"Did you ever notice the way he looks at *you*?" Charlie countered.

I took a blade of grass out of the ground and threw it absently.

"Cal, that's the news I had to tell you. Girls all over camp have been asking Brandon to the dance and he's been saying no to them all."

"So? That could mean a lot of things. It can especially mean that he's waiting for *you* to ask him."

"But Cal, I already asked him about it and he told me-"

"Just stop it okay? I know what I know."

"She's just in denial, give her time," Lane smiled at me.

"Geez Cal, are you this stubborn with your parents?"

I was messing up big time. I really didn't know how to have friends. This must be how I'd start losing them.

"She's spacing out again," Saliesha announced.

"Charlotte, quick, take a picture of her face, it's absolutely hysterical." Sheila laughed.

"I actually agree with you about something," Charlie snapped a picture of my face.

I blinked when the flash got in my eyes and when it cleared I saw everyone staring at me.

"You okay girl?" Saliesha asked.

I took a deep breath. I had to admit it. "I uh…I have no friends back home." Maybe they'd understand why I was the way that I was.

"Well join my magnificent club!" Sheila exclaimed. "I, unfortunately, have no friends back home either. However, my friends remain here, at Camp Eerie."

"Geez Sheila, you sound like a commercial," Charlie muttered.

"Well I *was* featured in the commercial two summers ago," Sheila bragged.

"Forget I said anything…"

"Callie, I do not have any friends back home either," Sofia admitted softly.

I looked at the beautiful princess and shook my head in disbelief, "Really?"

"I guess I do not click with a lot of people."

"Well you sure enough click with us," Saliesha announced, her braces shining in the sun light.

"I have only one friend back home," Lane admitted and glanced at Sheila. Sheila glanced back but quickly looked away.

"I'm sorry to say girls, but I've got tons of friends back home," Saliesha bragged, "I'm just a people person."

We looked at Charlie and she furrowed her brows, "What?"

"Any friends back at your home?" Sofia asked.

Charlie admitted. "I'm what they call a 'tom-boy'. I mostly hang out with my brother and his friends. Girls don't usually skateboard and play hockey."

I was surprised that so many of my new friends were just like me, save for Saliesha and Charlie. I once thought that I was alone, that I was the only one in the world with no friends and no hope. But here, at Camp Eerie, I made five great friends; each different in their own way.

And now I was sounding just like Sheila.

"And my brother is extra protective since we only have our mom now," Charlie continued. "My dad died when I was really little."

The girls said they were sorry and I was in shock. "I'm so sorry Charlie, I had no idea."

Charlie shrugged. "It's cool. I'm good. My mom, brother and grandma give me lots of love." She finally smirked. "Kumbayah everyone!"

"My dear mother passed when I was a baby," Sheila admitted softly. We all started saying sorry, but she stopped us. "It's perfectly okay. I never really knew her nor do I remember her."

"So you and Charlie have something in common," Saliesha said in a soft voice and a smug smile.

"We do," Charlie looked at Sheila.

Sheila faintly smiled back. "Well then," Sheila announced. "Now that that's all settled, I should be off to my rehearsals. Come along Charlotte."

Charlie groaned. "Sheila, you don't even know my lines."

"Piffle! Part of being a brilliant actress is that you remember *everyone's* lines," she stood up.

Charlie's jaw dropped and she said dryly, "You never cease to amaze me."

"I know," Sheila fluttered her lashes. "Off we go!"

Charlie hesitantly stood up. "Yeah, here we go." She looked at me and mouthed, 'Help me', tripping on her small heels.

The girls started going off on their own and Sofia stood behind with me as we gathered our trays. "Callie?"

"Yeah?"

"I know it took a lot for you to admit that you do not have any friends back home."

I shrugged. "It's okay. I actually feel a lot better about it."

"Well it helped me too because I have never admitted that I have no friends. My life of a princess is very controlled…this is the most free I have been and it felt wonderful getting some things out."

I was so touched. "I'm glad I helped you out." And not just anyone; a princess!

"Oh and there is one other thing," Sofia's green eyes glowed.

"What's up?"

"I know you are searching about the camp ghost…"

It must have been the wind, but I really thought I heard giggling somewhere. I turned around and saw the bushes rustle, but I shrugged it off and smiled back at Sofia. "I don't believe in ghosts. I thought I did, but it's not true. It really *is* just a story to scare off new campers."

"Good for you. Because what I saw was not a ghost at all. It was a reporter from my country, trying to snap pictures of me here at the camp. The will do anything to get a good picture. Brom stopped them."

Whoa. "Seriously?"

Sofia nodded. "Have fun fishing next period."

"I've done it loads of times with my dad. I think I'll feel right at home."

We walked up the hill and I was curious to know what else this day would bring. It was far from over.

Chapter 13

Um, excuse-moi, but it's horrible enough that I have to rest my fashionably gorgeous head on a non-satin pillow in a bunk numbered *thirteen*. It's also outrageous that I happen to be *thirteen* years young. I simply refuse to allow a chapter with that same horrid number. Onwards to chapter fourteen please! Oh and thank you.

~ Sheila Penelope Ann Van Housen

Chapter 14

How Did She Do That?

Note to Self: Keep one eye open when you sleep.

THE REST of the day flew by. I met up with Lane for the obstacle course practice since she was Saliesha and I was still Sofia.

"I must tell you that I am not a physical person and I will most definitely slow you down," Lane explained. She wore goggle glasses that wrapped around her head.

"All that matters is you try and have fun," I said firmly as I tied my sneakers.

"I'm usually out with the nature group at this time of day. The forest is full of so many pretty plants."

I smiled as I stretched my legs and arms. "I'm sure Saliesha is whining and groaning by now."

Lane grinned, "Probably."

We got started on the practice and by the end of the hour I thought Lane was pretty good. "You're faster than Quinn in some areas." I downed the bottle of water.

Lane took off the goggles and put her normal glasses back him. "That's a huge compliment, thanks." She cleared her throat. "You have a lot to work on."

I groaned. "I know. That wall is the killer."

"It would help more if I pulled you up."

"No. I just have to do it on my own."

"Callie," Lane said softly. "It's okay to have help once in a while." She drank some water and pointed out, "Quinn might make you work harder if you don't want help."

"Yep, she always tells me that," I mumbled.

"And not all partners are willing to help each other on that wall."

As we fixed the course back up and grabbed our backpacks, I asked Lane, "Did you and Sheila ever make up?"

She sighed as we limped to the restroom to freshen up for dinner. "Not really. You know, for all of her vanity, she really was a great friend and I miss her, but she isn't willing to forgive me for the mean things I said to her. And I guess I deserve it."

"But not if you feel bad about it and apologized. It's not like you're still gloating about it."

She took a deep breath and pushed some sweaty hair away from her forehead, "I know."

Right after dinner, the recreation center was crowded. Campers wrote names on pieces of paper and shoved them into boxes. I stuck with Charlie as we made our way around the circle of tables.

"Camp Clown…" Charlie tapped a tiny pencil against her chin in thought and said with a twinkle in her eyes, "Sheila Van Housen."

I giggled and wrote in the name of a boy I'd seen act goofy a bunch of times.

"Hello ladies!" Sheila called out to us over the loud chatter of the crowd. "Just an F.Y.I., 'Camps Most Beautiful' is a few boxes ahead of you." She patted her hair. "Be sure to write my last name correctly. V-A-N H-O-U-S-E-N."

"Sure." Charlie nodded with a tight smile and then made a face when Sheila turned away. "She actually meant C-L-O-W-N." Charlie looked giddy, "This is more fun than I thought it would be." She shoved her small paper in the box and moved on to the next box. "Cutest couple…"

"Oh," I pointed my pencil at her. "That's an easy one. Tom and Lois."

Charlie stuck her pencil in her open mouth and pretended to gag. "Don't think so. They are *way* too smooch-woochy, kissy-wissy for me." Someone bumped into her and she said happily, "Oh hi Tom, hey Lois." They replied happily and moved away. Charlie whispered, "*You and Brandon are a shoo-in for cutest couple.*"

She better not! "You better not!"

Charlie tried to find room on the table to quickly scribble our names. I tried pushing her hands, but there were too many campers around me to really get her, "Don't you dare! We are *not* a couple!"

Charlie spun around and wrote it really quick and then she spun back around and stuffed it into the box.

"I can't believe you did that!"

"That's what friends are for," Charlie winked.

"Fine," I said smugly, angry now. "Then you won't mind if I enter you and Edward as a couple."

Charlie laughed; which really irritated me, and said, "Fine. But it will be the *only* vote in the box."

"What do you mean?" I asked in a warning tone. "You're not saying that there are *more* votes for me and Brandon?"

Charlie turned to Sofia and Saliesha, who were on the other side of the room. I looked in horror as they gave Charlie a thumbs-up.

I saw red.

"Four votes are not as good as over one hundred for Tom and Lois," I argued.

Charlie clucked her tongue, "We'll see."

That night at the bonfire, my bunk-mates and me sat together on a log in front of the big ancient tree. Charlie was still in character, knowing that all of the junior counselors were paying close attention to all of the girls.

"…and imagine my surprise when I realized I am great at the part of the queen." Charlie imitated Sheila perfectly.

Sheila sat there laughing and cheering on. She spotted me and beamed, "Charlotte is clearly the best choice to play me in an upcoming movie about my life."

Saliesha laughed, sitting next to Sheila. "Yeah right, she just really wants that edible reward the winner gets." Her braces sparkled from the fire as she laughed.

Charlie's eyes landed on me and her dark blue eyes brightened, "Calliope! How wonderfully charming it is to see you!"

I knew my face was red when I saw everyone look at me. "Uh…right." I sat down between Sofia and Lane and whispered, "I want Charlie back."

"Oh that Calliope; always embarrassed about something. I don't know why with all that beautiful brown hair. But it really isn't as good as *my* curls," Charlie touched her hair.

The girls exploded with laughter and Sheila proudly applauded and pointed, "That's me!"

I grabbed a stick and jammed a few marshmallows on top. "So how did rehearsals go?"

The color of Sheila's face matched her hair and she seemed to shrink, "Let's talk about something else. S'mores anyone?!"

Charlie reached over Saliesha and patted Sheila's hand. "It's certainly okay." She looked at me. "She sprained Brandon's ankle."

"*She what*?!"

"I didn't sprain it! I just bruised it…a little," Sheila said weakly.

"She got a little too excited while singing the princess' song 'I Won't Break Your Heart' and ended up breaking something anyway." Charlie smirked and I was relieved to see some of the real Charlie come back.

"How did she do that?" I asked as I started to roast my marshmallows.

Sheila explained. "Well at the end of the song, the princess is supposed to run into his arms…"

"She more like tackled him." Charlie finished.

I think Sheila's face was *redder* than her hair at this point. "I got a *tiny* bit excited."

"Brandon was taken to the nurse and was told to rest."

"I apologized profusely," Sheila insisted.

"And that's when she broke his other ankle." Charlie announced.

"*What*?!" I screeched.

All of the girls giggled and Charlie's face cracked into a big smile. "I'm only joking."

"Har, har," I said in a dry voice.

Fifteen minutes later Charlie was proclaimed the winner of 'Be Your Bunk-mate Day' for bunk thirteen. Madison and Mary proudly presented their camper with a tray of freshly baked chocolate cakes made by the camp chef; who happened to have once been a pastry chef in Paris many years earlier.

As envious campers looked on, Charlie happily shared her winnings with her bunk-mates.

"I'll be happy to take the white chocolate red velvet one," Sheila said enthusiastically and turned red again, "If that's okay with you Charlotte."

Charlie laughed. "You're already drooling, how can I deny you?" She gave the happy Sheila the small cake.

"I certainly am not!" Sheila proclaimed and then wiped her mouth.

We giggled and Charlie handed out the rest of the goodies, making sure she kept the double milk chocolate buttercream cake for herself.

As I swallowed my dark chocolate raspberry cake without chewing, I enjoyed laughing with the girls. Even Sheila was laughing; with Charlie of all people, the two that hadn't gotten along the most in the beginning.

"Charlotte," Sheila began to lick her fingers, "is it safe to be *moi* again? I mean, now that you've won?

Charlie breathed a huge sigh of relief. "You know being you wasn't all that bad."

All of our jaw's dropped.

Charlie rolled her eyes. "I'm just joking! Give me back my hockey shirt."

"Gladly," Sheila exclaimed with her own relief and took off the hockey jersey. Everyone's eyes grew big when she revealed a very gold and glittery shirt that sparkled in the fire light. She handed the hockey shirt to Charlie and set her wild curls free from its ponytail prison.

"There can only be one Sheila," Saliesha said with a grin.

"And one strawberry chocolate cake," Sofia said as she held up her half eaten pink cake. "This is too pretty to eat."

"I can eat that for you," Sheila said carefully with her eyes rounded.

"She's drooling again," Saliesha pointed.

"I am *not!*" Sheila defended and wiped her mouth anyway.

All six of us laughed into the cool night air.

*****

A little squirrel scurried across the front porch of the old bunk. A branch from the old gnarled tree tapped the side window as soft wind pushed it gently. But not a single noise stirred the six sleeping girls who were safe and snug inside. Soon, a loud tapping noise began hitting two windows at once. Lane stirred from her bottom bunk and looked around. She heard the tapping turn into banging. Putting her glasses on, she slipped out of bed and clumsily walked around in the dark to find the noise.

We woke up to Lane's screams.

Saliesha even fell off the top of her bunk, ending with a loud *bang!* on the floor. Charlie rushed over and with her sleepy eyes saw glowing green hands tapping on the windows. "*Wha...?!*"

We were all in between sleep and awake and only knew fear. I screamed and ran for the door, followed by Lane and Sofia. Sheila (with her hair rollers) and Charlie followed along as soon as the glowing green hands started to open the windows.

"*Daddddyyyy!*" Sheila cried.

I swung the door open, but before I could get to the screen door, I bounced off of an invisible wall and fell backwards. The other girls fell back like bowling pins and landed in a big heaping tangle of arms and legs.

"Someone get the lights!"

I didn't know who shouted it, but I scrambled up in the dark and hit the light switch as fast as I could. I was now fully awake and saw Sofia, Lane, Sheila and Charlie thrown on the floor. I looked at the windows and the hands were gone. I turned back to the door, wondering why I flew backwards, Charlie got up and joined me.

"Saran wrap?" She touched the wall of thick clear wrap.

"Thumb-tacked to the ceiling and floor," I noticed.

"We've been bamboozled again!" Sheila squealed and suddenly ran to the mirror to make sure her face wasn't painted.

"That's it. This is war." Charlie proclaimed.

Sofia and Lane tore down the plastic wrap and threw it into the nearest trash.

"Let's not give them the satisfaction of a successful prank anymore. I'm shutting off the lights," I was so angry!

"They're most likely out there right now, hiding behind that ugly old tree and laughing at us." Sheila said with outrage.

"Um Callie, wait. I think I know why we were tricked so easily this time." We all followed Lane's gaze and saw that Saliesha was snoring on the hard floor.

I shook my head and folded my arms, "So much for our lookout."

Chapter 15

Who Cares What We Think?

Note To Self: The mirror doesn't lie.

A RED head popped out from behind the bushes. Glittery fingernails came up with a pink flashlight and flicked it on twice, signaling that everything was "all clear".

Sofia flashed her light three times, pulled down her binoculars from her lookout on the hill and spoke quickly into her dark green walkie-talkie. "*Clear.*"

"Ten-seven," Saliesha whispered back.

"It's ten-*four*," Lane corrected.

"Oh right. Ten-four."

Lane turned around from behind the trees near Madison and Mary's bunk house and ran to me and Charlie. We were holding big buckets in our arms. "Everything's all clear."

"Go, go, go," Charlie said quickly and we both ran to the bunk house.

Lane and Saliesha grabbed the two large remaining buckets on the ground and followed along. Three windows were wide open, letting in the cool early morning breeze from the lake behind. In the distance, the sky was starting to turn pink and orange, signaling the coming of the morning.

Charlie quietly emptied the contents of the bucket into the window, Saliesha followed after.

I took care of the other window and Lane, the third. We quickly took the now empty buckets and ran as fast as race cars. Saliesha whispered furiously into her walkie-talkie as she ran, "*Cover tracks! Now! I repeat; cover tracks* now!"

Sofia's excited voice came through, "Ten-four!" She flashed her light twice and Sheila jumped over the bushes, quickly closed the three windows and smoothed over the sneaker marks we left behind.

She quickly jumped back over the bushes, flashed Sofia once and ran away. Sofia left her spot on the hill and ran away as well.

We all tumbled into our bunk house in fits of laughter. I was on the floor laughing so hard I was in tears. Charlie held herself up against the wall as she laughed. Saliesha and Lane gave each other high-fives.

Sheila plopped on a blue bean bag chair and put her hand dramatically over her head. "I cannot believe we actually did it." She said breathlessly.

"Sheila, you were amazing," Sofia praised.

"As long as I didn't have to touch those slimy little frogs, I was fabulous." She put her finger to her chin and wondered for a second before saying, "Then again I'm *always* fabulous."

I gasped for air. "Can you imagine the looks…on their…faces…when they see *hundreds* of tiny…frogs in their bunk house?"

An explosion of laughter erupted and Sheila cringed. "Yuck!"

"It was fun catching them." Charlie teased Sheila, who made a horrified face.

"We better hurry up and get into bed before they get here," Saliesha stated and quickly pulled off her sneakers.

"Yeah and I have a feeling they'll be here earlier than usual." Charlie said and quickly got ready to go back into bed.

Charlie had been right because ten minutes later Madison and Mary came barreling into the bunk house without even knocking. Madison's curly hair was up in a high bun and she was still wearing her fluffy pink robe.

Mary's face was green from an overnight face mask, her white eye mask was pushed up to the top of her head and she was wearing her bunny rabbit robe with matching slippers.

We all pretended to sleep, but felt Mary and Madison's furious glares. "Well played ladies…well-played."

"Well we can't prove it was *them*." Mary sang.

"No we can't," Madison knew that we were listening. "But they just better watch their backs."

"We'll get the janitors to get the frogs out of the bunk."

Someone snorted and Madison turned back to us suspiciously. "We'd better go Mary," she announced, "before we wake the sleeping beauties." She paused again for a few extra seconds and then, "*Hm*."

And then they were gone.

And we couldn't help but erupt into another round of laughter.

*****

It was officially seven weeks since I've been at camp. We were sitting in a circle for our weekly talk with Madison and Mary. Madison had sneaked in some cakes from the chef and each of us ate a piece and looked really greedy doing it.

"So campers," Madison said as after she settled in her chair, her long curly hair touching the seat, "what's new?"

We were quiet until Charlie let out a loud belch. We couldn't help but giggle while Sheila made a sour face, "*Disgusting*."

Charlie shrugged. "When you gotta, you gotta."

"Okay," Madison said slowly. Mary covered her mouth to hide her own giggles. "Does anyone want to share something about themselves that no one knows about?" She wiggled her thick eyebrows.

Sheila raised her hand but spoke right away. "That depends on what you mean by the term 'no one knows about'."

"She *means* what kind of snacks have you been hiding in that high hair of yours," Saliesha shook her head in the way only she knew how.

"No, no, no," Charlie put in. "She meant what have we been hiding in our hearts," she pounded her own heart, "right *here*," she whispered dramatically and smirked.

Madison tried to pipe in. "Well actually it's somewhat of Saliesha's theory, but-"

"*What*?! I beg your pardon! I am outraged!" Sheila ranted.

Saliesha raised her eyebrows haughtily at Charlie and she made a funny face in return.

Madison explained. "Don't worry Sheila, I didn't mean it quite that way. Let's try this again. Does anyone want to tell me what they wished they had?"

I raised my hand halfway. I felt comfortable enough to admit my biggest flaw. "I envy people with blonde hair. I always imagine myself with it."

"And what's wrong with red hair?" Sheila asked indignantly. And the only reason I know the word 'indignantly' is because she taught it to me.

"What's wrong with brown hair?" Charlie asked with a smirk on her face.

"There's nothing wrong with it! Sometimes I just wish I had blonde hair."

"And I wish I even *had* hair," Saliesha muttered.

"What was that Saliesha?"

We all looked at her and she was in shock. "Did I say that out loud?"

We all nodded.

"Elaborate please, because last time I checked you *had* hair." Sheila crossed her arms.

Saliesha squirmed a little then shut her eyes tight.

"You don't have to share or explain if you don't want to," Madison said softly.

Saliesha sucked her teeth in attitude and exclaimed, "I wear fake hair okay?!"

No one spoke, we just studied her. Her black hair was straight down and up to her chin in a shiny bob. She sucked her teeth again, "What?"

"You can't even tell," Lane explained.

Saliesha looked up to the ceiling. "That's kind of the point, *duh*."

"Well Saliesha, the question is why do you wear it? Do you wear it for others or yourself? Think about that," Madison's gray eyes watched her carefully.

"I think it boosts my self-esteem yeah, but...sometimes I wish I could just pull it off and jump in the water. I don't go near water sports because I don't want to get it wet."

"Come to think of it, I haven't seen you in any water activities," Sheila added.

"I was wondering why you dropped out of swimming," Sofia wondered aloud.

Saliesha nodded. "And I feel left out because I want to go wind sailing and swimming and kayaking."

Madison looked at her with sympathy. "That's the problem. You should accept yourself for the way you are."

"I'm sure your real hair isn't bad at all," Mary said in her sing-song voice.

"Yeah," we all agreed. Charlie put her hand on Saliesha's shoulder.

"Saliesha, do you mind taking it off and showing us what your hair really looks like?" Madison asked, leaning forward.

Saliesha took a deep breath, "Yeah."

She got up slowly and went to the bathroom, locking the door.

Everyone was silent for five full seconds until Sofia blurted out, "My eyes are not really green!" The words had come out so fast that they were almost jumbled.

"What?" I couldn't help but ask in disbelief. I always admired her big green eyes.

Sofia's white face turned pink and she said miserably, "I've always wanted my father's eyes. My mother bought me contacts because I continued begging for them. My eyes are really brown." She said the word 'brown' as if it were a deadly non-curable disease.

I've said it that way too.

Sheila raised her hand and spoke at the same time. "I feel deceived! Bam*boozled*!"

"Oh come on Sheila, aren't you gonna tell us that you dye your hair red?" Charlie asked with an evil grin.

Sheila's face matched her hair and her freckles turned white. "Why, I've *never* been *thus* treated in my *entire life*!" She snorted in outrage.

Mary clapped. "Okay girls! That's enough persnickety business!"

Madison looked at Sofia with understanding, "Do you mind showing us."

"Of course," Sofia said softly and got up. She went to her bunk in the corner and her back faced us.

"Anyone else?" Charlie asked dryly, one foot was up on her seat while she leaned on her knee with an elbow.

Madison looked at the rest of us. "You have to understand how hard this is for Saliesha and Sofia. They are very scared to show their true selves."

A few minutes later, Sofia came back and sat down on her chair quietly.

"Sofia?" Madison encouraged since her head was face down.

She looked up and Sheila gasped. Sofia looked even more beautiful than before. Her dark black lashes framed her deep chocolate brown eyes. I studied them more and noticed that they were more an amber color with gold streaks in the center.

"What is wrong? Is it that bad?" She closed her eyes in shame.

"No!" We all shouted at once and she looked up in surprised shock.

"I must admit they are *almost* as pretty as my light brown hue." Sheila said haughtily.

Sofia smiled; the small dimples on the sides of her lips came through. "I will take that as a compliment."

"They're absolutely gorgeous," Mary sang.

"Personally, I like these better than those fake ones," Charlie shared honestly.

"I thought I was jealous of your eyes before…but *now*…" I couldn't believe I admitted that. I briefly realized that I was really envious of a lot of people.

Madison nodded, "They are beautiful Sofia."

"Thank you," she replied gently. "That is what my parents told me."

The bathroom door opened and every head swung to the right. Saliesha had ringlets of thick black curls all over her head.

"Oooh," we all marveled.

"What?" Saliesha asked in defense and crossed her arms in that signature attitude.

"Those curls blow Sheila's out of the ballpark," Charlie exclaimed.

"*Humph!*" Sheila snorted and grabbed her red curls.

"Please tell us why you've been hiding those spectacular-riffic curls!" Mary proclaimed while getting up and passing around sticks of chewing gum.

Saliesha grabbed a piece and popped it in her mouth as she sat down, "Because it didn't look like everyone else's."

I shook my head. "But can't you see? This is what makes you, *you*. You don't need different hair to be beautiful." Everyone gave me knowing looks and I asked, "What?"

"Maybe you don't need blonde hair after all," Madison winked.

Charlie touched a lock of my hair, "Or a certain shade of brown. This is what makes you, *you*."

And that's when the light turned on. Everyone was right. I *could* accept my brown hair and my brown eyes. I bit my lip and looked down.

Saliesha touched her own hair. "You all really think this is good? For real?"

Sheila uncrossed her legs and blew out a frustrated breath, "Who *cares* what we think!"

Madison smiled with pride.

Charlie was smiling too. "I'm gonna have to agree with Sheila." We all looked at her in surprise. She put her hands up, "Just this once…again!"

"I don't know…but I'll try it."

Madison spoke. "There will never be anyone like you in the world. Embrace yourself, embrace your everything. From a freckle to a beauty mark to a scar…this is what makes you who you are."

"Lyrics from Zipporah, love her!" Sheila exclaimed.

We nodded and chewed our gum.

"This is how God made you. Now pull out your mirrors."

We each went under our chair and pulled out a long mirror Mary had given us at the beginning of the meeting.

"Now before we part, give yourself a big smile: I mean a *big* smile, teeth and all!"

We all smiled and then Sheila screamed in terror.

"What happened, Sheila?" Madison asked innocently.

We all ended up screaming in horror.

"*Myyy Teeeetttttthhh*!!" Sheila shouted.

Charlie put the mirror down and looked at the counselors in mutiny.

"Don't look at *us*!" Mary said in innocent amusement.

"You *gave* us *black* dyed *chewing gum*?!" Sheila screeched.

"I did?" Mary asked and shrugged. She got up with Madison. "I didn't even realize."

Saliesha and Sofia ran to the bathroom to brush their teeth and fought over who was going in first. I turned around to watch the fray as Lane pushed the both of them and jumped into the bathroom first. When I turned back around, Madison and Mary were gone.

"Oh this is far from over!" Charlie fumed.

I looked at her. "Nice teeth."

*****

The next morning we were all busy doing our designated chores. I was busy sweeping the floor. As I gathered up the dust and dirt into the dust pan; Sheila sang out, "Oh Calliope! You've got some visitors!"

"Huh?" I moved the broom and pan aside and hurried to the screen door. "Hi Carrie and Liz," I walked out onto the wide porch. They both looked refreshed since they never got a prank pulled on them in the middle of the night.

Carrie smiled brightly and held out a big box. "Here are the yearbooks."

I knew my face lit up as I took the box into my arms. "Thank you guys so much!"

"Sorry it took so long. We've just been really busy," Liza said as she played with her long hair.

"We're like in every activity." Carrie shook her head, "And we've been going crazy organizing this year's yearbook with the committee."

"We've gathered nineteen-eighty through nineteen-ninety." Liz added.

"We hope you find what you're looking for."

"Thanks!"

"Oh yea and thanks for the chocolate cakes," Liz said happily.

"When Brandon delivered them, I wanted. To. Die."

"They were so amazing!" Carrie remembered fondly.

I was confused, but said, "You're welcome."

They waved goodbye and skipped down the porch steps. I looked at the books and bit my bottom lip in anticipation.

I headed straight to the library after lunch. I had sent Brandon a note to meet me there during the free period. I set the pile of yearbooks neatly on the table and a few minutes later Brandon came in.

"Hey Cal!" He greeted with excitement. His eyes were so bright blue today that it was almost scary!

And I definitely mean scary-handsome.

"Look what I have," I sang as I lifted a book up.

"Awesomeness," he lifted up a yearbook.

"By the way, how did you get those cakes to the twins?"

Brandon lifted his ankle. "I'm sure you've heard about the 'ankle incident'."

I made a sorry face. "Yeah."

"Well after that I took a little visit to the kitchens. Chef felt so bad that he made me an entire tray of his mini cakes to make me feel better." He waggled his brows.

"Genius!"

"I know," he blew on his nails and polished them on his shirt, "I'm *that* good. And I felt better too after I took a cake for myself to enjoy."

I couldn't help but laugh and pointed at the books. "Let's get started." We sat at the table and started in the early eighties. "These books feel so ancient," I thumbed through the pages carefully.

"Yeah, I can't believe people from this time are still alive," Brandon said in astonishment.

We only had a half hour for free period and wanted to be able to look through every book before the time was up.

"Let's make a plan," Brandon pointed off with his fingers, "Look for the group photo of every bunk thirteen since we know that's where F stayed. We also look for the camps cutest couple and swim teams since the picture was taken by the lake."

"Right," I started looking carefully for any clues.

I was starting to feel helpless after a half an hour, but I still had hope. I grabbed the nineteen eighty-seven book and looked through it, going straight to the girls living in bunk thirteen. I read the names aloud and looked up at Brandon, "No F."

"Well remember, F could probably be a nickname."

"Then how on earth will we find out who she is?" I asked in frustration. I put my hand through my hair angrily.

I couldn't believe how he could still smile through this. "Just check out any girl who has a flowery name."

I took a deep breath. "Right, okay." I remembered the other names and didn't recall seeing a 'flowery' name. "Cutest couple of eighty-seven Peter and Emma," I read aloud. "This is going to be impossible."

We were busy looking through the yearbooks for a solid fifteen minutes before I got distracted. I kept glancing at Brandon's face and looking back down. There was no way that Brandon liked me. The girls were crazy to say that baloney! It was just too obvious that he liked Charlie.

What would Charlie say if he asked her out? Would she be interested? So many confusing thoughts started spinning in my mind and I wasn't paying any attention to the yearbooks.

"Uh...Callie?"

I looked up quickly. "Huh?"

He smiled. "You've been staring at the same page for like five minutes. You okay?"

I looked down, "Oh. I just got distracted, sorry." There was no way I'd tell him *what* exactly had me distracted. I turned the page. I had to know exactly how he felt about her. There had to be a way...maybe I could talk to the person Sheila hired to follow Brandon around.

I put down the eighty-seven and picked up the eighty-nine. "I'm just wondering how Charlie did in her rehearsal today. She's actually been practicing really hard."

He nodded as he looked through the book. "I'm sure she did fine."

"Yeah, but she's not really a singer." I looked at him carefully, trying to see if his face would light up at the mention of Charlie.

"I'm sure she'll do okay since she's been practicing so much," he said casually and shrugged.

Geez! I wasn't getting anything out of him! He showed no signs that he was *really* interested in Charlie. How could I get him to say it without asking?

I tried a different tactic. "So...the camp dance next week is sure to be a great time. Thought of anyone to take?"

He looked up quickly. "Well, the girls are supposed are supposed to ask the guy so..." he gave me one last look before looking down and turning the page.

Ugh! How did I forget that vital piece of information? I roughly turned the pages, not really looking at the people. *Ask him!* My mind screamed at me. *Ask him if he wants a certain girl to ask him. No!* I fought myself. *Then he'll know I like him! Is that really such a bad thing though?*

My mind spun and I didn't realize how hard I turned the pages. *Yes it is a bad thing because he likes Charlie! But I can change his mind and* make *him like me. No! I'd* never *do that! What kind of girl do you think I am?*

I'm you, *you dummy!*

"Ugh!" I shouted and accidentally tore a page. "Oops…"

"Hey…you okay?"

"I'm sorry. I just think of a million things at once…" I looked down at the torn page.

"I'll go grab some tape." He got up.

Great! I slammed my forehead on my hand and looked down at the photo I tore. Now he thinks I'm a weirdo. I looked at the tiny smiling faces and automatically looked through the names, reading them off in my head to distract myself. *Bunk thirteen girls…Hailey, Jenna, Sara, Rose, Kimberly and Felicia.* My eyes narrowed as I focused on one name in particular. Felicia. An F "Okay…" I straightened up and rustled through the pages to find the cutest couple and found nothing but a torn out page.

I slumped back down and looked for the swimming team photo and found one with about twenty campers. The picture was taken from far and was a little fuzzy, but I went straight to the names. Two names stuck right out, "Christopher…Felicia…" I gasped and looked up.

Brandon came back with the tape and gave me a funny look. "You tore another page?"

"I found them!"

"What?" He put the tape down and quickly sat next to me.

"Look at the swim team," I pointed. "C is Christopher, there it is right there and F is Felicia." I turned the pages back, "And *look*! Felicia was in bunk thirteen too."

Brandon's eyes scanned the pictures quickly, "Whoa…what about cutest couple?"

I took a deep breath and shook my head as I turned to that page, "It doesn't make any sense. The page was torn out."

"What?" He asked in disbelief. "What year is this?" He got up and walked back to his side of the table, checking out the yearbooks.

"Nineteen eighty-nine."

He grabbed nineteen-ninety and went straight to the same pages. He was still standing as he held up the book. "Felicia isn't in bunk thirteen this year." He turned some pages, "The cutest couple page is torn out here too. But look here, Felicia is Camp Clown."

"What?!" I grabbed the book from him, "Hmm…"

"Why are these pages torn?"

I shook my head, "Something smells fishy."

"It doesn't help that these yearbooks have no last names." His eyes lit up, "Looks like we've stumbled on an even deeper mystery."

"This is *so* not cool. It will be impossible to find out why the pages are missing from these two yearbooks."

Brandon nodded. "I agree. It's gonna be hard but," he shrugged, "I think we can figure it out."

"How on earth can we do that?"

He shook his head and crossed his arms. "I can't believe you already forgot. And you call yourself an investigator."

"What on earth are you talking about?"

"Mrs. Bijou. We have faces now."

"That's right! I stood up quickly, but not before bumping into the table, making a heavy book fall right on my toe.

And to think I almost saw Brandon without getting hurt.

"Hey, you okay?" He came around and picked up the book.

I was frozen to the spot. My toe was on fire! It hurt so, so bad! I couldn't take it! "I'm perfectly fine!" I gave him my biggest smile.

I was sure I looked crazy.

He put the book back and straightened them.

My toe was just starting to feel a tiny bit better so I found the strength to ask, "Were you checking out eighty-eight?"

"Yeah, but I barely got through it when you ripped the page."

I felt my face turn pink and grabbed that book. "Sorry." I looked through it. "There's a cutest couple page in this one…Paul and Hannah." I shuffled through the pages and only saw Christopher.

"What's wrong?"

I sat back down. "So they only went to camp together for the summers of eighty-nine and ninety. This definitely has to be them."

"Take out the picture from the box," Brandon said, curious.

I handed it to him, "What's up?"

"I just want to make sure we're looking at the right girl…" He looked at the photo and compared it to the Felicia under the Camp Clown photo, "No, totally different hair."

"Let me see that." I grabbed the book and compared it to the smudged photo. "Felicia's hair is straight blonde. The girl in the picture has brown, wavy hair, kind of like mine."

"So Felicia may not be the F we're looking for," he frowned.

I was completely confused now. "I don't understand. Are we back at square one again?"

We heard the bugle over the intercom, signaling a change in activity.

"Agh, I gotta go."

"Yeah, I have swimming," I said distracted.

Brandon put all the books back into the box. "Listen Cal, whatever you do, don't over-think this. We found a lot, well not too much more but actually more than I thought we would."

"Huh?"

"Exactly. Just focus on swimming class and see how Charlie did at her rehearsals," he came up closer, "Now I know why Charlie reminds you to do stuff."

"Why?"

"Because you constantly need reminding," he laughed and winked at her. "I'll catch you later."

"See ya."

I tried not to faint, which was easy since I never fainted. It wasn't that he winked or smiled at me…it was because he actually cared about me. And best of all, best of everything…he called me Cal.

My smug smile turned into a frown when I thought about what we found. Felicia stayed at my bunk. The initials were outside on the tree. She had to be the F we were looking for. Before I got dizzy I thought about Brandon's advice, don't think about it so much!

We were getting so close to solving the mystery. It wasn't going to be easy to do, but I never *ever* give up.

Chapter 16

It's The Best Music Ever

Note to Self: Don't chew gum in class.

WE GRUMPILY got up for the raising of the flag. Lack of sleep was something I did not appreciate. I noticed dark purple circles under my eyes and when I looked at the other girls; they had the same thing. Except for Saliesha, who slept like a rock. We were all so terrified to sleep because of Madison and Mary.

"I'm in dire need of some cucumbers," Sheila whined as she looked into the mirror that hung on the wall. She stretched her face out sideways and then pushed her cheeks together to resemble a fish. "I'm going to have a talk with the kitchen staff. Surely they could spare a few."

"Why do you need cucumbers?" Saliesha asked as she tied her sneakers.

Sheila kept playing with her face and rolled her eyes, "*Because* the cucumber has a cooling effect that soothes the savage beast that is puffiness."

"I think you're gonna need more than cucumbers for that. Maybe some big fat pork will do the trick." Charlie smirked and we giggled.

Sheila rolled her eyes *again*. "I am in no mood for your tasteless dry humor today Charlotte. By the by, that isn't how a princess should act."

"When I'm *here* I'm Charlie. When I'm on *stage* I'm the princess, got it?" she made clear as she put her hair up into a sloppy ponytail.

"As an actress, you must let the role consume you in your everyday life." Sheila stated matter-of-factly.

"I should have known." Charlie said cheerily. "I was wondering why you're playing the evil queen so good. Besides, the only real princess here is Sofia," she grinned, knowing how to push Sheila's buttons.

Sheila scoffed and we giggled as Mary and Madison strolled in. "Good morning campers," Madison called out. Her beautiful curls were tied up high in a ponytail, making her gray eyes even more noticeable.

"Having a fantasti-cal morning?" Mary sang.

We all grumbled a 'good morning'.

"How did everyone sleep?" Madison asked smugly.

"Like you don't know," Sheila replied dryly.

"I don't know!" Saliesha raised her hand cheerfully. Sofia threw a pillow at her head.

"We each have to take turns to guard the bunk house at night," Sheila whined.

"We don't know what you're talking about," Madison said with fake innocence.

"I'm hungry." Charlie announced. "Let's just go to the raising of the flag so we can eat."

"Not so fast Camper Charlie!" Mary chimed, catching Charlie and dragging her back.

Charlie closed her eyes and counted to three before opening them and looking into the impossibly cheerful face of Mary.

"Today happens to be a certain camper's awe-so-riffic birthday!"

"What?" Some of the girls asked.

Madison walked out onto the porch and brought in a handful of colorful balloons, handing Mary a shiny blue birthday hat.

Mary walked to Charlie and placed the hat on her head; she and Madison both sang, "Happy birthday Camper Charlie!"

We laughed in surprise.

"Girl, you didn't say it was your birthday today!" Saliesha accused with her hands on her hips.

"Happy birthday Charlie," Lane clapped and slid her glasses up her nose.

Me and the other girls wished her a happy birthday and Charlie couldn't have looked anymore embarrassed. Her face turned bright red.

"Saliesha's right, why didn't you say it was your birthday?" I asked.

"Nobody asked."

"We set a special place for you in the dining hall," Madison declared.

"You didn't."

"We most certainly did!" Mary sang with disgusting cheerfulness.

"It's even a bonus day," Madison announced.

"Someone else has a birthday?"

"We're not that lucky," Madison answered Saliesha. "It's inside-out day, so wear your clothes and socks inside out."

"And don't be quick to take off that birthday hat Camper Charlie!" Madison exclaimed. "You have to keep it on *all* day."

Charlie groaned and planted her face in her hands. The counselors laughed and Madison announced, "We'll see you at the flag pole, get moving."

I patted Charlie's back. "It's not supposed to be a bad day."

She shook her head, "I just associate it with kiddie birthday parties."

"Whatever do you mean?" Sheila asked. "I absolutely love my birthday parties. It's on Halloween so I always get to dress up like my true self; a princess. My daddy throws me a huge costume party. It's an annual event."

"Your birthday is on Halloween?" Saliesha asked in disbelief.

"It's not really as horrible as everyone thinks," she fluttered her lashes.

Charlie groaned. "It's not as scary as mine. Just last year my mom had a clown, a balloon maker and a face painter like I'm still nine or something."

"Ouch," Sofia added.

Lane nodded. "That's pretty bad."

"I'm actually kind of glad I'm not home for my birthday," Charlie said gratefully.

"My birthday is on Christmas," Sofia shared softly.

Sheila's jaw dropped. "You're a princess *and* your birthday is on Christmas?"

Sofia nodded happily.

"Well…my birthday is on Christmas too," I shared.

The girls reacted in shocked amazement with Saliesha exclaiming, "Say *what*?"

"How wonderful!" Sofia said in delight. "We're lifetime birthday friends!"

"Yeah!" I gave her a high-five.

Sheila flipped her hair behind her shoulder, scoffed and walked away to slip on her pink sneakers.

Charlie shook her head and walked to the bathroom. I looked at Saliesha and she gave me a knowing look.

"What?" Sofia asked curiously.

"Girl, we are throwing Charlie a *party*," Saliesha whispered.

Sheila squealed with delight.

"Shhhh!" We shushed her.

Sheila's eyes grew large and she held her hands together excitedly. "I can't help it. I simply *love* throwing parties. Tell me what to do. Give me an occupation please, please!"

"Okay, this is what we do…" we circled together and quickly made plans.

*****

The entire class sat quietly as we sewed woolly socks. I couldn't think of anything but the questions I was going to ask Mrs. Bijou.

"Great job Camper Calliope," Mrs. Bijou said as she walked by. "It actually resembles a sock."

I smiled with pride as I looked at my fluffy blue sock. "Really?" It was kind of shocking since I wasn't really paying any attention to what I was doing.

Mrs. Bijou's red lips turned upwards and she nodded, "Really."

As she turned to walk away, I stopped her, "Uh, Mrs. Bijou? Can I ask you a question?"

"Surely," she patted her hair, which was in a fancy little braid with a flower sticking out.

"It's about-"

"MRS. *BIJOU*!" Someone screeched from the other side of the room.

We both turned and I shook my head as she gasped. Rachel the Gum Smacker's braces were being pulled from a piece of thread in the sewing machine.

"It's being held together by her gum!" The same girl who shouted for Mrs. Bijou, Belinda, exclaimed.

"I told you about that gum Miss Mathis!" She rushed to help.

"Iiish na ma faauuu!" Rachel tried to talk.

I think I actually understood what she said, but shook my head. I sat there in shock as Mrs. Bijou, Belinda and another camper named Haley tried to get Rachel's teeth free from the thread.

By the time the class ended, Rachel was pulled away. She was banned from coming to class with any gum in her mouth and taken straight to the nurse to see if they could fix her braces.

Mrs. Bijou looked flushed and was fanning herself when I approached her. "Mrs. Bijou?"

She looked at me, grateful for the distraction. "Yes darling?"

"I had a question…"

"Oh right, yes." She leaned on her elbows and looked at me with attention.

I took out the eighty-nine yearbook and turned to the picture of the camp clown. "Do you recognize this girl here? Her name is Felicia."

She looked carefully at the picture and adjusted her oversized glasses. "Oh yes! I remember her. Felicia Fedora." She gloated. "I told you I never forget a face."

I turned the page and showed her the swim team photo. "I noticed that Felicia was in the swim team. Do you remember anyone in this picture named Christopher?"

Once again, she examined it carefully and shook her head. "This picture is too blurry. I can't really make out the faces."

I was worried about that. I took the book and tried to find another picture with him in it; maybe his bunk picture…

"Camper Callie, I'm so sorry to cut you short, but I must go off to lunch. All that shouting I was doing at Camper Rachel made me too hungry for my own good. I'm not a fan of brouhaha." She let her glasses hang down around her neck. "Was there anything specific you wanted to know about Felicia Fedora?"

I continued to look through the book and nodded. "Yes…was she really popular? I mean, did she have a boyfriend at this camp? Was his name Christopher?"

"Christopher…there were many Christopher's in my years here at Camp Eerie. I would need a picture of him for sure. But as far as Felicia…well I don't recall her having a boyfriend. I do remember that she was very funny and everyone liked her very much. She was always laughing here in class," she explained fondly.

"Aha!" I found a picture with the name Christopher at the bottom. It was the boys from Bunk Four. "Any Chris here?"

She took the book one last time. "Oh yes, handsome boy. This is Camper Christopher right here."

I peeked to get a good look.

"Now *that* was a fun bunch of campers." She looked right at me, "But I'd never seen him with Camper Felicia. I believe there was another girl he was fond of."

My face fell. "Really?"

"Yes, I saw them together all the time."

"Her name didn't happen to start with an F, did it?"

"You know I don't remember. Maybe if I had a picture…" I said the last sentence out loud with her.

"Well if you could look through the book and point out-"

She stood up. "I'm so sorry, but a headache is coming on. I think I need to lay down for a spell."

"Oh yeah. Sorry. Thanks for your help."

"You know who's good with things like this? Mrs. Copperpot." She nodded. "She can remember the color you wore on the first day at camp twenty years ago, believe me."

"I can't remember what I did this morning, let alone know what camper dated whom twenty years or so ago," Mrs. Copperpot explained to me outside of the dining hall.

"I'm sorry for bothering you-"

"Oh don't be sorry dearie," she said with her British accent. "I'm not sorry about my memory. However, let me take a glance at these pictures and see what I can do to help."

I happily showed her the picture of Christopher and his friends outside of bunk four.

"Hmmm…" the elderly teacher looked closely at the picture. "As a matter of fact dear, I believe you are in luck because I happen to remember this group of campers. Fun campers, they were."

I turned the page to the girls of bunk thirteen and she looked carefully again. "Oh yes!"

"Yes?" I asked eagerly. "Yes what?"

"Camper Christopher definitely dated a girl in this picture," she tapped on the page.

"Was it this girl here? Felicia?"

She frowned and chuckled, "Oh no. Camper Felicia was too busy making everyone laugh. No, no, he dated this girl here."

I quickly looked at the fuzzy picture and saw her point to a girl with brown hair. "What's her name?"

"You know…I don't remember."

*****

I was so frustrated with the mystery and the names; I decided to go to the entertainment room during my free period after lunch. I'd sit down and plan out Charlie's party with my notebook and pen. It was simple and I wouldn't have to think so hard.

Even though there were movie posters taped to the wall, a huge flat screen TV and an entire section for music, campers had so much fun outside they didn't have any desire to go in.

When I entered the bunk, I was greeted by the smell of movie popcorn. I saw someone's head behind the big sofa watching an action movie from the nineties. A few campers were playing darts in the corner and another camper was reading a magazine and wearing headphones. I walked over to the back and thumbed through the music CDs.

"Callie?"

I turned around and saw that it was Brandon sitting on the sofa. His foot was propped up on a small footstool.

"Hey Brandon," I walked over to him. "Are you okay?"

He smiled. "It's nothing." He moved some hair away from his eyes. "I actually fell on the same ankle that was sprained a few weeks ago. It's nothing really but my counselor suggested I rest it during the free period.

"I hope it feels better." I knew a lot about injuries this summer.

He had a faraway look in his eyes for a moment and then nodded at the notebook in my hand, "Taking a break?"

"Yeah. I don't want to interrupt your movie, so…"

"No," he shut it off and hobbled over. "I'll join you."

"You need any help?" The question was silly since he easily walked to the back with me. He laughed and scooted into a chair at the table.

I turned red and hurried back to the CDs. I found one of my favorite swing CDs by Glenn Miller and popped it into the player. Once the first strands of music started, I closed my eyes and smiled. I almost felt like I was back in my room at home.

"So you like this kind of music huh?"

I opened my eyes, turned around and sat across the table from him, "It's the best music ever."

The campers playing with the darts started to dance really goofy, but I didn't mind at all.

He nodded and stuck out his bottom lip, "Sounds pretty good." He tapped on the table. "So you've been pretty busy."

"Yeah, I don't really have time to think about a whole lot. Our counselors have been pulling pranks on us really good."

He sat back and whistled. "You should see our side of camp, it's basically chaos. One morning we woke up in the forest. I still can't figure out how that happened." He scratched his head and then looked like he remembered something, "Hey, did you get a chance to talk to Mrs. Bijou?"

"I completely forgot to tell you about it!"

"What?"

I told him everything I learned about Felicia.

"Are you serious? Wow." He rubbed his face in his hands. "We'll figure this thing out. I have hope."

"Hope?" I shook my head. "That's about the last thing I have right now."

I tapped my feet and he smiled at me. "Tell me more about this kind of music. Who's the band?"

I was taken by surprise. Besides my mom, no one ever talked with me about this music. I got excited. I was totally going to make him a fan. I told him all about the era and the music. He actually looked hooked on every word I said! I glanced at the clock and realized that I'd spent almost the whole time talking.

"I'm sorry. You were probably hoping I'd shut up," I laughed.

He opened his mouth to say something when a girl with straight red hair came over to us. She had a face full of freckles and really light eyelashes. "Hi, I'm Molly."

Brandon leaned back. "Hey."

"I couldn't help but hear this music," she said with a notebook and pen in her hand.

"I'm sorry, is it too loud?" I turned to lower the radio.

"No, I'm the head of the camps dance committee and we're stumped on an idea for this year's theme." She waved her friends over. "We're kind of pressed for time. This is Mindy, Chloe and Lauren."

"Hi."

The girls were silent for a moment as they looked at each other and listened to the music.

"What do you think?" Molly asked them.

The blonde Lauren nodded. "It's definitely different." Just then, one of Glenn's most famous songs came on, 'In the Mood', one of my faves.

The girl named Chloe tapped her toes. "This is called swing music right?"

"Yeah, it's great."

Mindy pointed out, "We don't have time to be picky. The dance is next week!"

Molly nodded as she started bouncing up and down to the music. "I think we have this year's theme."

"Are you serious?" I asked excitedly.

"I'm dead serious." Molly's light green eyes widened at the possibilities this option opened.

"We have to hurry and let Ms. Tremaine know," Chloe nodded.

"We have to make the announcement," Lauren added.

"We have to get the decorations," Mindy announced.

The girls all turned in a hurry to grab their things and Molly turned back to me. "Thanks for the idea!" She ran out of the building.

Brandon chuckled. "Wow Cal, you're just a big ball of inspiration."

"I wouldn't say that," I laughed. "Wow, a swing dance! I can't wait."

"It's next week." He sat up. "We actually only have one week left here, do you believe it?"

I got nervous every time his blue eyes looked at me. "I..." I cleared my throat nervously. "I know. This time has gone by so fast." I tapped on my notebook and avoided his eyes as much as I could.

I was never able to jot down notes for Charlie's party, but it didn't matter. Charlie was going to have a great time.

"So…" I felt Brandon's gaze on me as he asked, "Did you ask anybody to the dance yet?"

I must have been really super nervous because I started laughing. "That's a good one Brandon."

"What? I'm not joking."

I was a little confused. If I wasn't mistaken (and ninety-nine percent of the time I was) it almost sounded like he hoped *I* would ask him. I opened my mouth to ask if anyone (namely Charlie) asked him yet, but stopped when the bugle sounded. "I have hiking right now," I rushed and stood up. "It was nice talking to you Bran."

He winked at me. Insert blush here! "Don't have too much fun out there. I'm supposed to take it easy for the rest of the day. I'm going to sewing next."

"It can't be all that bad," I replied tongue-in-cheek as I took the CD out and put it back in its case.

"Tomorrow, I'll be back in action," he followed me to the door. "And the first thing I'm going to do is hand glide."

I laughed as we walked out of the air conditioned bunk and into the sticky summer air. "Oh. We're throwing a surprise party for Charlie tonight. It's going to be at the rec center. You're invited."

He smiled and it was devastating. "Thanks. I'll be there. You mind if I bring Edward?"

I'm sure my dimple deepened, "The more the merrier. Charlie is going to freak out."

Thinking about it now, those were really ominous last words.

Chapter 17

Everybody Likes *You*

Note to self: Arguing with your best friend is *not* fun.

AS WE left the dining hall after dinner, Mary jumped out and exclaimed, "Hey girls! I'm ready to decorate for the surprise party!"

We were stuck in shock as Mary noticed Charlie. "Oops...I guess I got a little too excited. I'm sorry, okay I've gotta go."

"What surprise party?" Charlie asked accusingly.

"Mary!" Sheila whined.

Mary ran off and we started backing away from Charlie.

"Wait, what party? Not a birthday party, right?" We started to run after Mary, Charlie followed, "Because I remember specifically saying no parties! Get back here so I can pound you!"

After a while, Charlie finally gave in and accepted that she was getting a birthday party. We forced her to stay at the camp fire by herself while Mary and Madison helped us decorate the party. Mr. and Mrs. Reeves let us use the beautiful terrace outside of the rec center, facing the woods. Mrs. Reeves even brought balloons and punch. We hung up lights and set up goodies on the table. The chef even prepared his special chocolate cakes just for the birthday girl.

We hurried back to the bunk to dress up. As we picked out our outfits, Charlie jumped onto her top bed and relaxed.

"Na-ah girl," Saliesha snapped her fingers and tilted her head. "Everyone needs to check out this chick over here."

Sheila and I looked up and I sighed. "What are you doing?"

Charlie propped her head on her hand and asked defensively, "What?"

"You *must* dress up for this party," Sofia explained.

"It's *your* party!" Sheila complained.

"Exactly. And I can wear what I want." Charlie smirked. "I can even cry if I want to."

"Charlotte Louise Mackenna, if you don't get yourself off of the bed and get dressed right now, I will finish you like a cupcake! Do you hear me?!" Everyone went silent as they looked at me in shock. Well, the girl had it coming! The girls slowly looked back at Charlie.

Her face cracked into a huge smile and she cheered. "Well that's more like it!"

Sheila clapped and squealed, "Makeover!"

We all clapped along and Charlie bolted up right away, "Ohh no. Keep Sheila and her feather boas away from me!" Me and Sheila pulled her down and we all worked together to make her look fancy for her birthday.

Saliesha and I decided on a cute summery pink dress. Sofia dotted on very light makeup that didn't add color to Charlie's face but enhanced the color she already had.

We decided that she didn't need any necklaces or bracelets because her natural beauty was enough.

Sheila took the curling iron and curled Charlie's thick chestnut brown hair and then swept the long locks over the front of her shoulder. When we all stepped back, we were amazed and more than satisfied with our work.

"You look beautiful," Sofia announced.

Charlie gave a dry face, "Do I?"

"Girl, you got it going *on*!" Saliesha exclaimed.

"Let's hurry so we can take pictures," I said quickly.

"Photo-shoot! *Yes*!" Sheila patted her hair. "You will learn from the best, my dears!"

We all scattered, leaving Charlie by herself on the chair. "So now I have to sit here and wait? Some birthday," she complained. I noticed her stand up, stomp to the mirror and freeze.

I smiled and walked over to her. "You *are* beautiful Charlie."

She jumped in surprise and turned around. "Yeah. I didn't even know I could be a girly girl sometimes. It's easy to forget when I'm shooting hoops."

I snapped a picture and handed her the camera. "A picture is worth a thousand words…but a thousand words can never be enough."

Charlie smiled and her thick brown eyebrows spread over her sparkling deep blue eyes. I was really starting to understand what being a friend was all about.

"Geez Callie, is this how you get your dad to buy you stuff?"

I laughed.

Twenty minutes later we were all dressed up in our summery dresses. I had so much fun when we went to the porch and took turns taking pictures. Of course Sheila *had* to be in every one. She wanted to show off her long pink sparkly dress and she put in extra hairspray to make the red curls even higher than usual.

"I didn't think to bring a camera with me," I said glumly. I wore a pretty dark blue summer dress. The instructions from camp said to bring at least two dresses for special events and I just pulled anything out of my closet. Sofia convinced me to let my hair down and it honestly felt really good.

"It's okay," Charlie replied. "I'll send you all the pictures and remember to bring one next year. Hey Saliesha," she started to hand her the camera, "this next one is just for me and Cal."

"Hold on girl my eyes are hurting me, I'm about to break out my sunglasses again!" Saliesha explained. She wore a bright yellow party dress and placed a small yellow bow on the side of her short curly hair.

"What's wrong?"

"Sheila's dress is blinding me!" Saliesha complained.

Sheila gasped in return. "This is fashion! *Something* you know *nothing* about."

"I know enough not to blind my friends-" Saliesha argued but Sheila stepped right in and argued back. The other girls were too fascinated by the argument to stop it.

"Smile!" Charlie put one arm around my shoulders, held the camera up high with the other arm and snapped a quick picture.

A few minutes later Lane, who was wearing a summery white dress and matching headband, announced that we had to hurry to the party. Madison and Mary were waiting for us.

"Laney," Sheila said on the way down the porch. "Your dress is so fetching."

Lane smiled. "Thanks Sheila."

"Am I going crazy or did they just speak to each other?" Saliesha asked.

"You might be crazy Saliesha," Sheila said haughtily. "However, we have joyfully made up from that ugly non-necessary spat."

Sofia smiled. "When did this happen?"

"Just today," Lane replied happily. "We realized that even though we argue and say things we don't mean, we'll always be friends."

"A friend loves at all times, no matter what," Sheila called out.

"Hey guys go on ahead," I told everyone. "I forgot to use the bathroom," I turned pink and did the potty dance. "I'll be there soon." I bolted into the bunk house.

When I came out, I checked myself in the mirror one last time and liking what I saw, I finally left. But after leaving the porch I realized that I forgot my present for Charlie.

I darted back inside, grabbed the tiny silver gift bag from under the bed and ran right back out. I knew the party had to have been in full swing and I was so excited to just get there already.

The path was empty since most campers were either still at the camp fire, or at the entertainment bunk hanging out. Thankfully, it was lit by the full moon and the billions of stars in the sky.

I looked ahead as I passed the bunk houses and headed to the part of the path that had a forest on either side. It turned a little bit darker and I felt a slight chill. I decided to run.

But I stopped and my feet froze to the ground. There was a light in the distance. And not like the firefly light; this time it was different. It was bigger. And it wasn't just a light…it was a human *form*.

I felt my feet again and moved my dark blue flats as fast they could go, following the light. I don't know why in the world I decided to go for it, but I had to get a closer look. The form was definitely one of a girl and it disappeared into the trees, deeper into the forest. I left the path and ran right after it.

The trees in the forest were thicker, but it didn't stop me from trying to get closer. What was the form? Was it a secret spy from Sofia's country? If it was, I wasn't going to let him or her ruin this night.

A few minutes later, the form flew through a thick bush and I wasted no time following behind with speed that would have made Brandon jealous. When I came out of the bushes, I was greeted with a flash of light in my face, making me wince.

When I opened my eyes, I was met by horror.

Gwen stood there with a camera in her hands and her face was smug. That form had led me straight to the party where all of my friends and invited campers were standing and talking. But no one said a word as they stared at me.

"Hey Callie! Did you get a good look at the ghost?" Gwen asked with a revolting look of smugness and she giggled.

When I turned to the side, I saw the "ghostly" girl still running and collapsing of laughter in the darkened distance.

"Callie?"

All I could see was the blurry form of Charlie. I couldn't blink, everything was in slow motion. I'd never been so humiliated in my entire life. I spotted the girls from the dance committee; Molly, Chloe, Mindy and Lauren. My *own* friends were staring at me. Why wasn't anyone saying anything?? That made things worse! I finally blinked and looked up and saw Brandon staring at me. He was next to Edward and Brom. What was that look on his face? Was it pity?

He looked really angry. He was probably mad at me because he thought I was chasing the ghost of the missing girl. He told me to give it up and I did! I was tricked! But I couldn't talk…couldn't move.

He suddenly turned and ran off. He had a sore ankle…he shouldn't be running. Was he that embarrassed by me? Madison ran off in the same direction as Brandon…I wasn't too sure.

I finally cleared my eyes from the blurriness and noticed that everyone's mouths were moving at once, but I still didn't hear anything. I heard voices far away in the distance.

The voices became heated and I thought there was an argument going on, but I wasn't sure. I felt something wet on my hands and realized that in my shock, I'd been crying.

I looked up again and saw Carrie and Liz staring at me. Great! They saw it too! I thought I felt tugging on my arms but wasn't sure. I just knew that I had to get away. So I started running, not knowing where, just wherever my feet took me.

I don't know how far I ran before I tripped on a tree root. At that moment I couldn't stop the sobs from coming out. I cried and cried until I was sure my eyes ran out of water. This was beyond humiliated. This happened in front of my friends, in front of my counselors…in front of Brandon.

I took a deep breath, smelled water and looked up. I was at the lake. I was on the dock that led out to the vast expanse of the water. There were no fireflies here to even comfort me. My face felt puffy from crying and I touched it. I looked down and saw the initials that had captured my mind for the entire stay at camp.

C & F

I wiped my swollen eyes and turned around and jumped when I saw Charlie standing by the tree. "This is why I don't have friends," I called out.

Charlie looked concerned. I'd seen her serious before, but never this serious and it was all my own fault. "What are you talking about Cal?" She crossed her arms.

"I just ruined your birthday party!" I shouted and walked closer.

"No you didn't," she argued. "Just come back. Gwen was just pulling a really messed up prank-"

"*Just* a prank?! I was humiliated in front of *everybody*!" I pointed to the forest behind Charlie.

"Everyone knows it's not your fault," Charlie stood up straighter.

"Easy for you to say Charlie, everybody likes *you*!"

"You say that like it's a bad thing."

"It *is*! Because I can never be as popular as you! I can never be as pretty! I don't know why I get close to anyone!"

"Excuse me Callie, but I think it was you who invited everyone to this party. So that means you have a good amount of friends. And did you even look at yourself in the mirror tonight because you're gorgeous! I'm so *sick* of hearing you talk about how ugly you are when it isn't true!"

I never heard Charlie yell before. But I didn't care because I was just so angry and hurt. "I'm sorry I make you sick. You have no idea what I'm going through!"

She shook her head. "You're wrong."

I choked on a sob. "Did you see the way Brandon ran away from me?!"

"Cal, he wasn't-!"

She was cut off by Madison, who had just come out of the forest and was running towards us. Her face was really concerned. "Callie! Are you okay?"

I ran into Madison's arms and couldn't stop myself from sobbing.

*****

It was Monday, the beginning of the last week at camp. The obstacle race was the next day and me and Quinn had been practicing for a half an hour. Quinn was frustrated. Her hair was up in a high ponytail and her pointy nose faced the sky. "We are *never* going to win this!"

I hunched over and put my hands on my knees as I tried to catch my breath. "You're too hard on us Quinn. We improved by two whole minutes."

"It's not enough!" She growled. "And you still can't climb over the wall!"

"We're trying our best. That's all that matters," I reasoned and stood straighter.

Quinn ignored me and demanded, "Again!"

"You're pushing yourself too hard-"

"I said *again!*"

I sighed and got into position. I had been avoiding Charlie and the girls for the entire weekend, which was hard since I lived with them. The girls knew that I wasn't in a talking mood so they didn't say anything to me, wanting to avoid a fight or confrontation.

That morning I said I was sick and went to the nurse with a fake belly ache just to avoid everyone at the raising of the flag and breakfast. I was quiet during my morning activities and ate a granola bar while hiding out in the library during lunch.

I began to spin on the baseball bat and was barely able to tap Quinn. She ran so fast, I couldn't believe it. I hurried to the end of the tires when Quinn tripped and shouted in pain. "Quinn!"

I ran over to her. She was groaning on the ground. "What's wrong?!"

"I think I just twisted my ankle!" She howled.

I felt horrible. "Come on," I hoisted Quinn up and supported her firmly. "I'll take you to the nurse."

Quinn looked very upset and I said nothing as we slowly made our way.

Half an hour later the camps nurse, Mrs. Wilkins, confirmed that Quinn had a broken ankle.

"Oh dear," Quinn fretted and looked at me in shame. "Don't worry one wit. I'll be fit by tomorrow."

Mrs. Wilkins, who was a kind woman with a Texan accent looked at Quinn in sympathy and explained, "I'm sorry Camper Copperpot, but a broken ankle won't heal in just a day."

Quinn looked devastated. "*No?*" She asked weakly.

"'Fraid not Sugar Plumb. You'd best take it easy and rest. I'll have my assistant grab some good books for ya to read. You'll be shacked up in here for the rest of the day." Mrs. Wilkins' shiny black hair was up in a bun held in place by a pencil. "I'll be gettin' your cast ready. I called up your counselor Jenny so she'll be on her way."

The nurse had big brown eyes with very long eyelashes and they looked at Quinn sternly, "And I don't wanna hear anymore complainin' because if I do I'll take you right out back and give you what for." She winked at Quinn and moved the curtain aside so she could leave.

Quinn twiddled her fingers anxiously. "Callie, I'm so terribly sorry."

I shook my head. "Don't worry about it Quinn. We gave it our all and we know it. That's all that matters."

"Where is my darling?!"

We heard her grandmother, Mrs. Copperpot, shuffling into the room.

"The good thing is now you'll be spoiled," I whispered.

Quinn smiled for the first time in a long time. "It's so wonderful being with my grandmother."

The curtain was pulled aside and the white-haired older woman came over. "Oh my dear Sybil!"

"Grandmother, it's me, Quinn! Sybil is still in Chipping Campden, remember?" She said in outrage, obviously used to her grandmother's forgetfulness.

"Oh well I know where your sister is! How's your finger?"

"It's my ankle Grandmother."

I smiled and left the nurses' station, heading into the big courtyard in the middle of the office buildings. I wished that I could see my grandma too. I wished I could see my entire family for that matter. Camp turned out to be a disaster and it was all my own fault.

I didn't know how I'd spend the rest of the day avoiding my *ex* friends. Oh that *Gwen*! I was so angry I could spit! They all probably thought I was crazy. I hadn't even seen Brandon since the night of the disaster. He was probably avoiding me too and I didn't blame him. Charlie probably hated me at this point and probably never wanted to see me again.

That's why I was so surprised when I looked up and saw Charlie standing right in front of me.

Chapter 18

Life Is Too Short For Grudges

Note to Self: Fighting is not as fun as making up.

CHARLIE WAS leaning on a tree, her arms folded and wearing that familiar smirk on her face. "Hey," she nodded casually.

"Hi," I replied weakly. I missed her so much. I missed all of the girls, even Sheila. And the fact that this was our last week together made the silent treatment worse.

"How did you know I was here?"

Charlie had looked like she'd been standing here for a few minutes. "I heard what happened to Quinn."

"Word travels around fast." I turned red when I realized how fast news of my embarrassing humiliation must have flown around.

Charlie stood straighter. "Listen. We need to talk. This silent treatment has to stop."

"What silent treatment?" I pushed some hair behind my ear.

Charlie let out a breath. "Cal, you've been avoiding all of us all weekend."

"That's because you're all mad at me for making a fool of myself!"

Charlie looked around and then back at me, "Uh, no Cal. No one thinks you're a fool."

I tried to process that, but it sounded impossible.

"We miss you," she said simply and that made me crumble.

"I miss you too." I ran to her and gave her a big hug. She hugged me back and I said, "I'm so sorry for ruining your birthday party. I'm so sorry I fell for Gwen's prank."

Charlie pulled away and whistled. In a matter of seconds Sheila, Lane, Sofia and Saliesha came out from behind the side of the main office building and ran towards me, all hugging me. I was overwhelmed by the emotions inside.

"My party wasn't ruined." Charlie said in the circle, standing across from me. "It was just really boring without you there and we were worried about you."

"We wanted to go to you but Mary said that you needed some time for yourself," Saliesha added.

"And we wanted to talk to you during the weekend but you avoided us like the plague," Sheila *humphed!* and crossed her arms.

"I thought you were all mad at me," I said weakly.

"You are such a wonderful friend Callie," Sofia explained, her beautiful brown eyes were full of emotion. "We could never be angry with you."

Lane pushed her glasses up the bridge of her nose before saying, "But we decided to give you the space you wanted."

"And it truly killed us!" Sheila shouted.

"It did," Charlie nodded.

I wiped a tear that just couldn't help but fall. "I've missed you all too. I'm so sorry."

"Stop apologizing!" They all shouted at once and I laughed.

"We got Gwen and Miranda back," Charlie said firmly.

"Wait, Miranda?"

Saliesha nodded. "Mm hmm, *she* was the one running through the forest." Her head shook with attitude.

"Miranda and Gwen heard us talking about the camp ghost." Sofia shared.

"But how did they...?" I remember now hearing giggling and seeing the bushes rustle that day when I was talking to Sofia.

"Miranda would have gotten away with it if Brandon hadn't gone after her and grabbed her," Sheila explained dreamily, "Ever the hero."

"What?" I asked in complete surprise. "But I thought-"

"That's what I wanted to tell you that night," Charlie answered. "Brandon wasn't running away from you, he was so angry that he ran after Miranda and caught her. Madison was right behind him."

Sofia continued the explanation, "Since the prank was meant for humiliation and harm rather than for fun, Mr. and Mrs. Reeves took all of their special programs away."

"Which means that they aren't in the obstacle race anymore," Saliesha elaborated.

My eyes widened in shock, "Oh no."

"Oh yes," Charlie nodded. "And that, my friend, is the ultimate way we got them back. And we didn't even have to lift a finger. Bad things will come to people who deserve it." She gave Saliesha a high-five.

I actually felt bad for Miranda and Gwen because I knew how hard they worked for the obstacle race. "So Brandon doesn't hate me?"

"Why would I hate you?"

We all turned around and the girls had smiles on their faces. I stood there, knowing that I looked like shocked prey facing its predator. I swallowed hard as Brandon walked up to us. He didn't smile, but his light blue eyes sparkled.

The girls stepped back and I said, "I'm sorry-"

He shook his head and cut me off, "There's only one thing I want to know from you."

I swallowed nervously again. "What's that?"

"When are you going to ask me to the dance?" A small smile crept over his face.

I heard tiny squeals and gasps from the girls, but I didn't look at them. I smiled really bright and my heart leapt from my chest. "Brandon, will you go to the end of the year camp dance with me?"

He looked as if he were thinking about it very seriously before finally saying, "What time should I meet you there?"

Sheila clapped her hands in excitement. "Don't worry Calliope. I gave him *special* permission!"

Brandon's handsome face lit up in laughter and I rolled my eyes.

I felt wonderful that I had all of my friends back, but my adventure was nowhere near over yet.

*****

During sundown, before the sun completely left the sky, the entire camp met in the middle of the main field. There was a huge thick rope on the ground. I stood chatting with my friends as Mr. and Mrs. Reeves approached everyone.

"It's boys against girls!" He shouted. All of the campers began to cheer.

Sheila groaned as she looked at her finger nails, half of her big curls were held up high in a ponytail.

"Worried about your manicure?" Saliesha teased.

Sheila smiled politely. "Beating the boys is worth it to me."

"That's my girl," Charlie gave Sheila a high five.

All of the girl counselors rallied up our side of the camp into a long line and we held up the rope. The boys cheered themselves on as they did the same. They just knew for sure that they were going to beat us.

Mr. Reeves counted down from five and we all pulled as hard as we could. Sheila was in front of me and really wasn't trying too hard at first, but as soon as the boys tugged really hard, Sheila pulled back harder than ever before.

"Pull!" One of the girl counselors cheered us on from the sidelines.

"Come on you sunny-riffic campers! You can do it!"

It was a hard struggle, but a few moments later we all pulled really hard, making the boys lose their grip and fall. We cheered and celebrated and the boys were ordered to congratulate us.

As I cheered along with my bunk mates, I noticed that Gwen wasn't looking like her usual smug self. Everyone started to head to the bonfire, but I stepped away from my group and went to Madison.

She was laughing with a few other counselors, "Hey Madison? Can I ask you a question? Well...it's more like an idea."

Twenty minutes later Madison and I were standing in front of Gwen and her bunk counselor, a pretty black girl named Towanda. Ms. Davies joined us, standing with her toned arms folded in front.

"So Gwen, what do you say?" Towanda looked at Gwen in question.

"I personally think it's a great idea," Madison said as she stuck her thumbs in her jean pockets.

Ms. Davies nodded and looked at Gwen. "Since Miranda has gotten into trouble for other things and this is your first offense, I approve of you participating again."

Madison told me how devastated Gwen was when she heard that she wouldn't be allowed to be in the race. It was a fair punishment for what she did, but I forgave her.

Gwen's chin went up high. "We don't stand a chance. We haven't even practiced together." Her black shiny hair was held away from her face by a gold headband.

"But you both know the course right?" Towanda asked us.

I replied, "I can do the course backwards."

Gwen shrugged. "I guess I can too."

"It's settled then." Ms. Davies clapped once. "I'll fix up the paperwork tonight," she nodded and walked away.

Towanda turned to talk to Gwen and Madison's gray eyes sparkled as she said, "I'm really proud of you Callie. This is very big of you to ask her to be your partner."

My face twisted in thought. "Well, I figured life is too short for grudges. And camp life is even shorter."

Madison nodded with an astonished smile on her face. "Your parents are doing a great job raising you."

I never thought I'd say this, but it just came out. "I have the coolest parents in the world."

*****

The next day, many games were happening throughout camp. There was the annual camp swimming race, the art contest and an endless list of fun activities campers could have competed in. The one that counted was about to start in a few minutes.

I was gathered with the girls in a circle. The sun was extra bright and the weather was extra hot and sticky. Sheila stood there with oversized black sunglasses, a huge straw sunhat and she held a small battery operated fan which was pointed at her face.

She sighed dramatically, "Good luck Saliesha and Sofia." She turned to me, "Extra good luck goes to you Calliope." She looked at Gwen in the distance and gave a twisted face, "I wouldn't have been so gracious to *her*."

"That's why *she's* Callie and *you're* Sheila," Charlie said dryly.

"More's the pity," Sheila scoffed, flipped her hair and tried to find a comfortable seat in the bleachers.

Lane looked over to Gwen. "What is she doing?"

We all turned and saw Gwen waving me over angrily.

"May the good old fashioned force be with you," Saliesha said and nudged Sofia so they could prepare.

"Good luck Callie."

"Thanks Lane."

Charlie softly punched my arm. "You'll probably lose."

"You're probably right," I nodded happily.

"But at least you tried right?"

I took a deep breath as Charlie walked away. Oh how I'll try. Gwen looked frustrated as I walked over and asked, "Are you confident?"

"Not too much."

She shook her head. "This isn't like swimming class. You're going to have to trust me as your partner."

There was the T word again.

"Even though we haven't practiced together, we're still familiar with the race and we can at least try our hardest," Gwen explained.

Ms. Davies ran over to us, "You girls are last!"

"Thanks Ms. Davies!"

Gwen smiled. "This gives us a little extra time to make a game plan."

We started planning as Sofia and Saliesha went up first. Sofia was so dizzy after spinning on the bat that she fell twice! But she quickly got up and tapped Saliesha.

"What position did you practice in?" Gwen asked as she watched the girls intently.

"I was Sofia's position." I looked around and finally noticed how packed the bleachers were with campers.

"They've got good form." Gwen said competitively.

She kind of reminded me of Quinn. I was a tiny bit glad I didn't have time to practice with her too.

"Callie!"

I turned and saw Mrs. Copperpot happily pushing Quinn in a small wheelchair; her foot propped up in a cast. I walked over to them and smiled. "Quinn. How are you feeling today? Hi Mrs. Copperpot."

The older woman, who was still dressed as if she were about to walk in a blizzard, smiled brightly, "Hello my dear, lovely to see you."

"I'm so terribly upset that I can't be in the race," Quinn pouted. "But I've come to support you and I've heard you were able to get another partner."

I glanced at Gwen. "Yeah, I have no idea what to expect, just keeping positive because we'll try."

"You'll probably lose." Quinn said matter-of-factly. I noticed a pattern with that comment, but knew they all spoke some truth.

"Probably," I smiled and spotted Sofia and Saliesha rolling to the finish line. Gwen pressed her stopwatch and groaned.

"Uh oh," Quinn noticed Gwen's disappointment. "You'd better get back. We'll be watching!"

"Good luck on your game of rugby dearie!" Mrs. Copperpot said as she pushed Quinn away.

"Grandmother, it's an *obstacle* race."

"Thanks," I called out as they disappeared into the crowd. A little while later Gwen and I were ready. I turned to look at the girls in the bleachers and noticed that Brandon and Edward were sitting next to Charlie. They were all waving at me! Like I needed the extra pressure!

Sofia and Saliesha were in the lead with another team in a close second. All we had to do to win was beat them by one second.

The crowd was on its feet since our team decided the winner. The tension in the air was really thick. Ms. Davies stood hunched forward with her stop watch and whistle. "Are you ready?"

"I guess I have to be!" I exclaimed.

She blew her whistle.

I quickly ran to the bat and spun around five times. I fell once, but got up to tap Gwen's hand. I quickly got up, grabbed the scuba slippers and waited for her at the end of the tire run. Gwen was actually quicker than Quinn because we both made it there at the same time.

I slipped into the slippers and waddled over to the large broom. Gwen hopped on and I dragged her to the table. We quickly ate the candy bar. Ms. Davies was already there waiting and we showed her our empty mouths.

We grabbed the potato sacks and hopped over to the wall. That dreaded wall looked scarier as I got closer. Gwen was fast as she hopped out of the sack and jumped on the wall, pulling the rope for help. I followed behind and tried to hoist myself up but I couldn't do it.

I started to sweat and my foot kept slipping. I needed to try harder but I really needed more than that! I needed some help! I needed…

I looked up and saw Gwen's hand reaching out for mine. "Come on!" She encouraged. "You can do it Callie!"

I reached up and grabbed her hand firmly. She helped me over the wall and together we jumped off. Falling to the ground, we reached over our heads to grab hands and rolled all the way to the finish line.

Ms. Davies' whistle blew in my ears and Gwen jumped up quickly, eager to know what she would say. "Winners!"

An ear piercing scream came into my ears and I realized that it was me. Gwen jumped up and down and her friends ran down to cheer her on.

I felt hands spin me around and Saliesha pulled me into a hug. I almost fell down when everyone else came to hug me. There were 'Way to go's' and 'We knew you'd win' and lots of other encouraging words, but none of them were better than what happened next.

I felt a tap on my shoulder and as soon as I turned around, Gwen hugged me tightly. I quickly did the same. "Thank you Gwen."

"I'm sorry," she whispered in my ear. "For everything I've done."

I pulled away and looked at her. "It's okay. I forgive you."

Gwen smiled and then flitted some jet black hair behind her shoulder. "Just don't think we're friends now or anything." She spoke in a high-handed tone of voice, but then she winked at me and turned around back to her friends.

I became distracted by the girls as they surrounded me in delight. I thought this was a great end to my stay at camp. Little did I know that I was in for the surprise of my life.

Chapter 19

I Think You Should Sit Down

Note to Self: Things are not always what they seem.

THE NIGHT of the camps End of Year dance had finally arrived. For the entire day, the camp was laid back since everyone basically had free period all day. Charlie and Sheila spent the day at final dress rehearsals for their play and I stayed at the bunk house with the other girls, reading letters from home and picking out clothes for the dance.

Madison and Mary surprised us before the dance when they brought in boxes from the drama department. The two girls were dressed in twenties evening wear. Madison's curly hair was straightened and pinned underneath up to her ears to make it appear shorter. She had a shiny red headband that went over her hair and on the left was a large red feather. Her dress was the same red color and it was full of layers all the way to the knee. "Well girls, you'll all be the best dressed bunk."

We ran to the boxes and looked inside. They contained costumes from the roaring twenties. I couldn't believe my eyes. Sheila squealed in delight when she took out a red feather boa. "I've fallen in love!" She continued to go on about her undying love for costume jewelry.

"The absolute moment we found out the theme for this year's dance, we jumped on the opportunity to get these amazing-tastic costumes!" Mary sang. Her hair was in its usual French braid. She wore a blue fill skirt and collared white shirt.

Charlie pulled out a hat that resembled a bowl and planted it on her head. It was a little tight and she complained.

"It's supposed to be a little tight," I tucked her hair under the hat. "They wore their hair short. It went with the hat."

Everyone started to take out the costumes, deciding who was wearing what. "Callie," Madison whispered as the girls spoke loudly. "I've got something for you."

I walked to the corner with Madison and noticed that she held something behind her back. "What is it?"

Madison pulled out a very pretty and elegant pink dress. It had thin straps made out of costume diamonds and was smooth all the way down to the toes. There was a large pink bow on the back, complete with a train that fell down to the floor. My eyes grew large and I gasped.

It was the same dress I usually imagined myself in. The girls noticed and came over to us. "Ooh," they sang in wonder.

"Does this mean that I made bunk mate of the year?" I asked.

"No," Madison said with a smile. "I just thought you'd like this one a whole lot, especially since Molly tells us that the swing dance was your idea."

"Speaking of bunk mate of the year..." Mary sang. "We've come to a decision."

Madison went back to the box and pulled out the red feather boa Sheila had been petting (and basically named) a few minutes earlier. "You've all made so many improvements over the summer. We're proud of all of you. But the camper who we think deserves this title is..." she looked at Mary.

Mary looked like she was about to burst. "Sheila!"

We clapped and congratulated Sheila who covered her mouth with her hands. "*Me*?!"

"Yes you," Madison pointed at her. "Come on don't be so shy about it."

That was all Sheila needed to hear. "You *shouldn't* have! *Really*, you shouldn't!" Madison put the boa around Sheila's shoulder. "Oh, there are many people I'd like to thank..."

We groaned.

"But to all of the little people, I hope I didn't step on you *too* hard to make it to the top."

Charlie slapped her forehead in agony.

"It *does* get lonely all the way up here in the stars…" Sheila continued.

"What were you two *thinking*?" Saliesha complained to the counselors.

"But the view is *spectacular*!" Sheila went on.

"Okay, okay!" Madison stopped her. "It's time to get ready for the dance!"

We cheered and ran off to get ready, leaving Sheila alone in the middle of the room.

She grumbled. "The winner always gets cut off."

Madison and Mary stood on the porch protectively in the nice warm breeze while our dates waited by the stairs. Lane wore a bright yellow feather dress that came down below her knee and a matching yellow hat. Her glasses were proudly on her face as she walked down to greet a fellow nature-walker named Josh, who also wore glasses.

Saliesha asked a handsome soccer player named Arnold. He waited with some purple flowers as Saliesha walked down from the porch wearing a purple dress that tied at the waist. She wore a few layers of beaded necklaces with the longest one swopping down to her knees. She took the flowers and the moonlight glinted against her braces as she smiled and stood to the side.

Sofia wore a layered green dress and instead of pinning her hair up, she let it flow down to her waist freely. Her heels clicked on the porch as she walked down to her date; a handsome boy who was half Scottish and half Japanese. He handed her yellow flowers and she smiled, "Thanks Rei."

Madison and Mary smiled as Charlie stepped out in a pretty deep blue dress. She pinned her hair up like I suggested and wore the blue bowl hat. Edward stood there next to Brandon and both of them smiled at her.

Edward stepped forward and Charlie walked down asking, "Where are my flowers?" Edward had a look of panic and tried to look around the ground for a flower. Charlie started to laugh and punched him in the arm, "Dude, I'm joking."

Sheila swept out next, wrapping the red boa across the front of her neck. "Sheila?" Madison asked. "Is your date late?"

Sheila laughed really loud. "A star like *me* needs no escort." Nose in the air, she carefully walked down the stairs with her heels and stood next to Charlie and her date.

I came out last and was surprised when the girls gasped. Sheila had taken the time to crimp my hair in waves and pin them underneath, creating a bob. Charlie pulled out costume diamond earrings and clipped them to my ears. The dress completed the look along with heels I borrowed from Sheila.

Saliesha wolf-whistled and I turned as pink as my dress. Brandon walked over to me with pink flowers. "You look really pretty."

I smiled brightly and took the flowers. After I sniffed them I replied, "Thank you."

"Okay!" Mary sang and walked off of the porch. "Off we go!"

Madison walked down the steps and Brom offered his arm. She smiled and took it graciously.

Our big group started to walk down the long path and joked and laughed the whole way there.

When I walked into the recreation center, it was as if I walked into a different world. Everyone was dressed in the old fashioned clothes. Lights hung everywhere and the radio in the corner blasted Billie Holliday.

It was so exciting!

Molly, Mindy, Chloe and Lauren walked over to me. "Thanks for the idea Callie. This all turned out amazing!" Molly exclaimed. She wore a glittery black dress and matching black headband with black feathers, making her light green eyes more vivid in color.

"Thanks!"

We enjoyed the rest of the dance. It was just a dream come true! I was laughing with friends, I was having a great time and Brandon was there with me. And the best part of all was that they liked me for who I was. I didn't have to be blonde or have blue eyes. I just had to be me!

Brandon and me took a break from dancing and drank lemonade by the table. He smiled, "Remember the last time we drank lemonade in here?"

I smiled over the rim of my cup and let it down. "It seems like that happened years ago."

"I can't believe the last day of camp is tomorrow."

I couldn't believe it either. "I don't want to leave."

He pointed at my wrist. "You're wearing that bracelet."

I looked down at the charm bracelet resting comfortably over my gloved hand. "I'm thinking about burying it back where it was. Whatever it means, it's obviously just for C and F."

A lock of hair went over Brandon's forehead as he turned his head to the side. "I forgot to tell you. Mr. Mendel wanted to talk to you. He said he knows something about Chris and Felicia."

My jaw dropped, "Really?"

"Yeah," he took a sip of lemonade. "As soon as I started asking him questions and mentioned your name, he said he'd rather talk to *you*."

I turned and saw Mr. Mendel in the corner talking with Ms. Davies and another camp teacher.

"Go ahead," he suggested.

"Okay." I set down my cup, took a deep breath and walked over to the teachers in the corner, Brandon was somewhere behind me. "Um, excuse me Mr. Mendel?"

He turned his friendly dark brown eyes in my direction and smiled, "Camper Callie!" He excused himself from the other teachers and turned to me. "How can I help you?"

"Brandon told me that you wanted to talk to me about Christopher and Felicia?"

"That's right." He nodded happily. "I was a junior camp counselor when they were in camp." Mr. Mendel still had his youthful looks. With his full head of black hair and athletic build, the only signs of his true age were the laugh lines around his eyes and mouth. "As a matter of fact, Chris was in my bunk."

Excitement tore through me, "Really? So tell me, was it *really* him who wrote the initials all over camp?"

He nodded again and crossed his arms as he remembered. "He was really an easy-going camper. I remember that group of campers really well. He got into trouble from a few initials he was trying to make in more obvious places. He and his girlfriend were inseparable."

"Who was his girlfriend?"

Mr. Mendel gave me a secretive smile and I wondered what that was all about. "Callie, what's your father's name?"

"Well...it's Chris." I furrowed my brows. "But what does that have to do with anything? It's just a coincidence."

"Did you get a good look at the Chris in the yearbook?"

"Not really. The pictures were a little fuzzy."

"It's too bad the yearbooks didn't include last names."

"Mr. Mendel, I have a feeling you're trying to tell me something really important."

He hesitated for a moment and then, "This Chris you're trying to find out about...his last name is Thornton."

"Thornton? Wow, that's cool, that's the same last name as my dad too."

Mr. Mendel laughed patiently. "Callie, he *is* your dad."

Light switch.

I froze.

"You mean...*my* dad came to this camp? He's the C? The same Chris?"

He nodded with a friendly smile.

"But you must be wrong. My mom said that her and my dad were together since they were teenagers. This Chris was in love with *Felicia*."

He shook his head. "Absolutely not."

"Then who is F? I wanna know." I said angrily in defense of my mother.

"I knew your mom too...Rose."

Mind. Blown.

"I think you should sit down."

I fell backwards onto a folding chair. He sat down opposite me and I didn't take my eyes off of him for one second as he began, "It all started by the lake..."

"Felicia!"

Felicia ran to the large tree by the lake and sat on the log facing the water; her face in her hands. "Go away Rose," she muttered, her blonde straight hair covering her hands.

"No." Rose replied and sat down next to her friend. "What's your damage? You're totally tripping if you believe those girls."

Felicia looked up, her green eyes water. "They told me that I was totally ugly and I should like totally bag my face."

"That was way harsh, but who cares what they said? They were just being mean. It makes them feel totally righteous about themselves."

Felicia's face, which was dotted with acne, frowned as she accused, "So easy for you to say."

"Yes it is because it's true. I have braces and I don't like, let it bother me." Rose shook her head; her hair was in a high ponytail on the left side of her head, held up by an electric blue scrunchie. "*You* know you're pretty and *I* think you're pretty. But the best part is that you're totally slamming on the *inside*. Those girls? Cheeuh. They're totally ugly because they're so ugly inside. Grody to the max."

"You really think so? Like seriously?" Felicia sniffed and played with her neon green knee-high socks.

"You're totally the funniest person I know."

"I'll never be as beautiful as Isabella Davies."

"Isabella Davies will always be Isabella Davies. And you'll always be Felicia Fedora. We all like you for *you*. You're rad. Don't ever change. You're totally not a wastoid or space cadet."

Felicia smiled and gave Rose a hug. "You always like totally know how to make me feel better. That's so radical on so many levels."

"Felicia!"

Rose and Felicia looked up and saw their bunk-mate Hailey waving.

"Rehearsals for the play, I like totally almost forgot! I have to book it." Felicia jumped up.

"You're going to be the most kickin' Court Jester Camp Eerie has ever seen.

"Thanks Rose! You know, you're totally going to make a rad mom one day."

"You think?" Rose asked thoughtfully.

"No duh! For sure!" Felicia laughed. "You're totally my homefry for life!" She ran off.

Rose stood up and thought about what Felicia said. Just then she heard a crack and screamed when something big fell down and knocked her over. Jumping up, she looked wildly around and saw a boy with torn blue jean shorts and a red camp shirt groaning on the ground.

"Hey!" Rose touched her arm. "You're like from another planet, watch what you're doing!" She looked up at the broken tree branch and then down at him. "What were you doing?"

He groaned again and stood up, rubbing the back of his chestnut brown hair. "I'm really sorry-"

He stopped talking and she made a face. "What's your major malfunction? Why are you staring at me like that? It's totally wigging me out."

He shook out of his stupor and then pointed at her. "You're bleeding."

She jumped and her dark blue eyes went to her hands, "Where?!" She scanned the rest of her clothes.

He grabbed her forearm and showed her the large thorn stuck in her skin. Her deep blue eyes grew large. "Whoa. That is *so* not cool!" She squeezed her eyes shut, "I *so* can't look at it!"

"I'm sorry dude, it's all my fault."

"*Well*," she said helplessly, "pull out the thorn!"

"Why can't you do it?!" He dropped her arm and stepped back.

"Because I trip around blood! *Especially* my own."

He wasn't too sure, but he thought the blue color in her eyes looked like volcano lava. He put his hands up in front of him and raised his brown eyes, "Hey that's your problemo."

She gritted her teeth. "I. Will. Like. Totally. Chuck. On. *You*."

"My bunk counselor says that girls like to exaggerate." He crossed his arms. "And he knows *tons*."

Rose nervously and painfully moved her eyes down to the thorn sticking out of her skin.

Then...

Rose threw up all over his sneakers.

Half an hour later they were both leaving the nurse. Rose had a large neon orange band aid on her arm. "Thanks for staying."

"I had no choice," he said, walking barefoot, "one look at that up-chuck and my stomach went out the door." He ran a hand through his thick brown hair.

"What *is* your name anyway?"

He pinched his shirt by the shoulders quickly and said proudly, "I'm Chris Thornton, in the flesh."

"*Thorn*ton?" She laughed. "So someone like totally falls on me from a tree, I get a thorn and most outrageously maybe a scar and all by a boy named *Thorn*ton! Most triumphant. *Not!*"

"Hey, it could be worse," he winked at her.

"*Thornton!*"

They both turned and saw Chris' counselor Abram run over to them. "Here's your extra shoes," the tall, older teen handed Chris a pair of yellow flip-flops.

Chris looked at them in disgust. "Mendel! These aren't mine, their Mathis'!"

Abram shrugged. "Just give them back when you make it to the bunk house."

Chris planted his hands on his hips and looked up at his counselor with an attitude only friends could pull off with each other. "Yeah right. Mathis wears shoes three sizes smaller than me!"

"Are you talking about Rupert Mathis?" Rose asked curiously. Both guys turned to her and nodded. "Oh I totally know him! He chews gum a lot right? Nice guy, but I have a gnarly feeling that he'll pass down that habit to his kids one day."

Silence.

Chris turned back to Abram. "Thanks anyway Mendel." He looked at Rose and scratched the back of his head again, "Watch out for counselors. They prank every chance they get."

Abram looked firmly at Chris. "You've got obstacle course practice in ten minutes Thornton. Don't be late again or Merchant is gonna pound on you." He walked away.

Chris made a face. "I forgot."

Rose smiled. "Too busy climbing trees huh? So okay, like what were you doing up there anyway?"

Chris winked. "Waiting to fall on pretty girls."

Rose blushed because he called her pretty.

"I've gotta get to that practice. Merchant is giving me grief." He walked in the direction Abram left.

"I'm going that way," she called out. "I'm headed to hiking and the trail is that way. Do you like, mind if I walked with you?"

He leaned his head to the side. "What was your name again?"

"Rose Flowers."

His jaw dropped. "You're gonna shout *sike* right? You're joking."

She laughed. "No! I'm totally serious, stop bugging. It's a big joke in our family. My mom totally loved that her last name would be Flowers when she married my dad so she named all of her daughters with flowery names. I have two sisters named Daisy and Hyacinth."

Chris raised his brows. "Well Flowers, you can walk with me as long as you don't ralph.

She shook her head, "As long as you don't stick those grody thorns in me *Thorn*ton."

He held the yellow sandals in his hand and laughed as they walked up the hill.

"...after that day, they were inseparable. Voted camps cutest couple two summers in a row," Mr. Mendel recalled as he was sitting; a faraway look in his friendly brown eyes. He finally looked at me. "Your dad and I...we were really close." He sighed. "I haven't seen him in over twenty years."

"Why did he stop coming to camp?"

"Maybe that's something you have to ask him yourself." He winked at me. "You know Callie; you look just like your dad."

I moved some hair behind my ear, forgetting about my fancy hairstyle, it didn't seem to matter just then. "Everyone tells me that."

"It's not a bad thing."

"I thought it used to be," I looked at Mr. Mendel and smiled brightly, "but now I know it's not."

"You know, you're just as popular as he was."

"Me? Popular?" No way.

"You're always traveling around camp with an entourage of friends so I'd say so." He nodded behind me and I turned around. Brandon and my bunk mates were staring at me with excitement. I turned back around. "Thank you Mr. Mendel."

"Anytime Camper Callie."

We got up and I walked over to my friends.

"Cal, this has to be the coolest thing I've ever heard," Charlie shook her head.

"Yeah," Brandon raised his brows. "I'm blown away."

"C is for Chris," I explained out loud, "and F is for Flowers." I looked at them in amazement.

"How romantical!" Sheila burst forward with stars in her eyes and held her hands together tightly.

"Oh no," Charlie groaned.

"The most popular boy at camp dating the most beautiful swan!"

"Flower," Charlie corrected and we giggled.

"It turned into forbidden love as they were abruptly torn apart by society!" Sheila placed the back of her hand on her forehead. "The pages were torn out of the camp books and their love buried in the cold muddy dirt of the dark forest!"

Charlie stuck a finger in her mouth and pretended to gag, making us giggle again.

"…only to be found *hundreds* of years-"

"Twenty years."

"-later by a descendent of their future love!" Sheila opened her eyes really wide and looked at me. "*You* are a reminder of the love they started here at this *very camp*." She whispered the last two words.

I felt Charlie behind me. "Sheila, you really freak me out when you look like that."

I smiled, rolled my eyes and asked, "So why were their pages torn out of the camp books?"

"Maybe someone did not want them to be together," Sofia said softly.

"Maybe they had a sworn enemy," Saliesha added with a nod.

"Maybe they didn't want their parents to see that they were together." Lane shrugged.

I looked at Lane, "But why would their parents ever look at the camp library?"

She shrugged. "You never know. Things were probably really different at camp all those years ago." She pushed her glasses up the rim of her nose.

"It's either they tore it themselves," Charlie added, "or someone else did it."

"Sworn enemy," Saliesha smiled.

"Someone who wanted to tear their love apart!" Sheila shouted dramatically.

"Yeah, that." Charlie nodded towards her.

"This just explains why my parents really wanted me to come here."

"So you can find love?" Sheila fluttered her lashes.

"No," I said slowly and then smiled, "So I can find hope."

Saliesha nodded. "Yeah girl, I like how you think."

"That is very sweet," Sofia added

"Were you so very hopeless back at home?" Sheila asked.

"I thought I was once…but not any longer."

Just then, a popular big band song from the thirties started to play and at the same time the camp chef brought out his famous chocolate cakes. Lane, Saliesha and Sofia walked out to the dance floor with their dates.

"Charlie, you want to dance?" Edward walked over and asked.

"Hold that thought Eddie. I think I'm gonna be busy for the rest of the night." She ran over to the large trays before anyone else got to it.

"Charlie! What about your figure!" Sheila shouted after her. "If you can't fit into your princess costume tomorrow than *I* can!" She sang.

Edward looked at Brandon. "Charlie is the coolest girl I've ever met," he followed after Charlie and Sheila.

I smiled at Brandon. "You've been quiet."

He smiled back at me. "You may not realize it Cal, but you're a great friend."

My heart leapt out again. I had made so many great friends I needed at Camp Eerie, but the best part was that I became friends to people who *needed me*.

Chapter 20

Hello

Note to Self: It's not so hard to say goodbye.

ARE MY eyes tricking me or have I seen a real angel?"

"You haven't been deceived. I am Princess Dulcet...beauty of all the lands and real as could be."

Edward squinted from the sun shining in his face, "Are you really real?"

"Dude, I just said so," Charlie said dryly, out of script.

Thunder clapped and the stage crew turned on the fog machine. Sheila swept in wearing a big black sparkly cloak and a large golden crown. "Ha, ha, ha! *I* am Queen Minacious! Ruler of all the lands!"

Edward, as Prince Handsomely Charming, raised a finger, "Uh, well my father, the king, kind of owns this land. And when I say kind of, I mean he does. So this land doesn't really count."

The large audience, filled with campers and parents, laughed. Sheila's red hair was covered in glitter and it sparkled against the sun as she shook her head and said very loudly, "It matters not! I shall take Princess Dulcet as my prisoner!"

"Not if I say so!" Edward stood protectively in front of Charlie.

"She will be mine!" Sheila sang along with a piano, signaling the start of another song.

"Never!" He shouted.

"She will be mine!" Sheila sang again.

"Not if I have anything to do with it!" Charlie sang.

I was sitting next to Saliesha in the audience and with both giggled with astonishment since it was the first time we'd ever heard Charlie sing.

They sang the song and just before the end, Rachel the Gum Smacker as Queen Gracious jumped into the scene. "She will be no one's-" she started choking uncontrollably.

Sheila sang out of script because according to her, the show must go on, "Queen Gracious! You should stop chewing guuummm!" The audience laughed, thinking it was part of the show.

During intermission, I walked out to the concession stand with my mom and dad. They had arrived with Adele just a few minutes before the play started. I was so happy to see them. Even Adele.

"So what do you think of the play so far?"

My dad smiled. "We love it." He put his arm around my mom's shoulders and I hid my smile. They had no idea that I knew.

"You're not even *in* the play. What do you care?" Adele asked with her loud voice filled with attitude.

"My best friends are in it." I said with pride. There was no way I'd let Adele bother me...

"Friends? Ha!"

...it was going to be really hard.

Saliesha came over with her parents by her side. "Hey girl!"

I turned around and felt my hair fall around my shoulders. I let it loose today because I got so many compliments when I did it before. "Hey."

"These are my parents Michael Senior and Georgina."

"Hi," I greeted and they returned it. "These are my parents Chris and Rose." Both sets of parents shook each other's hands and introduced themselves.

Saliesha's big dark eyes grew round, "*The* Chris and Rose?" My parents looked at each other curiously and I nodded. "Dang that's too cool!" Her braces shined in the bright sunlight.

"And what am I chopped liver?" Adele crossed her arms and demanded.

"Not too loud Adele," I whispered. "I don't want everyone to know that my little sister is a piece of chopped liver."

Adele made a "mean" face.

"Have you seen Sofia's parents?" Saliesha asked me quietly.

"Yeah, they came in a limo. They looked so glamorous, like right out of a magazine."

"I don't think her being royalty will be a secret for long."

"I'm still interested in what she meant by saying she's from a 'magical world'."

Saliesha nodded. "Maybe we'll find out one day."

Laughter was very much part of the second half of the play; mostly due to the camps actors rather than the actual story. Carrie and Liz as the Sinister Witch Sisters were hilarious, even though they were supposed to be scary.

Sheila continued to speak off of the script and the surprise of the play was Charlie's singing. It was bad, yes, but way better than anyone thought it would be. They received a standing ovation at the end and during the curtain call, Sheila's short and stout father marched down the bleachers and to the stage and handed her two dozen roses. A delighted Sheila blew kisses to the audience.

After the play was officially over, I found myself in the middle of my friends outside the stadium. We were laughing and hugging Charlie, Sheila and even Lane, who had a funny one-liner.

I happily introduced my mom and dad to my friends. Sheila adored Adele. "Look at her!" She patted Adele's head, "She's like a mini-makeover waiting to happen!"

Adele crossed her arms and grumbled and I couldn't have been giddier.

"Please no," Charlie complained, still wearing her princess costume complete with makeup. "We have one Sheila in this world and *that* is enough." We giggled.

"Look Sofia!" Sheila pointed towards her dad. "*My* father is speaking to *your* father about staying in your castle for a visit!"

Sofia's eyes sparkled. "There are a lot of events happening in the kingdom soon."

"I might just see you sooner than you think!" Sheila exclaimed.

Charlie patted Sofia's shoulder, "My condolences."

Brandon came over, congratulated the girls and then turned to me. "Well my Grandma's ready to take me home." He scratched the back of his head then put his hands in his pockets, nodding over to my parents, "Are they C and F?"

I giggled. "Yeah, that's Chris and Flowers."

"Cool." The sun was starting to lower in the sky, making the light blue of his eyes even more dazzling. "I had fun this summer."

I grinned and looked at the ground. "I'm not really good with goodbyes." I peeked up at him through my lashes.

He smiled and I got a really good look at his devastating dimple. "This is not goodbye. This is hello."

"Hello?"

"Yeah, if we say hello, then we won't have to say goodbye."
I laughed. "Well, hello."
"Hello." He didn't laugh, but stared at me.
"Brandon!"
He turned around, saw his grandmother waving him over and then faced me again, "See ya!" He shouted to everyone in the group. He looked at me one more time and then just like that, he was gone.

Everyone in the play had to turn in their costumes and Sofia introduced her parents to a star-stricken Saliesha.

"Mom, can you buy me a bag of popcorn for the ride home?" Adele whined.

My mom sighed, "Of course, sweet." She took Adele's hand and they walked over to the still packed concession stand.

"Well Callie," my dad gave me a knowing look, "still angry with us?"

I looked down bashfully and then back up at him. "I have to say dad, my summer was not supposed to be this fun. I have something for you."

"What do you have?" I felt him stare at me as I fumbled through my pockets and lifted up the charm bracelet.

"I think this might belong to you and mom."

I'd never seen my dad look more shocked. "Callie…" he was absolutely speechless! And I've seen a lot of his looks since Adele and I were always up to something. "Where did you get this?"

"Believe me dad, I have no idea how this happened." I reached into my backpack and handed him the box with all the special things inside. I told him about the initials I found. He looked shocked when I told him about my investigation and his face lit up when I talked about Mr. Mendel.

"I understand dad. You and mom wanted me to find the same thing here that you did."

He made a face. "Well we really weren't looking for you to find love-"

Last person on earth I wanted to talk to about that! "*Ew!* Dad, stop." I closed my eyes and opened them again. "I've learned that I can have friends. There's nothing wrong with me and if there *is* something wrong with me, who cares? There are people who like me for *me*, just the way I am. I even learned to trust someone I'd never thought in a zillion years I would."

He looked overcome with emotion. "I don't know what to say Cal…"

"Just tell me one thing. Why is your cutest couple pages ripped out of the yearbooks? I mean, everyone gets to buy a copy."

My dad looked over at my mom. The woman he'd been married to for fifteen years. He smiled, "My parents had put every cent they had together to get me into summer camp and there was no money left over for me to buy a yearbook. With much regret, I took the page so I could remember her…us."

He looked back at me. "I sent an anonymous letter with a donation to the camp." He put his hand on my shoulder, "I had no idea anyone would find this out, especially my own daughter. But I'm glad. Coming here to camp and meeting your mother was the best summer of my life."

I couldn't stop the tears from watering my eyes. I looked up at the sky, hoping the tears would go away. "Dad, I…"

He hugged me. "You don't have to say anything Cal. Sometimes it's okay to be speechless."

I closed my eyes and smiled into his shoulder.

"Okay, are you two having a talk show moment or something?" Adele asked in her usual attitude as she walked up to us with mom.

"Everything okay?" my mom asked.

I ran into her arms. "Everything is perfect mom, just perfect."

She was surprised, but then held me back really tight.

"Callie!" Carrie and Liz walked over to me, both holding huge boxes. I noticed my mom look at the box in my dad's hand in shock.

"Yearbooks are just in time."

"Here's your copy!"

"Thanks! Bye girls."

"See you next year!" They said at the same time and walked away.

It felt so great to hear that.

"*Thornton*!"

My dad turned and saw his old bunk counselor walking towards them. "Mendel!"

"Abram? Oh my!" My mom exclaimed in astonishment.

"Geez," Adele groaned. "Now we're *never* leaving."

I ignored Adele and smiled at the old friends reuniting. I turned and sat down on a nearby log to thumb through the yearbook. I breathed a sigh of relief to know that me and Brandon were not voted Camps Cutest Couple. Rachel Mathis was voted Camp Clown.

I looked below and there was a picture of Charlie on the day of the play auditions, juggling the fruit. The caption read, 'Charlotte Mackenna: Camp's Coolest Person'.

I froze when my eyes looked to the picture taking up the entire page. "*No way.*" Right there, there was a picture of me laughing and hugging Gwen when we won the obstacle race. The title below read, 'Calliope Thornton: Camp Beauty'. I could barely breathe.

"This camp is loony! Dad should ask for his money back!" Adele shouted from behind me, looking over my shoulder at the yearbook.

I shut the yearbook and stood up. "Mom, dad." My parents and Mr. Mendel turned to me and I announced, "I'm going to go say goodbye to my friends."

"Ooh! Can I come? I'd like to talk to the *freaks* who think you're a beauty."

"Not in a billion, zillion years!"

"Moooooom!"

My mom shook her head and sang in warning, "Adele."

My dad nodded. "We're leaving in a half an hour. Be in the parking lot by then."

I didn't waste a second. I turned on my canvas sneakers and ran down the long path towards my old bunk, holding the yearbook close to my heart. The sun was almost set and the sky was pink and orange and a brilliant purple. I sniffed in the air of the woods and dirt and quickly close my eyes to savor the smell.

Much to my delight, all of the girls were already there, taking one last look at bunk thirteen.

"Look at this place," Saliesha said somberly.

"It is so...*empty*," Sofia said softly, looking at the bare bunk beds.

"My flair for style really added a lot of color to this otherwise drab bunk," Sheila proclaimed, wearing oversized bedazzled sunglasses.

"We have a lot of memories here," Lane added.

"Dudes, enough moping around!" Charlie took out her yearbook and a pen, "You all better sign my yearbook."

We all giggled and signed each other's yearbooks.

"I want to thank you all," Sofia announced to us, "for making my summer so special and so…normal."

I put my arm around Sofia. "Thank you for making my summer unforgettable. A real princess at camp!"

Everyone agreed with me.

A few minutes later Mary and Madison walked in. "We thought we'd find you ladies in here."

"It's not such a fan-tabulous day," Mary wasn't very cheerful.

Lane ran into Madison's arms and we all said goodbye to the two best counselors in camp.

We all went outside and said 'so long' to the big scary tree. I passed my hand over the small initials carved on the bark.

"So we have a present for all of you," Madison announced as we slowly walked back towards the main camp grounds.

"Oh you do?!" Sheila exclaimed, "I simply adore presents!"

"Of course we do!" Mary sang. "You didn't think we'd let you leave without a token of our appreciation did you?"

"Well what is it?" Saliesha asked.

Madison and Mary looked at each other and ran to a tree, "It's back here."

"Something smells fishy," Charlie muttered and started backing away. Her guess was right when the two counselors pulled out water guns. "RUN!" Charlie shouted.

We all ran down the path screaming as Mary and Madison shot us with water.

"Not my glitter boa!" Sheila squealed as she covered her head.

I noticed that other remaining campers were screaming and running from their own counselors as well. "It's an ambush!" Carrie and Liz shouted at the same time.

"They don't know who they're messing with!" Charlie slapped me a high five and a second later we were on the main camp grounds.

Behind every tree and bush were safely hidden buckets filled with water balloons. "ATTACK!" A camper shouted.

All of the campers grabbed balloons and threw them at the counselors, getting soaked at the same time. Rachel the Gum Smacker accidentally got me in the head. She blew a bubble and when it popped she said, "Sorry!"

Rachel was then hit in the head by Charlie. "Like I said when we first met, I've got your back."

I laughed and someone shouted, "Every camper for himself!"

Before we knew it, everyone was hitting each other with water balloons. Gwen threw one at me and I got her back. We both laughed and when I looked up, I saw someone hit Mr. Reeves with one.

Everyone stopped and Mrs. Reeves put a hand over her mouth then crossed her arms.

"Uh oh…" someone breathed.

Suddenly, Mr. Reeves pulled his hands from behind his back and threw a water balloon back at the offender. Everyone laughed and the water fight continued with teachers getting in it as well.

It was even better.

*****

I exchanged addresses with the girls so we could write to each other throughout the year. After saying a heartfelt goodbye, I walked to the parking lot. I was wet from hair to toe and proud of it. Adele was leaning against the car, kicking rocks around and looking very irritated.

"Where are mom and dad?" I felt the hair plastered to the sides of my face.

Adele's jaw dropped. "What happened to you?"

"Something I've been dying to do to *you*," I replied.

Adele made a face. "This camp is so weird! You're acting all…*popular* and mom and dad are acting extra lovey-dovey. They went into the forest to "bury something" and said they'd be back in a few minutes." She lifted her hands in frustration. "That was twenty whole minutes ago!"

I smiled to myself and watched as our parents walked towards us, arm in arm.

"There they are! Are we ready to leave yet?!" Adele whined.

My dad nodded, obviously not letting Adele's attitude ruin his mood. "Yes pumpkin."

"Finally! Wait until I tell Jelly Bean about this place! Four hour drive for a clown show!" She jumped inside of the car.

"Callie!" My mom yelled in shock, just noticing my soaked clothes.

"I'm okay mom. It's hot enough so I won't get cold."

She chuckled. "You'll change at the first rest stop."

My dad opened the door for her and shut the door before walking to his side. I held the door behind his seat open and stood there for a minute. "You ready to go?"

I nodded and he got into the car. I looked around the big forest, smelled the not-so-far lake and felt the sticky air. Taking one deep breath, I closed and opened my eyes and whispered, "Hello."

Epilogue

One Month Later

"Are you sure this is going to work?"

Adele looked at one half of her two best friends in disbelief. "Just trust me. Once I count down to one this is so going to be work." Her dark blue eyes turned back into the window. Along with Leila and Jelly Bean, she sat outside on her knees, watching the living room intently.

The doubting friend, Leila, let her small pert nose rest on the window sill and said shakily, "Okay."

"Jelly Bean," Adele whispered and her small friend turned to her. Did you make sure she can't see the water balloons?"

Half of Jelly Beans face was covered with her overly large glasses. She nodded and half of her mouth lifted up into a smile. Adele chuckled like one of those wicked witches in a movie. "This is gonna be so good."

Leila gasped; some of her white blonde hair got stuck in her mouth. "*Here she comes.*"

"When she sits on that sofa, she's going to be sitting on a whole lotta water," Adele was giddy with anticipation.

Callie always fell for her pranks. It was even better that Adele almost never got caught. Today, Adele and her friends stuffed the single recliner with barely closed water balloons.

Callie always sat on that recliner precisely at four-thirty to watch her favorite afternoon teen soap opera 'The Locker Diaries'. Adele almost shouted with laughter just at the thought of Callie sitting down and getting a wet surprise.

She stopped breathing when Callie walked into the living room and looked for the television controller, her brown ponytail swinging to the left and right.

"It's on top of the TV," Adele whispered through grinding teeth. Callie looked around the floor and then walked out of the living room in a rush.

"It's four-thirty," Leila whispered. "She's angry because she can't find the controller."

"Why can't she just turn on the TV *from the TV*?" Adele asked in frustration, wanting the prank to be done so she could laugh until she cried.

"Look, here she comes again," Leila whispered.

They watched as Callie grabbed the controller from the top of the television. It was now four thirty-one and Callie was missing precious seconds from her show, but she didn't turn the TV on yet. She placed the controller back on top of the television and walked out again.

"What if it's a rerun and she just remembered?" Leila asked hopelessly.

"No way, I checked *myself*. *All* new episodes *all* week long."

They turned back and noticed Callie bring in a big bowl of popcorn. The three pair of eyes looked expectantly for Callie to sit down, but still, she didn't.

"Of course," Leila said as they watched her leave the room again, "soda."

"Four thirty-two," Adele noted. "This is taking forever. She is the slowest person on *earth*. This *has* to be some kind of record."

The girls waited patiently until the time on the cable box read four thirty-five. "What is *taking* her so long?"

"I had to use the bathroom."

Leila looked at Adele and then Adele looked at Jelly Bean. That voice didn't belong to any of them. It actually sounded like…the three little faces turned around and were greeted by a smiling Callie.

"I didn't spend eight weeks in summer camp without learning a *little* something about pranks."

"Uh…" Adele said weakly.

"Lesson learned girls," Callie said cheerfully. "Pranking me is not going to be easy anymore."

Adele looked at Callie's hands.

She couldn't see Callie's hands.

Callie's hands were behind her back.

Uh oh.

"Ah…Leila, Jelly Bean?" Adele's eyes never left Callie's. "Run!"

Callie took her arms from behind her back and started pelting the three running girls with the water balloons that had been stuffed under the sofa cushion. She got each one on the head before they made it into the house.

"Callie!" Rose called out.

"Coming mom!" Callie called out happily and walked in the kitchen.

Her mother was going through the mail and handed Callie a blue package and a large gold envelope. "Both of these came for you," she winked at her daughter.

"Alright!" Callie grabbed the blue one first. "It's from Charlie!" She ripped the blue envelope in no time and scanned the letter:

Hey Ca-lee-oh-pee,

Here are the pictures I took over the summer with my camera. I made copies and sent them to all the girls. Hope to hear from you soon.

Your bff,
Charlie

Callie quickly grabbed the pictures and looked over them, smiling to herself. There was Sofia and her at The-Most-Boring-Party-Ever. The very first picture of Sheila bragging about 'being in pictures' in the bunk. Her heart fluttered; there was one of her and Brandon sitting on a log. There was one with all of them looking crazy with colored hair during that horrible prank...and many more. Holding them to her heart, Callie closed her eyes in happiness. Callie quickly opened the gold envelope. It was sealed with wax and looked very fancy. She took out the card and her eyes widened in disbelief as she read on…

Lady Calliope Thalia Thornton,

Her Royal Majesty Queen Seraphina and His Highness, King Tristan,

hereby invite you…

Callie finished the letter and gasped for air. "MOM!"

For more on the Camp Eerie Series check out:

SuzetteEmilia.Com
Facebook.com/SuzetteEmiliaBooks
Twitter @SuzetteEmilia
And Sheila's very own facebook page!
FB.com/SheilaPenelopeAnnVanHousen

About The Author

When she's not plotting some adventure or finding a way to test friendships, Suzette Emilia is usually thinking about some other way to push her beloved characters. She's been writing stories since she was a young girl and is a huge fan of Jane Austen books. She currently resides in New Jersey with her high school sweetheart husband and three children.

Made in the USA
Lexington, KY
05 November 2014